Infinite
Yearnings

Of the HEARTS

The genesis of one's emotions

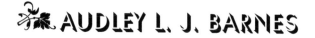

AUDLEY L. J. BARNES

Trafford rev. 10/29/2012

 www.trafford.com

North America & international
toll-free: 1 888 232 4444 (USA & Canada)
phone: 250 383 6864 ♦ fax: 812 355 4082

To my dear, deceased, mother Lucille Barnes
(Mama Luce).
I could never stop loving her.

In her honour, fifty percent of profit from sales of each
book will go to Campbell Castle church school, also to
May Pen high school.

They had something in common: a need for love, respect, understanding, security and expectations they wanted fulfilled. Each day they hoped, in their yearning hearts, that their needs would be met but that day came and went and nothing had changed. Then they looked towards tomorrow—the future, because tomorrow is forever. And they knew as long as they are alive there is always tomorrow. But although they hoped tomorrow things could be better they had no assurance what tomorrow would bring, because they had no control over their own destiny.

Then, too, doesn't one have to be absolutely fortunate to go through life without experiencing some of its pitfalls such as—life threatening incidents, traumatic incidents or otherwise?

CONTENTS

The Pilot Clipped Her Wings 1
Death by a Shingle 57
Dove in Blue 77
Before the Last Sunset 143
I Will Never Leave You..169
Lucky Child 207
Conversations..281
The Invisible Key 291
IF 301

THE PILOT CLIPPED HER WINGS

- I -

No one will trample on my heart again

SHE KNEW BOUNTEOUS HAPPINESS when life was like spring or summer. She knew pain because she'd suffered physically and had suffered great lost and so she mourned when life became bitter as winter. But with all the emotional and physical abuse she'd endured she stayed strong; because nothing but death could stop that soul from reaching her goals.

One of Joy Foster's goals was to get married and live the American dream. Her other goal, she was an executive, was to become the president of a large executive company. But Joy was yet to begin her earnest search for the person to help her fulfil her American dream. However, on a cool day in November, on Interstate 75, while on her way back home to Chicago from a couple of week's vacation in Florida, Joy's Buick Century got a flat tire.

Several vehicles flew by, while she struggled desperately to change the tire. But eventually a motorist stopped and assisted her.

"I had intended to pull in at the next stop," he told her, "for a drink. There they'll fix you tire. Why don't you join me for a drink while they fix it. I would be delighted. He stretched a hand to Joy, a hand that needed some cleansing. She was hesitant to shake his hand but she did so out of courtesy. Besides, if he hadn't stop to assist her his hands wouldn't get so filthy.

"David," he said with a broad smile.

Joy did not tell him her name. She only did so at the gas station's cafe while they conversed. They exchanged phone numbers, and that was the start of their relationship.

About a year after she met David, the Chicago girl moved to Toronto. In time she married him. And over the years she had tenures at several executive companies. But not until after she landed a position at Jacobson/Rand in Toronto's financial district, at corner of Bay and Bloor streets, did she begin her serious quest to become President of that company.

For years while Joy worked her way up the corporate ladder, to become president of Jacobson/Rand, she and David lived a life of bliss. All she'd hoped for in a marriage was just as she'd imagined it to be. But then things began to change gradually because of David's secret habits, to the point where it affected her ability to stay focused on her ultimate goal. So did that change in their marriage caused Joy to take drastic steps, after she'd done what she could to save the marriage? Did she have to abort her quest to become president of Jacobson/Rand? Therefore,

Joy did the only thing she could to keep her sanity, and stayed focused on her goal. She moved on.

So in the late evening of the sixth of July, on the seventh anniversary of her divorce, it was also on that date she got married, Joy Foster sat on the sofa in her living room on the nineteenth floor—of the apartment building where she lived. She'd been contemplating the course of events in her life, and she'd drifted off to sleep with a wallet size picture of David, her former husband, in her hand.

"David you're the root cause for all of this. Your brutally, your arrogance, and your coldness. David, especially your coldness."

Don't blame me for any of this. It's your fault.

Joy laughed bitterly. "My fault? I know what you want, as if the harm you'd done is not enough. Yes, you want blood. You want to read tragic headlines about my death, don't you? But why was I so dumb? Why couldn't I have noticed it? You fall in love with someone, married him, but not until you live with him permanently that you begin to see those hidden faults surfaced gradually."

Joy felt a light tap on her shoulder. Then she heard a distance voice. 'Stop! Don't. Wake up! Wake up!'

By the time Joy Foster stopped, she was leaning against the balcony's rails. She opened her eyes slowly; shook her head to dispel her grogginess. But she did not stretch one of those long lazy stretches she usually did when she first awoke. "What's going on here?" she said. "Where am I?" She shook her head again and she was more coherent. "The balcony. How did I get here? Did I sleep-walk like some people claimed they do?"

Joy shivered as she leaned against the railings of the balcony. Then she grabbed onto it quickly with one hand.

She was still not sure how she reached on the balcony, and whether she'd really sleepwalked or wandered onto it in some sort of subconscious state. She looked down. "Oh no," she said, "it's a long way down from here. But although I've been down many times, I'm sure happy I did not go down from here today." She heaved a heavy sigh. "Thank you, my dear father. Today my life could have ended but you saved me."

Among other things, Joy's father was also on her mind that evening. He had been dead for years.

In a trembling hand, she still clutched the picture of her former husband. She took one last look at it as she backed away from the rails. Then she ripped the picture to shreds. She threw them, the pieces, to the wind. She took a small step forward. "David," she rubbed her palms together, "today you almost had your satisfaction. But you didn't. And I give thanks I woke up in time. However, it's almost seven years. Goodbye, my darling. Goodbye forever and ever. But although, now, that I have forgiven you, I will never forget the beast you turned out to be. Anyway, regardless of whatever had happened in my life, up to now, I must admit life is still beautiful."

Joy took small steps back into her suite. She went into the kitchen and leaned against the kitchen counter, a hand to the side of her flushed face. "Whew," she said, with a blank stare, "a close call indeed." Then she caught some cold water, in a top-heavy glass. She took few small sips. David—and he was not in the suite or anywhere close so he could hear her—tomorrow I will order that car I've always wanted. Besides, being an executive it will reflect my push to rise to the top. I will continue to work hard, push even harder towards my goal: to become the first female president of my company—Jacobson/Rand.

And, as I had vowed on that unforgettable day, the day you gave me the unmerciful boot in the stomach, I still maintain that nobody will ever again trample on my heart the way you did."

Joy almost broke the glass as she stamped it on the kitchen counter. *And nothing, and I mean absolutely nothing—not even if I should (something I can't see happening in the near future), fall in love again, I swear, will get in the way of my main objective.*

A week later, the same month, Joy drove her two-door, silver Mercedes Benz home. She smiled from her satisfaction as she looked pleasurably at the Benz parked in the space allotted for her to park. "Now, this is more like me. This car is impressive."

Next morning joy readied herself for work. She looked stunning in her snugly fitting grey jacket over light-blue shirt; the jacket flared tastefully down to and over her finely shaped hips, over her grey pants. She wore a pair of fancy high-heel grey shoes, a perfect match to the rest of her attire.

Joy sat in the car and made herself comfortable. Then she'd start the car and adjust the rear-view mirrors before she left the parking lot. However, when she tried to start the car it would not start. "This is not good," she said. She formed a fist and viciously pound the steering wheel repeatedly. She rolled the window down. "My old car never did this to me. Now what do I do?"

Joy fiddled about in her pocketbook for her cell phone, to call the dealer. That's when she realized she had left her phone in her apartment after a brief chat with Maria, her bosom friend, the likable receptionist at Jacobson/Rand.

"Now I have a dead car . . . and no phone. This is like a nightmare."

The frustrated Joy got out of the car and she pound on the roof of the car in similar fashion as she'd pounded the steering wheel. She shook her head in disgust, and her shoulder-length wavy black hair flared around her head and face like an open umbrella. Then her hair settled in a similar fashion, like a closed umbrella. The thought of being late for work petrified her. Everything she had to do that day, and her main criteria were a brief with Chief Randal before going to Ottawa, could be in serious jeopardy. And, to lock up the account in Ottawa could be an extra feather in her cap towards the attainment of her main goal.

In the meantime, while Joy leaned on the car in her state of turmoil, she saw a tall man looking in her direction. With a finger of his right hand stuck under his nose.

The man had come out of the apartment building just in time to see Joy pound her fist on the roof of the car. And he had his finger under nose in an attempt to block the odour of gasoline that was prevalent in the air.

"Now what's his problem," Joy whispered. She turned her back towards him, and she heard the man whistled a low, long whistle.

The man's whistle was in appreciation as he looked with delight at the tall woman with a figure to make heads turn. He walked over to her. "Excuse me," he said, politely, while he looked her over from head to shoes without giving her the inclination he was. "Um . . . are you okay?" He was always quick to help anybody in distress.

Joy turned and faced him, with frustration and anger on her face. But what a face. Hazel eyes, under beautifully arched brows, warned him to be cautious. Her voluptuous lips, with a tinge of lipstick, were the colour of strawberries.

His charismatic smile was captivating.

"It's my car," she said. "It won't start."

He knew, from the smell of gasoline in the air that she had flooded the engine, also that the battery could be weak, lost a significant amount of its cranking power due to her failed effort in trying to start the car. "I'll get my car," he said, "then I'll come back and help you to get going. Don't try to start it again. I'll get my car and come back to help you."

Joy watched her tall would-be saviour, dressed in dark-blue suit, white shirt, and a blue cap with a yellow insignia emblazed on the front his cap, walked away. "Quite handsome," she whispered, "supremely masculine too. I like those regimental strides of his, and the way his shoulders fill his jacket. He seems kina likeable, I might add." She watched him weaved his way among parked vehicles until he was out of her sight. *He has such a soft, kind, caring voice.* Well, she did not care who he was as long as he got her car started.

Joy slid back into the car and closed the door. "This is such a beautiful car, my dream-car long before I met David; married him (that impulsive Gambler), and then I had to divorce him. It hurts so much to see him go. I loved him, but he was so repulsive." She sighed deeply. "Horses. I hop the horses they say is under the hood of this car, that is now silent, will serve me better than the horses he gambled on did for him."

With her eyes closed, in a moment of contemplation, Joy heard, "I'm back. Are you asleep?"

"No, I'm not. Just . . . you know?"

"Uh huh," he said. "Now you can give it a go. Try if it'll start."

Joy did as the man asked her to do, but the engine only cranked slowly.

Just as I had imagined, battery is weak. "Open the hood, please?"

Joy could not find the leaver to pull on to open the hood.

The man walked to the door and pull on the door handle. The door opened. "Please get out," he said. "I'll try it myself."

The man found the leaver to open the hood. He pulled on it and the hood popped. Then he walked back to the front of the car, released the hood's safety latch, and raised the hood.

"The smell of gas is still strong in here," the man said. "I should wait for a couple of minutes before I hook up the jump-cables."

In the meantime, Joy had gone back to sit in the car.

When he thought the time was right, he hooked up the jump-cables from his car to Joy's.

"To jump-start a car as this," he said to Joy, "is not advisable but we'll do it quickly." *I'd better try to start it myself.* "Please get out."

Joy hesitated as a whiff of disobedience entered her troubled mind. "Why should I get out again," she whispered. "Why can't he just tell me what to do?" But with the thought she could be late for work, without further hesitation, she got out of the car and watched the man slid into the red leather seat. He turned on the ignition key, and Joy heard all the horses they told her that's under the hood respond immediately—that sounded like the stampede of a heard of wild horses. She sighed, in relief, because the sweet sound from the roar of the engine that was silent was like sweet music to her ears—sweet music such as golden oldies; rock 'n' roll and sentimental soul classics which she had a deep passion for. Her brows rose from her instant gratification. The glint in her hazel eyes returned to its maximum brilliance. Her strawberry coloured lips parted slightly, and her brilliant smile could light up a city block.

The man got out of the car. "There you go," he said.

Joy slid back into her car.

"Better disconnect the jump-cables," the man said. He walked back to the front of the car, removed the cables and laid them on the ground. He closed the hood. Then he walked back to the driver's door; rested his left hand on the driver-side windshield-pillar post of the car, leaned the upper part of his six-foot-six frame forward, so he could speak without the slightest of strain on his voice. "By the way," he said, "I'm Terry Kennedy."

"Hi, Mr Kennedy. I'm Joy Foster."

"Forget about the, Mr Kennedy. Terry is OK with me."

"OK then, Terry it is. Thanks for your help. Terry, you've made my day."

Joy glanced at her watch, to see what time it was. She was not overly concerned about being late any more, because she knew now she had more than enough time to be early for her assignments, and should make it to Ottawa as planned. She would give Terry a minute or two, because she felt she had seen something in his chuckle—his carefree laughter—that aroused her curiosity, which she'd not seen in any of the men she had dated casually since she divorced David. *Darn. I am a frequent flyer, and I should've realized he's dressed in a Pilot's suit.* "So you're a pilot?" she said.

Terry showed her a banter smile. "What do you think?"

"You are, aren't you?"

"If you believe so, then maybe I am. Anyway, I'm glad I was able to help you, and even though I stopped to do a heavy job I won't be late for my flight to London. Joy, you said, I've made your day."

"So my guess was right. You are really a pilot."

"Well, yes, I am."

A heavy job. I wonder what heavy job he meant. "There's no doubt about it; of course, you have made my day. And I do appreciate it tremendously."

"Don't give it a second thought," he said. "Well, Joy, I hope you'll make my day, too."

Joy thought for a second or two. *Just like any other man. Always want something in return. I hope he won't ask for anything I can't or won't be able to deliver.* "In what way?" she finally asked.

"Could we go for a cup of coffee; take you to dinner or take you to the movies or to some other place of interest to you?"

"Terry, I'm an extremely busy woman. I have no time for dating."

"That busy, huh?"

"Yes, Terry. Anyway . . ." she stretched a hand to him, with her business card. "I'm in the investing and financial business. Maybe sometime soon we could talk about investing. Again, thanks very much for your help."

Terry seized the opportunity to hold onto her velvety soft hand, gave it three quick pulsating squeezes. He kissed the back of her hand gently.

That's such a firm, strong grip, Joy thought, and yet so gentle.

They gazed intently at each other, and Joy felt as if his brown eyes, with mysterious glint, were penetrating deep into her thoughts.

"You're a special lady," he said, as he released her hand slowly, and his face lit up with that warm, charismatic, friendly smile. "Joy, you'll be on my mind."

Joy felt a warm tingle ran through her veins.

"Nonsense," she said. "Terry, I'm sure you have better things to do than to have me on your mind. I must get to work."

Just as Joy was about to drive off she heard him say above a whisper, which sounded to her like the name—Zac or Jack, but she wasn't sure. So she said, "What did you say?"

"Never mind," he said. "Have yourself a pleasant day."

"And I wish you the same."

Joy drove off. *I hope I'll meet him again, so we could do some serious business.*

Terry watched the silver Benz until it went out of sight. Then he scrutinized the card Joy gave him.

"—oh, she works for Jacobson/Rand," he said light-heartedly, with a slight shrug. "I would never invest a dime with that company. Well I, too, must get to work."

"I'm positive," Joy said contemplatively, as she drove along, "I've seen his face somewhere before today. Maybe, while I was on one of my trips to Paris, London, New

York, or even California? He said he was on his way to the airport to pilot a plane to London, England. Anyway, no need to bust my brains about where I saw him before today. Oops! My phone; I have to get it. Again thanks, friend, for your help, because I can go back and get my phone and still be on time."

When Joy reached the building where she worked, she parked her car, grabbed her briefcase and walked with short-mirrored strides to the elevator that would take her to the tenth floor. She stepped out of the elevator and walked into office. "Hi there, Maria, how's it going?"

"Good," Maria said. "How goes your new car?"

"If it were not for the help of Terry I wouldn't be here now."

"What happened?" Maria said.

"I could not start the car, but thanks to Terry—my Good Samaritan—, he started the car, and he told me what to do so I won't have similar problem any more. Such a caring man, and he seemed kina nice. He is darn good-looking too."

"A good-looking . . . Joy, did I hear you say, a darn good looking Good Samaritan? Joy, you should listen to yourself. You speak of him with aura in you voice."

"Maria, if I am guessing what I believe you have on you mind, don't harbour that thought. You know, as well as I, that I have no time for the opposite sex."

"Maybe . . . but . . ."

"Maria, please let the chief know I'm here."

"Okay. But I know he's anxious to speak with you. Why don't you just knock on his office door and see what happens."

Joy knocked on the door.

The Chief said, "Come in."

Joy walked in and sat down.

"How are you doing this morning?" the Chief asked.

Joy was about to tell him of the problem she had with her car, but decided not to do so because she felt it was not necessary, anyway. "Um, all right, sir. Every thing is hunky-dory."

"Hunky-dory?"

"Yes, sir, I'm doing just great. It is such a beautiful day, isn't it?"

"I hope it will be hunky-dory and beautiful for you on this assignment. Anyway, before we go into . . . all right, I have a few last minute suggestions for you on the Ottawa trip."

While she listened to the Chief's suggestion, Joy had a few suggestion of her own, too. And as they conversed, it was as if their minds were coordinated. And as Joy was about to leave Chief Arty Randal's office after he'd briefed her, he bade her Good Luck. "I know it's a tough one."

"Yes sir, I suppose it is. But I've had similar, difficult assignments many times before and came out a winner more times than I'd lost. Sir, I'll be OK."

"Have a pleasant flight."

"Thanks sir." She closed the door behind her. Then she tapped meditatively on the file she held in her hand as she walked back to the receptionist desk. She opened her briefcase and stuck the file in it. "See you later, girl," she said to Maria. She lifted her briefcase, turned, and walked back to the elevator and took it down to the ground floor, and out the door to the taxi that would take her to the airport, where she'd get on the airplane to go to Ottawa to face her tough assignment.

Shortly after Joy left the office, Maria answered the phone, but the call she received had zero to do with Jacobson/Rand.

"Hi," the caller said with a soft, clear voice. "Did Miss Foster reach work, and on time?"

"Who is this?" Maria said.

"She had problem, um, couldn't start her car."

Maria thought quickly. He could be the Good Samaritan. "Yes, she made it on time." She was still curious to know who it was that was the source of such inquiry. "But . . . who are you?"

"Never mind," the person said. "As long as she made it without any further incident, that's all right with me. Have yourself a pleasant day. Bye sweetheart." He hung up.

You bet I will, Buster. "Of all my years spent in this place, nobody had ever made such enquiry about Joy. Well, there's always a first time. Mmm, he has such a sexy voice."

"How did it go in Ottawa?" Maria said to Joy about mid-day the next day, when Joy walked into the office.

"The Chief is the first to know. We'll chat later."

"Okay. But you'd like to know that yesterday shortly after you left the office; I had an unusual call about you, which surprised me!"

"Maria, you got an unusual call about me?" Joy said, while she contemplates. "What was it about?"

"After you're through with your report to the Chief we'll talk about it. I saw your car. It is beautiful."

"I'm glad you liked it."

"You did very well," Chief Randal said, after Joy, who was anxious to learn what the surprise call was all about, was through with her report. "I know I could count on you."

"I hope you realize I have to take another trip to Ottawa. I am more than positive when I go back we'll have this account in the bag. I have already secured our next appointment."

"Excellent," Chief Randal said. "Keep in mind that there's this California thing also. It could be another challenge."

"Chief, I'll be more than ready."

Joy went back to speak with Maria. "Now Maria, what surprised call you had about me?"

"First tell me how it went in Ottawa, then, we'll talk about the surprised call."

"It went well. The Chief said he's well pleased."

"Well then, I don't have the complete scoop on what happened yesterday morning with you, but someone called, a male, enquiring if you made it to work on time and whether you had any further problem with your car. I asked who it was. He did not give me his name. As far as I can recall, that had never happened before. But I thought it was your Good Samaritan, because he mentioned about the problem you had with your car. You could not start it."

"Maria, only one person knew about my car problem, and he was the person who helped me out. We had a brief chat and I gave him my business card. So yes, your assumption could be right."

"Joy, I think the Good Samaritan is interested in you."

"Nonsense, Maria. He assisted me when I needed someone's help, and I expressed my appreciation. That's all there is to it—nothing more. Anyhow," and she did not wait to find out if Maria had more to reveal to her, "the Chief gave me the rest of the day off. See you tomorrow."

"Okay, have fun. You lucky one. See you tomorrow."

Each morning Joy usually got to work about sixty to ninety minutes after Maria. And as they usually did each morning, they greeted each other with a smile, then, good morning friend. Even if they'd talked anytime during the night or even an hour in the morning before they went to work.

"Maria," Joy said, "it's coming down in buckets out there. It is such a terrible morning for driving. Anyway, what's up?"

"You tell me—"

"Oh, Maria, isn't that lovely," Joy said, when she saw a bouquet of roses in front of Maria, "someone sent you flowers. It is such a beautiful arrangement."

"Isn't it?" Maria said. "Would it surprise you if I tell you it's for you? The card is signed, *From the Pilot*. I know you're a globe trotter, but why didn't you tell me you're dating a Pilot? Why so secretive?"

"Me? Dating a Pilot? From where did you get such incredulous information?" Then Joy thought for a while. "Oh, I suspect Terry sent the flowers. I suppose I didn't tell you he's a pilot."

"No, you did not. Nevertheless, seems to me this guy really have an ardent crush on you, for him to send you flowers."

"Maria, he sent me flowers but believe me, it's a waste of his time. Anyway, we should find a container to serve as a vase so we can keep these beautiful flowers alive as long as we're able."

"Yes, of course. We should, shouldn't we? When I find a vase for it I'll put it on your office desk."

"Let it stay here Maria; a welcome change to the landscape of your desk. See you later."

A couple of weeks later, after Joy got the bouquet, she was on her way home from work when she saw Terry for the second time. He and a boy had just stepped out of one of the building's service elevators.

"Hi Terry," Joy greeted him. "So we meet again."

Terry smiled. "So we have. Are you on your way home from work, from one of your very busy days?"

"Yes," she said, while she looked at a boy at Terry's side. She smiled at the boy. "Hi there little fellow."

The boy smiled back at her. But before the boy, dressed in short sleeves floral shirt tucked neatly into his brown trousers, and a Blue Jays' baseball cap on his head, bill turned backwards, could answer Joy, Terry introduced him as Zacri, his son. "We, although he's not here with me most of the time, we moved to this building seven months ago, while he's on vacation we spend as much time together as is possible, and on some of the weekends during school sessions. Today we're on our way to the baseball game." "So we're neighbours!" Joy said. She reached out a hand and almost touched the boy. "Zacri, how are you today and how old are you?"

"Just fine," the boy said, "and 'm almost nine."

"So that's the name," Joy said in a silent whisper, "I thought I heard that morning in the parking lot just before I drove off. His thoughts were on his son. My child, whether it was meant to be a boy or a girl, would be just about his age."

At that moment Joy became nauseous as she relieved the horrendous kick to her belly as if it were instant, a kick from someone who had sworn he loved her, would protect her, and that "they" would be together until death forced them apart. Then she thought his son spends time with him while he's on summer vacation, and on some weekends. "So, his mother?" Joy said.

"His mother, who was my wife, died in an automobile accident."

That's similar to what happened to my dad. "It must be hard for you and your son," she said, while she gazed at the boy with deep affection. "I'm so sorry to hear of your loss."

"Awfully hard," Terry said, "and thanks for your empathy. But with the help of my mother who lives in Hamilton, the road we're on seems okay."

Joy saw pain in Terry's eyes when he mentioned about the loss of his wife. Then she said, "I appreciate what you did that day after you'd helped me; called my work-place to inquire if I'd made it to work without any further incident."

"I was just concerned?"

Concerned, she thought, I wonder why. "And the bouquet, of roses, you sent me was very beautiful."

By then both elevators came and went.

"We should care about each other," Terry said, as he pulled out a piece of paper from his pocket. He wrote his phone number on it and gave it to Joy. "I would appreciate a call from you."

"Are you sure?" Joy asked.

"Yes, I would be delighted to hear from you."

Should I give him my home number? Anyway, she pulled out a card from her pocketbook and wrote her home phone number on the back of it. "Here's my private number," she said to Terry. "You may use it if you wish."

She saw the expression of delight on Terry's face. *I hope I won't regret this.*

One of the elevators came back and the door opened. As Joy stepped in the elevator she said, "You and your son take care. I hope both of you have a good time." She barely uttered her last word as the door of the elevator closed. "Whew. It was such a hectic day. When I get in that apartment I'll kick off my shoes, get into something comfortable, make myself a snack and relax while I listen to some of my favourite music."

Joy reached her apartment and did as she'd said she would, then she lay back on the sofa. "It feels so good to be home." Terry entered into her thoughts. "Well, what do you know?" she said. "I have the same impression of him now as when I first saw him. He seems to be a nice person."

Later on that evening, after Terry and Zacri got home from the ball game, Terry sat by the phone and picked up the card Joy wrote her phone number on. He thought he should call her but gave up on that thought because he did not want her to think he was anxious to speak with her—but indeed he was burning with the desire to do so. In the meantime, Zacri engaged him. He saw the card in his dad's hand. He flung himself in his dad's lap and wrapped his arms around his neck, and said, "Dad, the Lady I met today seemed nice. I like her."

Could it, he thought, be love at first sight for both of us?

"Dad, did you call her? She gave you her number, didn't she? I know she likes you, from the way I saw her look at you."

"No son. I am yet to call her."

"Dad, you like her, don't you?"

Terry smiled. "Yes Zacri. I like her and I will call her in another couple of days or so."

"OK dad. Dad, do you think she'd want to be my new mom?"

"Son, I can't say. Only time will tell."

Terry and Zacri spent the rest of the weekend as they always do. And Sunday evening Terry took Zacri to his mother's home in Hamilton, where Zacri stayed permanently.

After Terry spent an hour or so with his mother, he said goodbye to her and to Zacri. But before he walk away he said to Zacri, "Oh, God's willing, if all goes well we'll get together next weekend."

"We?" Zacri said gleefully.

"Yes son, We. You and I."

Terry saw a curious look on his son's face. Then he heard him say, ". . . and not the Lady, dad?"

He'd only seen her once and he's so taken up by her. "Maybe one of these days the Lady could be with us."

"OK Dad. But you'll call her, won't you?"

"I will," Terry promised.

Joy shared intimate things with Maria that she did not share with her mother, who with one hand worked and put her and her brother through school after their father's tragic accident. And so, throughout Joy's crisis with her husband, Maria's shoulder was always there for her to lean on.

Monday at lunch, Joy said to Maria, "Last Friday afternoon I ran into Terry."

"You did?"

"Yes, I did."

"And—?"

"And nought," Joy said as she took a bite from her tuna fish sandwich.

"Come on Joy. Don't keep me in suspense."

"There's no suspense here; however, the high point of our social contact this time was that we simply exchanged our home phone numbers. The boy I saw with him he said is his son, and his son's mother, she was his wife, lost her life in an automobile accident."

"Just like your dad. So both of you have folks who suffered similar tragic fate; a common thread."

"I guess you could say that."

"Joy, you better embrace yourself for his calls."

"But—"

"Yes Joy, I know. You've said you are not interested in this person, or any other man because you don't want to get distracted from your goal to be president of this company, which is paramount in your life. So why is it that now and then you speak of him? Joy, are you in denial? And you are attracted to him but you won't accept it? Anyway, now you know how to reach him."

"Maria, I'm not about to get into any relationship!"

"You gave this guy, a widower, your home phone number. Therefore, don't you think, by this time he'd figured out you are single. So yes, embrace yourself for his calls."

"He lives on my apartment building. He knows my name, and he probably had figured out by now that I live there. He could've checked the resident's directory to find out my suite number. So, according to you, if he really have an interest in me, though he said he would be delighted to hear from me, don't you think he would've at lease knock even once on my door? And like he'd called here, at work, to find out if I had made it all right without any further incident, he would've called again, if as you say, he has an interest in me?"

"Maybe before long, out of curiosity, he would've done so. Or probably he did not call you here because he feared you might try to convince him to invest in some business venture. Business venture he probably does not care to do. Neither did he not knock on your door because he feared you'd rebuke him. It could be many different reasons why he'd not try to get in touch with you. However, as you've said, he knows you live on the building, therefore he felt he'd make contact with you eventually. Now he's privileged to call you whenever he wants—so be ready."

"We'll see," Joy said. She immediately changed the subject. "Oh, by the way, have you given much thought as to what we should wear to the function next week Saturday night? I should think something new this time around would do just fine."

Joy and Maria were not only best friends; they look like twins by their height, sizes, and natural hair colour. They dressed alike whenever they went to functions or places of interest. They liked the way heads turn in their direction, which also amused Maria's husband, Jade, an accountant.

"New outfits," Maria said. "And how about this, Joy? Why don't you," she teased, "ask the new guy—your so-so attraction—to be your date?"

"Maria, you and Jade have been my steady date for years. I am very content to keep it the way it is. Over the weekend, we should go shopping for our new outfits. Now back to work to earn money for purchasing those outfits. Maria, for the last time, he's not my so-so attraction."

Monday, the following week, Joy said to Maria, "Maria, you were right. Terry called me a few times; Friday, Saturday and Sunday night."

"So what did you expect? I warned you, didn't I? You open the door by giving him your private phone number and he's trying to get a foot in."

"He even asked if I'd be his date to go to a function Saturday night. I told him I had already made plans. Each time we talk the conversation gets longer and longer. I could tell by the tone of his voice, and conversation, that he wants to get to know me or would want me to be his lover."

"Joy, it could be all of those things."

"Maria, from the first time he called I should have made it plain to him we can only be casual friends. To get myself tangled in a relationship is the farthest from my mind. Maria, I'll tell him like it is the next time he calls."

"Well, it's your call," Maria said.

But Joy did not hear from Terry again. Neither did they cross path until the Saturday evening when Joy and company went to the function, held at the Royal York hotel in downtown Toronto.

That Saturday evening Joy and Maria's formal beige outfits got astonished gazes. They were ushered to their table. Joy sat next to Maria, and Joy was the first to scan the program that outlined the evening's activities. And the name Terrence Kennedy as the keynote speaker did not peak her interest. But when the MC called for Mr Terrence Kennedy, Joy was surprised as Terry walked onto the small stage. And in response to her surprise she tugged on Maria's arm.

Maria looked at Joy. "What's the matter?"

"That's him!" Joy said above a whisper. "That's Terry, the Good Samaritan—the Pilot."

"Wow!" Maria whispered back at Joy. "Well from what I could see of him as he walked on that stage, he's a knockout. Look at that warm-your-heart smile. He looks like the type of a man any woman who's on the hunt for a man would want—Oooh, nice!"

Jade noticed their behaviour. "What are you two being so secretive about?"

"Girl's talk," Maria said. "It wouldn't interest you, my dear husband." She turned back to Joy. "If I weren't married I would be in hot pursuit of him. I'd make it difficult for him not to want me—but you have your reasons, don't you?"

"Yes I do, and you know about them as much as I. So, let's enjoy the rest of the evening as we usually do."

Soon after Terry finished his speech, the floor was open for those who wanted to dance. Joy, the dancing executive as she's known, and Maria, hit the dance-floor as they'd done on several occasions. They danced to couple of tunes, took a break and went back to sit at their table.

Terry walked over to their table and said, "Hi."

They all returned, "Hi."

Joy introduced him to Maria and Jade, and said, "Your speech was very good!"

"Humorous too," Jade said. "Pull up that empty chair behind you and join us."

"Thanks for the invite," Terry said as he sat down. "Up there you could've knocked me over with a feather. Fortunately for me I had something to lean on."

"I know that kina nervous feeling," Joy said.

All four of them began to dialogue, but Terry had more than to talk on his mind; he wanted to dance with Joy. So after a few more tunes had played, he popped the question.

"When I hear what I'd like to dance to," Joy said, "I'll let you know."

Terry did not have to wait for long. Because soon after Joy made the statement she got up when she heard a tune to her liking. "Terry, shall we dance?"

Terry did not miss a beat while they were on the dance-floor.

Later on in the evening, organizers of the function had a 'Spot-the-best-dance-couple contest of some sort'. They promised to give a bottle of vintage Champagne to winning couple. Joy and Terry won the prize.

"Now we have something to shear together," Terry said.

"You can enjoy it to your hearts delight," Joy said.

"Maybe we won't share it tonight, beautiful Lady, but someday we may sit back and enjoy this bottle of Champagne."

You may be a good dancer. Don't hang you hat on it. "I'm sure you'll enjoy it."

Terry was careful with his respond to Joy. So he said, "Uh huh." He followed her back to the table.

They sat down.

"You should be proud of yourselves," Maria said. "You two were fantastic!" She nudged Joy with an elbow and smiled from the corner of her mouth.

Joy smiled back at Maria.

The function ended just before midnight. Terry wished he did not have to say goodnight to Joy. Nevertheless, as he looked in her hazel eyes, which beamed with tenderness and passion, he thought the look in her eyes gave him hope.

The next day, Sunday, Terry called Joy in the evening. She was more receptive to his call than ever before. She accepted his offer for a date.

"Wait a minute!" Joy said after she hung up the phone, "what've I done? Did I just agree to go on a date with Terry? Anyway it could be for one time only." She called her bosom friend. "Maria, I can't believe what I did."

"What can't you believe you did?" Maria asked. "You sound as if you are in some sort of trouble."

"Maybe, because I can't believe I've accepted to go on a date with Terry."

"So what's wrong with that?" Maria said. "From the day you told me what happened between you and him in your building, I had the strong notion it could be just a matter of time before you two hit it off. Also from the way, I saw you gazed at him the night at the function. So go ahead but tread softly. He could be the man for you."

"Well, maybe or maybe not. And I won't know because I am not on the hunt. Besides, I don't think one date will cause me to feel otherwise. Furthermore, I have no interest to hook up with any man. Anyway, since I've accepted to go on a date with him I'll honour it."

"Joy, you can't say how it will work out until you give it a try."

"Maria, I know already how it'll work out. Because with all you are saying, I am just going on a casual date."

It only took that first date and Joy was caught in Terry's web. From then on, they had regular dates. She got on nicely with Zacri, who felt Joy was like the mother he'd lost.

Besides being fond of Zacri, Joy had not made it known to Terry, neither Zacri, of other reasons why Zacri also won an interminable place in her heart.

And for someone who was not ready to get into any relationship, serious or otherwise, Joy became more and more comfortable being with Terry. Nevertheless, something that had haunted Joy before she met Terry, would come back to haunt her again.

-2-

Rewarded

"IF I SHOULD TELL you," Joy said to Terry on one of their dates, "that I want to be the first female Chief /President of my company Jacobson/Rand, what would you say?"

Terry knew the history of the company: When, where, and how the company was founded. Even though it happened decades before he came into being.

"Are you sure you can become president of that company?" he asked.

"That's my ultimate goal."

Terry had told her he had no interested in investing in her company but not why. Now she'd know. "Joy, my grandaunt and one of her male friends started that company in her living room. She did not become president because, after the company set sail and became prominent it was male dominated. If you should become president, my grandaunt would smile in her grave. Try all you want but you won't penetrate that male-dominated barrier."

"Just watch me."

"You sound so confident or maybe a little too cocky."

"Both," Joy said. "Very confident and cocky. If you think I don't have a chance then I am with the wrong man. And if you are around me long enough be prepared to eat your words, also to invest. Now, how is Zacri?"

"He's all right," Terry said.

One Saturday evening, and Zacri was not with them, Joy and Terry had dinner—grilled pink Atlantic Salmon with rice and vegetables—at a prestigious restaurant in down town Toronto. While they conversed, Terry's favourite music, jazz, played softly. At that particular time Joy was about to impart to him of previous happenings in her life. About the way her former husband treated her, when she heard Terry say, "I wonder how my horse—Jazz on the run—did today."

And at his mere mentioning of a horse on the run, Joy's body snapped to immediate attention. *His horse Jazz on the . . . ? No, he can't.* And the negativity surrounding what she was thinking of caused her heart to skip a beat. Because she remembered her father lost his life one day when someone was in a hurry to get to a racetrack, to place his bet. Also, her former husband's insatiable gambling habits.

"Terry, your horse?"

His answer was he'd laid out one hundred bucks on Jazz. If jazz wins, he expects to be better off by five grand.

"Terry, you bet on horses! Gamble on horses?" Joy felt nauseous as pimples of sweat suddenly invaded her body.

"Not all the time. I only bet when I get good tips."

Good tips! Now Joy felt her heart behaving erratically, as if it was trying to find a way out through her rib-cage. "Terry, will you take me home please? Suddenly I'm not feeling good."

"What's the matter? Terry asked, concerned of her well-being. "Do you think the food you ate have something to do with the way you're feeling?"

"No Terry. The food has nothing to do with the way I'm feeling. I just want to go home."

"Okay, but are you sure you're all right? Joy, I'm concerned. What's the matter?"

"Terry, please keep your thoughts to yourself. Nothing you say or do now will help."

Terry wondered what went wrong as drove along. Joy was not behaving like the person he'd been dating over the months.

They reached their apartment building and Terry parked his car. Then they went in the building and stepped in the elevator that was not engaged. Joy was expecting Terry would get of at his floor. When he did not, she said, "You've passed your floor."

"You're my date. I'll see you to your door like I've always done. Regardless of whatever is causing you to sulk, which you won't disclose, I will do as I always had."

"Suit yourself." Joy said.

As Joy was about to open the door to her suite, Terry said, "Should I call you later to see how you are doing?"

"No. Don't. I'll be all right. Terry, I will call you . . . I am so very disappointed."

This is so strange, very strange. "Disappointed about what, Joy?"

"Never mind," she said.

Joy shied away as Terry tried to hug her. "Good night Terry," she said, coldly.

Joy opened the door, went in, and then closed it. She kicked off her shoes. "He's an Airline Pilot, isn't he? Can't he be satisfied with what he's making? Why does he have to gamble?—No, not a chance in hell or even in heaven. Nobody who gambles have any place in my life."

"She's disappointed. About what?" The confused Terry thought on the way to his suite. "If the food had nothing to with the way she's feeling, then it must have something to do with what I'd said or did during our meals or afterwards. But what could I have done to upset her so much? Her behaviour is unbelievable. She is so upset she wouldn't even let me touch her. I just can't fathom it."

Those thoughts would be with Terry for a long time.

Sunday afternoon, the day after Joy's gut-wrenching discovery, the phone went ring, ring, and ring at Maria's home. They had phone extension in the kitchen, the dining room, living room, and the master bedroom but not in the bathroom. Jade, who was always slow to answer the phone, and that day he was much slower because he was browsing through some files and in the meantime sipped brandy, said, "Maria, answer the phone." *Oh she's busy in the kitchen, preparing our special Sunday dinner.* "Well, I'll do the honours."

Jade answered the phone. "Hello!" He though he heard the doorbell the said time he answered the phone.

"Jade, it's Joy. Afternoon."

"Hi Joy. Ha, it sure is afternoon indeed. What's up?"

You wouldn't want to know. "So far it's okay." She did not waste any time to chat with Jade. "Maria, please?"

"Maria, Joy is on the phone. I will get the door."

It must be important, Maria thought. Because she knew, that Joy knew about her, Maria's, Sunday routine. She could not remember Joy calling her that time on a Sunday.

Maria grabbed a kitchen towel. While she wiped her hands she said, "I'll take it in here. Hang up when I get it."

Jade did not hang up. He'd laid the phone on the telephone table to go and answer the door.

"Hi, Joy, what's going down?"

"Are you busy?"

"I'm never too busy not to talk with my friend. Anyway, I am busy in the kitchen. Why don't you come over?"

"Sorry to take you away from your task. I know I'm always welcome but today the time is not right."

I can tell something is bothering her. "Joy, what's up?"

"Maria, last night I was so upset I was tempted to call you."

"About what? Why didn't you?"

After I thought about it I had decided it would not be fair to wake you up at that late hour to trouble you with my discovery."

"Your discovery?

Maria heard, Click.

"Hold on," she said to Joy. She covered the mouthpiece. "Jade, what have you been doing? Listening in on my call?"

"Maria, are you crazy? I had put the phone down to answer to the door, but no one was there."

"I heard the phone but no door bell. You had better watch you intake of that brandy stuff." She uncovered the mouthpiece. "Joy, what's your discovery all about? Sounds to me you were on an adventure."

"Yes, a gut-wrenched adventure indeed. Because last night I found out Terry gambles on horse races."

"He's a gambler?"

"Yes, he is. Maria you know how much I have suffered because of some people who had gambled on horses. I am so disappointed in him. That's it for him and me."

Maria was not about to get between two lovers. She also thought of the effect such debilitating discovery could have on her friend, on the eve of her going to California on a very important mission. "Joy, you say that's it for you and him. Tell me this, is he an habitual gambler?"

"I don't know. But what difference does it make? Now you understand why I did not want to get involved with anyone after all I've been through. Just thought I would share this with you. You are busy so go back to whatever you were doing. I am yet to pack, and I should have an early evening because comes tomorrow I don't want to have bloodshot eyes. See you when I get back from California."

"Joy."

"I can sense what you're about to say. But don't worry about me. Because, as I had vowed, and you know that, too, I won't allow anyone or anything to throw me off track. I'll be okay."

"Well then, good luck, Joy."

"Thanks Maria."

True to her word, whatever she had discovered about Terry had no effect on her activities in California.

When Joy came back, she and Maria talked about her achievement in California. Nothing was said about her discovery of Terry's habit. In the meantime, too, Maria hoped the subject would not come up. Because she was not sure what to say to her friend, in regards to helping her to handle the situation.

And although Joy told Terry not to call her, but he already knew she would be going to California and for how long she'd be away, he called her when he thought she'd come back. He could not reach her. Nevertheless, his persistence paid off.

"Joy," Terry said, over the phone, "what did I do wrong? Would you tell me, please?"

"Right now I am busy. I will speak with you some other time."

"When?"

"When I am good and ready and decide what to do."

"Good and ready . . . decide about what?"

"About you and me. I said I would call you and I will do so in good time. I have to go."

"Maria," Joy said one afternoon, days after she came back from California, and after she had spoken with Terry, "although I am very upset about Terry because of his gambling on horse races I can't get him out of my mind. I go to bed thinking of him and I wake up thinking of him. He's constantly on my mind."

"Joy, tell him what concerns you about him then see what happens."

Maria did not have to tell Joy what she had to do, because all along she was thinking that she should tell Terry what ales her about him.

One Wednesday evening Joy called Terry. "Terry," she said, "are you still betting on horse races?"

"Like I've told you before, I only bet on horse races when I get good tips."

Joy spoke plainly, and in such a way that the dumbest of person could understand her. "Terry, gamblers on horse races have no place in my life."

"Why?" Terry said.

She told Terry, her voice quivering, how she lost her father—but not a word about what led her to divorce her husband. Neither that he was a gambler. She would share that devastated event with him another time, when she felt the time was right.

"I am sorry to hear that, how you lost your father," Terry said. "Joy, now I understand why you are so upset about those who gamble on horse races. However, I am not a habitual gambler. I only place bets when my friend, a ranked jockey, tells me what horse race to bet on."

"Granted," Joy said. "However, one starts off by placing small bets here and there and before you know it one is hooked."

"Joy, I am not one of those people."

"Well, Terry, you are not listening to me."

"Who says I'm not listening."

"Now, to be perfectly honest, and I hope it will sink into your cranium, which I think it should, because if you have one of those thick cranium I suppose you wouldn't be a pilot. Terry, Gamblers Disgusts Me."

If I want this woman to be part of our lives, I have to give up this hubby of mine. "Joy, I am really missing you. Could we meet and have a discussion about this matter?"

"Terry, I'll let you know when I am ready for further discussion."

Autumn came, then winter. Through those months, although Terry spoke with Joy sporadically, he kept hoping Joy would tell him when they'd meet. She didn't, so he had no other choice but to play out the waiting game.

Now, came the time of the year when melodious tunes such as Joy to the World; Tis the Season to be Jolly; Silver bells; Silent Night; Noel; I'm thinking of a White Christmas and many more tunes reminded folks that it's Christmas season. A season when some folks gave, received, or exchanged lavish gifts; had plenty to eat and a lot to drink. Yet there were others for whom that time of year were the same as any other meagre season.

Also that time of the year, customarily Joy had Christmas dinner with her mother and brother, in Chicago. While they sat at the table, to have their Christmas dinner, Joy's mind wandered on Terry and his son.

As well, as Terry and his son was set to have their Christmas dinner, Zacri, although he knew there was pause in his dad's relationship with Joy, said to Terry, "Dad, I wish Joy was here with us today."

"Son, so do I. I guess we both miss her. But—"

"Who is this, Joy, you're pining for?" Terry's mother interrupted.

Terry looked at his mother. A twitch formed at the right corner of his mouth, and he said, softly, "Someone we met and we are very fond of her."

"I see," she said, without prying any further. "Well, thank God we are here together to partake."

Although Zacri missed Joy's presence, he devoured his Christmas dinner. But for Terry, the last time he ate his Christmas dinner with less enthusiasm, was for a few years after his wife had passed away.

And, for Terry, the anguished wait continued.

However, it was not until early spring, on a Tuesday evening, when Joy called Terry. "Terry what are you doing next Sunday?"

Terry's heart almost jumped out of his body when he heard that question, but he subdued his excitement.

"I should be home," he said calmly.

"If you aren't busy then, why don't we get together?"

"That's fine with me," he said. *Next Sunday? I can barely wait until then. But I've waited patiently all these months for her to make her mind up. I can live with a few more days wait.*

"Terry, I was thinking we could go for a long ride. Maybe go to Niagara. We could explore the orchards: see blossoms of those fruit trees that will mature in fruits for us to eat, and inhale their different fragrances. After that, visit the Falls. You could place a few bets on the horses while we're there. What do you think about that idea?"

"Joy, taking a trip to Niagara is fine with me. However, there's more to life than betting on horse races. For instance, there is someone I've met who means more to me, and to my son, than betting on horse races."

He heard Joy's light chuckle, before she said, "There is? Are you telling me you are out of the gambling business?" *People tells you what they want you to hear. Something they think should please you when they really mean something else.*

"Yes, Joy, of course there is."

"Sunday, about eleven in the morning, we should be on our way."

Terry breathed a sigh of relief. "Joy, I'll be more than ready."

On their way to Niagara Terry listened to hear if Joy would bring up the subject of horse race. To his surprise, she said nothing about it on the way to Niagara or on the way back. Neither did he. He did more listening than talking. Because he felt—baring any discussion on horse races—that he'd gotten a second chance and he was not about to let it slip away. Each time he looked at Joy, his desire of wanting her grew stronger and stronger. They were almost back in town and Terry asked her to have dinner with him. "Some other time," Joy said. "I need to go home and relax."

"When will I see you again?" Terry asked in a soft, cool tone of voice as he walked her to her suite.

"I had a wonderful time today, but that depends," she said. She was still in doubt about his gambling.

"Depends on what? Oh," he said, his brown eyes had this hungry look as he looked into her endearing hazel eyes, "Joy, I know what you're thinking." He squeezed her hand gently. "Joy, I would never deceive you. I am done with betting on horse races. That's my solemn promise to you."

She looked in his eyes without blinking. And as he focused on her eyes he could tell her eyes were filled with questions.

Then Terry heard her say, "Are you sure? Terry, are you sure—absolutely sure? So many times promises made are broken."

"As long as it is humanly possible, I promise not to break my promise to you," he said with solemn conviction. "Trust me, dear Lady. Trust me."

Yeah, trust you. I loved and trusted my former husband and look what it got me.

Terry moved closer to her. She let go of his hands and backed away. "Perhaps I could call you or you could call me," she said, smiling only with her eyes. She opened the door to her suite. "Goodnight Terry."

"Goodnight sweetheart," he said, with a low voice.

She glanced back at him, and wagged the tip of her tongue slowly, seductively, between her lips. Then she closed the door.

Terry stood for a while and stared at the closed door. Nothing in the world, I promise, will come between her and me again. "Sweetheart, you may think you are alone tonight, but my heart is in there with you! Sweet dreams, sweetheart, sweet dreams."

Terry did not take the elevator to his floor. Instead, he walked slowly down the fire route escape, stopping momentarily, while thinking of Joy. "She's so loving," he said, "and gentle too. How could anyone hurt her? But I feel behind that gentleness there's one tough person. She couldn't get where she is in that company if she was a softy. Ha! Anyway, she'll never be president of that company."

That night, and as it were for many nights when Joy first spurned him, Terry had difficulty going off to sleep, because Joy was constantly on his mind.

In the darkness of her room, when Joy closed her eyes, the silhouette of Terry was as large as life itself. She imagined his soft fingers moving slowly from side to side over her face in his gentle caresses; imagined receiving his tender hugs, and his sweet kisses that had pleasured her delightfully; something she still yearned for. He'd disappointed me once and no way will I give my heart completely to him until I am assured he is cured from betting on horse races. And I still do mean what I'd said that, nobody and nothing will I allow to get in the way to impede my path towards reaching my goal. Nobody or nothing whatsoever."

"How was your date?" Maria asked Joy Monday morning, while looking up at her with a sneaky smile all over her face.

Joy's smile got broader, much broader than Maria's smile. "Mind your own business!"

"If you wanted me to mind my own business you wouldn't tell me you were going out with him. Did you kiss and make up?"

"Nothing like that, Maria, but it was a very pleasant date."

"Given your pining over this guy all those months—"

"Who said I was pining over him?"

"My dear if thinking aloud, or under your breath about him isn't pining after him, then I don't know what pining after somebody is."

"To be honest, I was. I really like him. There's a place in my heart for him."

"So are you about to give him another chance?"

Joy smiled, "Perhaps! Honey, later. Don't we have work to do?"

Maria shook her head ". . . Perhaps? Don't you try to fool me."

But Joy knew all along that, that perhaps was a resounding Yes.

That day Joy thought of calling Terry, but she did not want to give him the impression she was still overly anxious for his affection. "I will wait as long as it takes for him to call me," she said. "Let him sway on the rope of uncertainty."

Meanwhile, Terry was waiting anxiously to hear from Joy. And when a couple of days went by without him hearing from her—his heart in turmoil—he took the initiative.

"Oh, hi Terry," Joy said, when he reached her on the phone. Then, "What do you want?"

That "what do you want" staggered Terry like a terrific slap to his face. It had him wondering what next he should say to her. Because the way she answered him was not something he was expecting to hear.

Joy detected a quiver in his voice, as he said, "I was expecting to hear from you by now."

"You were?"

Terry could not think of anything else to say but a brave—"Yes!"

"Well, Terry, you know I am a very busy woman. My work is paramount in my life."

Yes, you want to be the president of that company but you'll never make it no matter haw hard you try. "Joy my heart is aching for you."

Let it ache. No way will I let anyone trample on my heart again. This time, whenever I give my heart completely to somebody, and that's after I reached my goal, it will be forever. "Terry, I'll let you know when I have time to share with you."

"Okay," he said, "as you wish!" He threw the cell phone down hard and looked at it with disdain. "Am I about to lose out again? What do I have to do to have her securely in my arms?" He would not rush her. He would wait, wait and wait.

Joy let Terry suffered for weeks before she called him again. "Terry, "what's up?"

"Oh hi Joy! Just turning the pages of a manual."

"What kind of manual?"

"I can't tell you about it over the phone. I could show you what it's all about when I see you." He was hoping desperately he would see her again, soon.

"Okay," Joy said. "Better be interesting. Are you . . . ." She paused.

Terry waited while his heart throbbed with anticipation to her what she'd say next.

"Are you free this weekend?" Joy asked.

Pretending he could be busy, the overjoyed Terry said, "I have to check my schedule."

"If you have to check—"

"Please, please give me a minute," he said quickly. "As a senior Pilot, a lot is expected of me. Most times when I am not on duty, as long as I make myself available, I am always on standby. However, they always give me enough time to make any necessary adjustment."

"That means," Joy said, "like me your work is—"

"Joy, I've check and I am free this coming weekend."

"Boy, that was quick."

"My schedule is never far from me."

That weekend was the renewal of their relationship.

One day when Joy, Terry and Zacri stopped at an ice cream stand, something Zacri did surprised Joy. Zacri tugged on her hand. She looked down at him. He had his index finger over his lips.

"I wonder what's on his mind," Joy said. As she bent to his level, she noticed he was looking at his father through the corners of his eyes.

"I love you!" he whispered. "May I call you Mom? I want you to be my new mom. It's a secret between you and me. Is that all right?"

"Zacri, I love you too. If it's okay with you, let's discuss this secret of yours some other time."

"I can wait," he said. "Do you promise?"

"Oh yes, my little darling; I promise to discuss it with you later."

Terry noticed their secrecy. From his curiosity he asked, "What was that all about?"

"Nothing to cause you any worry," Joy said.

Thursday evening of that week, Terry said to Joy, "Sweetheart, you, me, and Zacri have had breakfast, lunch and dinner at several restaurants. Next time how about us eating dinner at a completely different venue?"

"A completely different venue?"

"Yes, such as my place."

Joy had never tasted anything Terry had cooked. She wondered what kind of a cook he was. "Ha! Can you cook?" she said.

"I'll try my best. I promise you, you won't get sick. I know you like salmon steak, but how about fillets of red snapper?"

"That's another type of fish I love to eat."

"So then, I'll see you Sunday at four. And I'll make sure delicious sizzled red snapper fillets will be ready for you. By the way, red snapper fillet is Zacri's favourite. You know I like beef steak."

"Indulge in your steak," Joy said. "Red Snapper fillet for Zacri and I will be just fine."

Joy had never been to Terry's suite. She deliberately kept herself away because she felt, given the way she felt about him, being in that environment, in his den, she could be vulnerable. She probably would've declined the offer if Zacri wouldn't be there.

Would Terry find the time, when Joy was at his place, to show her what's in the manual as he'd promised?

As it so happened, Joy could not honour the diner date because next day, Friday, something happened at Jacobson/Rand, which shocked everyone.

Joy called Terry. "Terry," she said, "I can't have dinner with you on Sunday."

"Why?" he asked.

"Our Chief Arty Randal suffered a heart attack."

"Your boss suffered a heart attack? Joy, that's serious stuff."

"Yes, quite serious. We'll make plans for dinner some other time."

"Joy, don't worry about it. We have lots of time ahead of us. Changes do occur over which we have no control."

"I suppose so," Joy said.

Fortunately, for Chief Randal, he'd only suffered a mild heart attack. He was back to work within a week. However, upon considering his doctor's advice, he decided to relinquish his position. Even though everyone thought things were back to normal with him.

During that time, Joy kept contact with Terry over the phone. So on a Tuesday evening two weeks after the postponement of their dinner date, she said to him, "Things are back to normal. If the offer still stands, this coming weekend I'll find out what kind of a cook you are."

"You are on," he said. "Same place. Same time."

"I'll be there. Will Zacri be there this time too?"

"You bet," Terry said. "Your little darling will be here."

Meanwhile, unknowing to Joy, Chief Randal was having meetings with the company's executive board concerning his departure and, who should be his successor.

"My recommendation," Chief Randal said to the board, "as my successor, is Joy Foster."

"Joy Foster?" Arnold the head board member said. "Who is this Joy Foster?"

"This Joy Foster," the Chief said, "is the best there is in this company. She's hardworking, never shy away from anything that seems difficult. She gives her all to whatever she undertakes, and is very punctual. Besides me, of course, she's honestly the best there is."

"What about the vice president?" Arnold said. "Joy Foster had never been a vice president. Let alone for her to suddenly become the president of this company."

"Arnold," Chief Arty Randal said, "you are the longest serving member on this board. I guess that's why you're the head board member. However, Lester is getting on in years. He's not as energetic as he should."

"This company has never had a female president," another board member said. "We should keep that tradition."

Other board members agreed.

"This is one time we should forget about tradition," Chief Randal said. "I have been the president of this company for twenty-five years. Arnold have I ever given you, and the rest of this board, any reason to doubt anything I have recommended?"

"So for no," Arnold said.

"So I hope you and your colleague will listen to me. I want to leave this company in the hands of a young, healthy, capable, energetic person. All right?"

"Chief Randal," Arnold said, "my colleagues and I will sit on this suggestion of yours for a few days. Then we will give you our answer."

At the third board meeting, Arnold said to Chief Randal, "Chief, what really makes you think Miss Foster should become president of this company."

"Arnold, I have already told you. I was right to the point. I am not guessing about the leader she'll be. There's none in this company to top her."

"Okay," Arnold said. "Let's speak with her."

That afternoon Chief Randal asked Joy to attend a special board meeting. He gave her no hint of what to expect. At the meeting, he sat at one end of the table facing Joy; board members on either side. Several members took turns in questioning Joy, and she wondered what such rigorous questions was all about? In the meantime, she noticed small smiles from the chief each time she made a reply. When they were through, the head board member said to Chief Arty Randal, "Now it's your turn, Arty."

"His turn. For what?" Joy said meditatively. "What is this all about?"

Chief Arty Randal went straight to the point. "Joy," he said, "the day I interviewed you, you told me that one day you'd like to sit in my chair. Well, I am resigning and I am very happy to pass the reigns of this company onto you. You have earned it. My chair is now yours."

Overwhelmed, Joy said, "But Chief Randal—"

"Yes, I should've warned you. If I had, would it have made any difference?"

"I suppose not," Joy said with a nervous smile.

Her mother ran through her thoughts. *Mama, we've made it. You daughter reached her goal.* Then she thought of Terry. *Boy, do I have a surprise for you!*

Joy casts her eyes over the board members. "Today," she said, in the boardroom of Jacobson/Rand at the corner of Bay and Bloor Streets, chills running down her spine, "you and Chief Randal entrusts this company on my shoulders. I promise to do all that's in my powers to uphold the integrity of this company."

"According to the recommendation Chief Randal gave you," the head board member said, "and the way you handled yourself during our question period, we are confident you will." He shook her hand. "Chief Joy Foster, we welcome you."

"Thanks very much," Joy said. She fought to control her swirling emotions.

Then Chief Randal said. "Before we leave here we should introduce the new Chief to the staff." When he did, everyone except the vice president applauded and welcomed her as their new Boss.

After the meeting, Maria said to Joy, "I am so happy you're our new Chief. Nobody expected it."

Joy put her hands around Maria's shoulders, their foreheads touched. "Maria, today I achieved my main goal."

"Girl, you've earned it."

"I should tell Terry," Joy said, "but—"

"But what, Joy?"

"Maria, I will wait until Sunday after we have dinner. I know this will be a shocker to him."

Although the date for dinner was already sealed, Joy called Terry to make sure there weren't any changes.

"Only death could stave off our dinner date," he assured her.

Sunday evening, just before they were ready to eat, Terry said grace. Then he said, "Let's go for it!"

Joy took a bite of the red snapper fillet and exclaimed, "Wow, this is so good—splendid!"

Terry smiled a smile of satisfaction. "I was hoping you would like it," he said. He looked at the bottle of white wine in the centre of the table. "Should I pour you some wine?"

Joy usually had a drink or two with her former husband, but slackened off when she though if she stayed on that course she'd become an alcoholic. An alcoholic she came to realize her husband was. She told him to seek help; he refused to accept he was an alcoholic. "Not yet, my dear. You know I am not much of a wine drinker."

They were almost through eating when Zacri looked at Joy contemplatively, back at his empty plate, then at his dad. "My dad is a real good cook, isn't he?" he said.

Joy stopped chewing. "Yes indeed, he is!"

Zacri burped. "Oh, sorry." he said.

Joy smiled. "French cooks say if you eat the meal they prepare and you do not burp that means you did not enjoy the meal; an insult to them."

"That means I did not insult my dad?"

"No Zacri. Of course not. I haven't burped yet but I have enjoyed your dad's cooking."

"I know you have," Zacri said, "by the smile on your face while you ate."

"You are very observant. Yes, Zacri, I have enjoyed every bite I took."

Zacri rubbed his stomach. "I over ate. Dad, Joy, will you excuse me, please?" he said politely. "You don't mind if I go to my room?"

"That's all right with me, son."

The boy wanted to leave them alone.

"See you later, Zacri," Joy said. "Terry, the meal was splendid. I really enjoyed it."

"I am glad you did," he said. "This could be the first of many. I like to cook whenever I get the time to do so."

"If this is any indication, of your cooking ability, you could take up cooking as a second career."

"I hope I won't have to do that. I like being a pilot, but I don't mind cooking for my family and my friends whenever it's possible."

Joy burped. "Oh, excuse me!"

"Ha, ha," Terry laughed. "Now I know you really enjoyed the meal, according to what French cooks say."

"I suppose you could say that," Joy said.

Terry stood up. "Better finish the last part of my job—clear this table."

"I'll help you to clean up," Joy said.

"I never allow guests to help with chores. Even though sometimes some guest stayed longer than I thought they should. Nevertheless, stay I wish you'd do and watch me work."

"I'll think about it while you clear the table," Joy said.

She left from the table and sat on the sofa.

After Terry was through with his chores he engaged the CD player. He began to play jazz music. He sat beside Joy and put his right arm around her shoulders, lifted it periodically and soothed her shoulder-length black hair.

"Joy," Terry said, "I know you're not a wine drinker but would you share some wine with me?"

I suppose a couple of little sips won't hurt. "Do you have red wine?"

"Red wine it is for my beautiful Lady."

While they sipped chilled red wine from long-stemmed rose-colored glasses, Jazz music still playing at a volume where they could hear each other speak, their happy laughter filled the room now and then, but Joy had something more on her mind than what they were engaged in; something she was dying to share with Terry.

"Terry," she said, softly, then she paused.

"Okay sweetheart," Terry said without giving her time to continue, "you don't have to tell me . . . enough of this jazz. I'll play something else." He thought, at that particular time, she was getting weary of the jazz music. So he reloaded the CD player, went back, sat down beside Joy and continued caressing her.

"The jazz music was not bothering me at all," Joy said. "Now that you have changed the music to something I really like—golden oldies—the tune playing now, I hope you are listening to it, because it speaks volume of the way I feel about you. It is such a beautiful tune. I am sure you missed some of it. Could you start it over, and listen carefully to the words with me?"

Terry did as Joy had asked.

"The expression about love, in this song," he said, "is so vivid . . . exceptionally strong. I really like the way the song starts—'My love have no beginning, my love have no end'—so sentimental."

"Terry, please listen to the rest of it."

'No front or no back,' the tune continued, 'and my love is deeper than deep, wider than wide, stronger than strong, my love won't bend. I'm in the middle, lost in a spin—loving you. And you don't know how happy I am!'—Etcetera.

"Terry, love such as that, as the song says, and much, much more I have to give. Hold me Terry. Please hold me and never let me go."

Secured in his arms, she said, "Terry—"

"Yes sweetheart."

"I was about to reveal something to you that night in the restaurant. About what happened earlier in my life between me and my former husband, when you interrupted the conversation to say I wonder how my horse, Jazz, did?"

"And needles I say how much I have suffered mentally because of that. Anyway, what was that something you wanted to tell me?" he asked.

"My husband blamed me for everything that happened to us while we were together—even the loss of our unborn child, and the divorce, too."

"He did that to you?" Terry said.

"Yes, he did. Terry, I really loved him; trusted him to handle our financial affairs. We were almost paupers when I found out about his gambling habit especially on horse races. When at the same time he was counselling others with similar problems. I confronted him, and faster than the flash of lightening I doubled over from his horrendous kick to my belly. That day I lost my child, and my husband."

Joy felt Terry leaned off of her. And even though it was ever so subtle, it was enough to cast doubt in her mind. "Am I about to lose him? Should I have told him about this before now? What is he thinking? Is he now seeing me as someone undesirable? Is this a sign of rejection?"

While she was thinking of what she did not want to happen, she felt his strong arms tightened around her. And she heard him say, "Sweetheart," she detected emotion in his voice, "from what you've shared with me so far about your life, it is not comforting. You are a fighter and I love you dearly. From now on you won't have to worry about a thing because everything will be all right. You can count on it."

She looked up at his face. "Terry I feel so secure in your arms. I wish I did not have to leave. I truly love you. Every inch of my body is telling me I should accept your offer to stay, but—"

"But what, Joy?"

"But I have something else I want to tell you."

"Yes," Terry said, softly, "go on."

"Just before the Chief's heart attack, I went into his office to make a request. To ask him to give me stay at home chores so that I wouldn't have to fly from point A to point B, like going all over the globe. You know what I mean?"

"Why would you want to do that?"

"I was willing to take a desk job so I'd have more time to spend with you and Zacri. I was willing to do so because, the Pilot clipped my wings."

"The Pilot!" he said, forgetting at that time he was a pilot.

"Yes, you, the Pilot have captured my heart. Instead, the Chief and I talked about other things. I got cold feet. Mind you, my main objective would still be front and centre."

"It's a good thing you got cold feet because—I don't think you'd be happy doing that? Didn't you say you like

51

flying from point A to point B because it's an important part of your job? And you're happy doing so?"

"Terry, I would still be happy with a desk job because I love you. Anyway, I don't have to worry about that anymore."

"Why is that?" he said.

"If I should tell you the male dominated barrier you'd said existed at Jacobson/Rand is broken, and a female is now president, this time what would you say?"

"I'd say it is nothing short of being impossible. No, a darn miracle."

"Well, Terry, your grandaunt is not only smiling in her grave, I hope she's laughing."

"Your company have a female president? Joy, are you sure?"

Joy wriggled out of his embrace. *I want to look squarely in his face, to see his reaction when I deliver this message of my achievement.* "Terry," she said with an animated smile, "in your arms is the new president of Jacobson/Rand."

From his shocked surprise, Terry's arms around her suddenly went limp.

"What's the matter, dear?"

I don't believe this. Is she really the new President of her company? Wow! Now I suppose I have to eat my words. Grandma, I was so wrong. She's done it, for you, and for herself.

"Are you with me, dear?" Joy asked.

"Of course, Sweetheart. But I am, so—"

"So shocked! Surprised?"

"Both. Nevertheless, I am so happy for you achieving you ultimate goal. I never thought I would witness the day you become president of Jacobson/Rand. Joy," he reinstated his hug, this time much stronger than ever.

"Careful," Joy said. "You are suffocating me."

"I am sorry, sweetheart. For a moment, my exuberance on your behalf got the best of me. You' are a phenomenal woman. I will never again doubt you or any other woman striving to reach her particular goal. No matter how difficult or impossible it may seem to me. I am so proud of you. We should celebrate."

"There's no need for it," Joy said. "It's only another meaningful milestone in my life."

Terry released her from his embrace. "Put you wine away," he said, "I'll be right back."

Terry walked briskly into the kitchen, smiles all over his face. When he went back in the room, he had a bottle of champagne in one hand and two champagne glasses in the other.

"Remember this bottle of champagne?" he said.

"Should I?"

"This is the bottle of champagne we won at the function that Saturday evening, because we were the best dancers. Remember?"

"Oh, that."

"That night, remember, I wanted to share it with you but you were not interested. I told you I would save it for a special occasion."

"You did?"

"Yes, I did, and now is as good a time as any. It's a bit on the warm side, not as chilled as it should be but I suppose it will do."

The cork of the champagne bottle went pop! as Terry opened it. The sound from the cork startled Joy.

Terry poured. They touched glasses.

"Sweetheart, to you for achieving you goal," Terry said.

Joy kissed him. "It's so pleasant to celebrate my ultimate achievement with you, the man I love."

"And I feel very fortunate to be the one to celebrate such a wonderful milestone with you."

Joy took a few small sips of the champagne, and said, "Terry, by now you know I had many pitfalls and disappointments in my life before I got this far, but I've had help along the way, especially that of my mother. Reaching my goal is a wonderful thing. Besides that, something else happened to me that surpassed the achieving of my goal."

"And what is that."

"You and Zacri. Terry, Zacri had asked me to be his new mom."

"He did, did he? He'd asked me the day he saw you for the first time if I think you'd like to be his new mom. I didn't know he'd also asked you."

"Now I know the reason for him wanting it to be a secret between him and me. He didn't want you to know he'd asked me."

"What was your answer to him?"

"I did not have any specific answer for him then."

"I knew from the first time he saw you he took a liking to you. And it didn't sit well with him either, the time we had our little misunderstanding."

"I was and I am still fond of him, too. However, after carefully contemplating the situation I told him I wouldn't mind being his new mom. He's the child I never had. I love him as if he's my own flesh and blood."

"I know he loves you very much; probably not as much as I love you."

Again they touched champagne glasses and the glasses made a fine high pitch sound of—Cling! Which resonated sweetly in the air and then it slowly faded, leaving a tingling effect on their brains.

And as if she was hypnotized by the high pitched sound, Joy, glint in her eyes, and she also saw the glitter in Terry's brown eyes, said, "Today I can safely say—I hope I can safely say—these days are some of the most wonderful time in my life; that could only get better as we go forward together."

So, now that Joy Foster who had suffered great loss and mourned when life became bitter as winter, and who had achieved eventually; would she again have bounteous happiness? Would life again become like spring or summer as she, Terry and Zacri walked a new path in life?

DEATH BY A SHINGLE

The Flower Queen cried Murder! Murdered! You'll pay dearly

THE TALL, THIN MAN in khaki clothing, emphatically promised Mary, The Flower Queen, he wouldn't, but as he danced merrily on the roof in the middle of the afternoon he became an assassin; something he could not believe and neither could Mary when she witnessed what he'd done. She buried her face in her hands and yelled, "Murderer! Murderer!" She vowed death. To the assassin.

Mary Pinkerton, who had three children, David, Robert, Grace, and a husband, James, and a brother Harry, was passionate about flowers. She'd go to any length to collect rare flower plants, healthy or withering, and nurse them until they matured. Her flower garden was the talk of the village. She did flower arrangements for weddings, conventions, graduations and other special occasions. She had won many first-place prizes at flower shows. They dubbed her The Flower Queen. Nevertheless, regardless of her love, her passion for flowers, so far not a single flower hasn't yet been created that could cause her not to be unfailingly attentive to her beautiful family.

In her endeavour to collect rare flowers, Mary visited flower gardens far and near. But the Queens Botanical Garden—the Mecca of flowers, was her favourite place to visit every three month, where she was certain she'd find rare flowers. Six month had passed since she last visited the Botanical Garden. When she did, a rare red flower got her undivided attention. She was awestruck as she looked at the flower.

"Wow!" Mary said, as she moved the palm of her hand to and fro softly against her forehead, "this is the most beautiful flower I've ever seen. It is so majestic. It stands head-and-shoulder over the rest. The King of the garden. Nothing would please me more than to have a flower like that standing in my flower garden."

Mary, who maintained God put beautiful flowers on the earth for all to enjoy, always furnish her neighbours with freshly cut flowers. The desk of the Headmaster of her children's school was always lavished with beautiful bouquets; her place of worship always had arrangements of beautiful flowers on the Sabbath day. Even so, Mary thought if she had a flower like that, she would not share a petal of it with anyone. She thought of Harry, who always teased her about her love for flowers and the trouble she usually went through to collect rare flower plants.

"Harry only like red roses," Mary said. "This flower would send his head spinning like a top. But if I don't have it in my garden he might not know it exists."

Meantime, while Mary, eyes still open wide, mouth agape, contemplated the rare flower, she saw a man in blue jeans, shirt out of his jeans pants, opened the gate of the garden where the awesome flower stood. He went in the enclosed area and closed the gate. His silver beard was bushy. His head shaped like an egg. He was partially bald but he had enough hair hanging down the back of his head, which he tied in a ponytail. Mary knew he had some authority. She did not waste anytime to begin a conversation with him.

"Hi there," she said to the man, her grey eyes gleaming with excitement.

The man, long face with narrow set eyes, a bump almost the size of a small marble on the crown of his broad nose, looked at her. "Are you talking to me?" he said.

"Yes, of course I'm talking to you."

"What do you want?" he said with gravely harsh voice.

"What do I want?" Mary whispered. "You'll soon find out. Lord, he sounds so crude. Not a friendly voice at all." Nevertheless, she said to him, "Um, may I come in and touch that beautiful, rare red flower? I've never seen one like it before today."

"No, you can't," he said. Authoritativeness evident in his voice.

I hope it's not showing on my face how disappointed I am, Mary thought, as the gleam in her eyes began to wane. "Why can't I? Now don't be difficult."

"Are you blind?" he said.

"From your observation do you think I am?"

"I don't suppose you are," he said, "because I can tell you are looking at me." He gestured with his right hand as he swayed it horizontally from left to right. "See the eight feet high chicken wire fence around this area? It's here for a reason; to keep intruders suck as you out."

59

Mary was wearing a floral dress much bigger than her size, and if one should look below her shoulders one could not readily guess her actual size. Her auburn hair was hanging loose under her broad rim straw hat. And with the excitement she'd felt almost non-existent, she looked at the man with contempt. "Mr., the fence is obvious, isn't it? So why waste your breath." She pushed back her hat, and the man had a full view of her face.

The man studied Mary's oval face. "Her face looks familiar," he whispered, "but I am not sure she is the person I am thinking of or where I've see her face before. Anyway, let me test my guess." He began stroking his beard, reflecting. "Um . . . Lady, you're," he said, his lips bore a small smile and they barely move like lips of a Ventriloquist, "you're the one dubbed the Flower Queen, aren't you?"

"From the look on your face," Mary said, "I can tell you are not sure."

"I guess you could say that."

"Well, your guess is right. You are looking at the Flower Queen. Who are you? What's your name?"

"Lenny," he said.

"Lenny, now that you know who I am, will you let me in to touch that rare flower? If that flower was human, I swear my husband would have a fight on his hands. I get hot just by looking at it. I am yearning Lenny, yearning to touch that beautiful flower. Have you ever heard the song My Heart Years for You? So it is, my heart is yearning to touch that flower. That tells you how much that flower affects me."

Lenny's brows furrowed from his mild astonishment. *She gets hot by looking at a flower. It's even affecting her heart. Wow, well blow my mind.* He leaned his head towards his left shoulder. Then, with a slight shrug, he said, "They can't keep me away from this flower. Since this plant first bloomed, I've made all kinds of excuses so that I could come here and touch it each time I'm on duty. Whenever I am not on duty I sit here and have an eye full of it. You're perfectly right. It is such a beautiful flower. At nights it has a delicate aromatic fragrance like the fragrance Bellflowers gives off at nights but not quite as strong."

Mary had Bellflowers in her garden. She imagined how much more aromatic the night's air could become with the addition of a flowering plant such as the one she had in her sight, whenever they are in full bloom at the same time.

During their conversing, Mary had only one thing on her mind: how to get a rare flower plant such as it in her garden.

"What do you think?" she asked Lenny, "now that you know who I am. Don't you think a flower such as that would look great in my garden?"

"You won't find this flower anywhere in this region but here. It was flown in, from where I can't say. In the next five years, according to what I've heard, it may become accessible to the general public."

Five years, Mary thought, that sounds like a lifetime. I cannot wait that long. "You said this plant—what's it called anyway?"

"Cockscomb," he said. "This beautiful rare flower you're staring at is called a cockscomb. Seeing you're the Flower Queen, and even though I am not suppose to go against company guidelines, I'll make an exception. You can come in and touch it."

Mary was elated as he opened the gate. She went in quickly. "Ah! At least he showed some compassion," she whispered.

A mischievous look came into Mary's eyes as she touched the flower. "I feel like plucking it off," she said, "and take it home with me."

Lenny gasped, as he thought of the forbidden rule not to let anybody in that fenced garden. "You won't do it, would you? If you should I'd surely lose my job."

Mary looked at him. "No, I won't, even though I have a severe urge."

Lenny felt relieved from those reassuring words, "Whew. I really felt trouble."

Now that he felt at ease by Mary's reassurance, he gave her sketchy information about the flower. "It is the second time," he said, "this plant bloomed. See those three small plants standing under it?"

Mary looked down. "Yes I see them."

"They are offspring from the first bloom."

"If those are reproduction from the first bloom there will be more," Mary suggested. "What do you suppose they'll do with them?"

"Keep them, I suppose. Maybe establish another flowerbed consists only of this type of flower. Who knows? That's my guest."

"Could be," Mary said while she gazed at those small plants with glint in her eyes. "I don't care what their plans are or what you are guessing," she whispered. "Comes hell or high water I am not leaving here today without one of those wee, tender looking plants." She would test his authoritative power. "You don't suppose," she said, "I could have one of those wee plants that looks like any ordinary plants."

Lenny squint his narrow set eyes. "Are you crazy? They would miss it for sure. What would I do or say when they find out one of those plants is missing." He began to think he shouldn't have let her in. "Tell me this. What would you tell people when they ask you where you got this rare flower from when it blooms in your flower garden?"

Although Mary's jaw dropped like an autumn leaf, she had a question and answer she thought might please him and set his mind at ease. "Lenny, are you the only one who comes in this garden?"

"No, there are others."

"So you see, Lenny, think about it. If you let me have it no one would know where it came from. I could even say the wind brought it there. Anyway, no need for that. If you can keep a secret, so can I. I am also certain no one could say 'they' are sure one of those small plants went missing on your watch. So what do you say? If you let me have one of those plants I could make it worth your while."

"How?" he said.

Mary pulled something from out of her pocket. "Here," she said. "I hope nobody is watching us."

Lenny eyes opened wide when he saw how much the bribe was.

"I don't have anything you could use to dig the earth," Lenny said. He thought by saying that it would dither Mary from her quest.

Mary observed the ground. It looked soft. She though she wouldn't have much problem digging with the tools she had. "Who said you have to have something for digging," she said.

She was not afraid of getting her hands dirty; neither was she afraid of getting dirt under her fingernails because, she did not only cultivate flowers but she was also an avid gardener. She had never gone to the market to purchase vegetables to feed her family. Now all she wanted to hear Lenny say was go for it, and she'd dig with her bare fingers until they bleed, as long as she left that place with a cockscomb plant.

"I will only let this happen," Lenny said, "because you're the Flower Queen. This you must also remember, I did not give it to you. I pray to God no one finds out anytime soon that one of those plants is missing."

Lenny turned his back towards Mary. "I don't care how you do it, only get it done fast."

Mary got down on her knees and dug carefully with her fingers as fast as she could. She dug as a dog would dig to hide a bone for later use. When she pull the cockscomb plant out of the earth, and hid it in her bosom, she carefully covered the spot it came from, so it would appear as if the area had never been disturbed. Because she did not want to leave any obvious signs of disturbance in the ground that could lead to early investigating and possible trouble for Lenny. "Thanks Lenny," she said, "for allowing me to do this."

"I swear," he said, "if you weren't the Flower Queen I wouldn't allow it to happen."

"Lenny, you couldn't even begin to think how much I appreciate what you allowed me to do."

"Where's the plant?" he said, when he turned around and looked at Mary.

"I have it where nobody will ever see it."

Lenny even gave tips to Mary on what she should do when she's planting the plant so that it had maximum chance to survive. He wished her good luck and, "Cherish it. When it matures I know it will bring you much happiness."

"Thanks again Lenny, for everything." Mary hurried out of the garden.

She took the wee plant home and planted it in her flower garden, below her bedroom window. She nurtured the plant and watched it grow until it matured into a robust plant that bloom a beautiful flower. She also realized the fragrance from the flower, that was now her pride and joy.

One day Mary noticed water dripping through the ceiling of a room in her house. James, her husband a self-employed accountant, also a handy man, thought he could do what was necessary to stop the leak. He did not have the necessary equipments. They called on Harry, Mary's brother, who was a carpenter to come and assess the damaged area in the low-rise roof, and the cost to have it repaired. But the slender, lightweight Harry had not been to Mary's home since she got the wee plant of that now special flower. Therefore, when he went to estimate the roof, Mary's special flower in full bloom got his attention. "Wow!" he said. "Mary, that majestic red flower, what's it called?"

"Cockscomb, Harry. It's a Cockscomb."

"I've never seen a flower like that anywhere. From where did you get it?"

"Top secret my brother, top secret."

"I know I've teased you often over the years about your love for flowers and the length you'd go through to collect rare flower plants, but whatever you did to bag this one is well worth it. I like my red roses; my sister this one is tops."

Mary had a satisfying smile on her face as she said, "The first time I saw a flower like that you and your teasing of me about my collecting of rare flowers blossomed in my thoughts. Right there and then I knew I had to have a flower like that. I knew you'd like it. So, tell me, do you like it?"

"Like it?

"Really, really like it Harry?"

"Mary I love it. Anyway, although that flower captivates me I am not here to talk about flowers. Where in the roof is the leak?"

She could not take him on the roof so she showed him the ceiling of the room where water dripped in.

Harry assessed the roof. He told Mary how much it'd cost and the time it should take him to complete the repairs.

Mary agreed to his terms.

The day Harry went to do the repairs, Mary, in long plaid skirt, brown short sleeves shirt, her hair tied in a ponytail, showed him a fascinating smile. But don't be fooled by her smile because, although she did not get heated under the collar quickly, it was not advisable to upset her unnecessarily. Or her full wrath would be unleashed upon you. And that Harry knew too well. Anyhow, she walked Harry over to her special flower and warned him sternly. "Harry," she said, "be very careful while working not to let any of your tools or loose shingles slide off the roof and damage my flowering plants. Harry, especially my cockscomb, the flower I idolize."

"I won't let anything happen to damage any of your flowers," Harry said. He knew if he should damage any of her flowers she could make his life awfully miserable.

"I will finish the job without any of your flowers know I was here."

"Harry, I went through a great deal of trouble to obtain the plant of that flower. When I brought the wee plant home and planted it, nobody thought it would survive."

"Puny, was it?"

"Yes, very. However, I nurtured it and watched it grow. As you can see, my effort was not wasted. So this beautiful cockscomb flower that looks like the red, fleshy part on a rooster's head . . . gives me much pleasure every time I look at it. Harry, this particular flower is my pride and joy. I'd die if I should lose it prematurely. So, please, work carefully."

"Don't worry. I'll be as careful as can be."

"Harry, you know that from my garden I share my flowers with my neighbours. The desk of the Headmaster of my children's school I lavished with beautiful bouquets; our church always had arrangements of beautiful flowers on the Sabbath day. However, Harry, although I love to share, and you know I share generously, I am not prepared to share a single petal of my special cockscomb flower with anyone. Harry, nobody unless it meant life or death."

Wow! "Um, you are very serious about that cockscomb flower, aren't you?"

"Yes, I am very, very serious about it. And you can guess what could happen if—"

"All right I know; if it so happens that I should damage your special flower?"

"Well, Harry, do your best not to find out. Um, come to think of it, if it weren't for that tool box in your hand I would swear you were on a visit."

"Why?"

"Because that crisp khaki coverall with so many folding creases looks like it just came out of the package you bought it in. Did you paint that yellow hard hat recently, polish that laced up ankle high brown boot this morning?"

"Gee whiz Mary," Harry said, as he put the toolbox on the ground. He felt Mary was pressuring, and needling him. "I'm a carpenter and not a ruddy construction worker." He pushed his hard hat back and looked at his sister contemplatively. Now he was wondering whether he should bother to do the job. However, after he reassured Mary again, and then himself, that nothing could possible go wrong, he decided he'd go ahead and do the job as planned.

Mid-day the second day, while harry ate lunch, Mary asked him if he'd be finishing the job that day. He said he would by about five o'clock in the afternoon.

"Well then," Mary said, "so far you have lived up to your promise not to damage any of my flowers, which I appreciate very much. So I'll see about getting some funds to pay you."

Harry, who always hummed or whistled a tune while he worked, or laughed at himself about some silly things he'd done in the past, was also pleased that he had almost completed the job and nothing had gone wrong. So with him having only the last shingle to put in place, what could go wrong? And so as he'd done sometimes, do a little fun dance to celebrate his premature completion of previous jobs, so did he on the low-rise roof. But as he did his little dance he was not prepared for the sudden gust of strong wind that almost blew him off the roof. In his endeavour to steady himself he kicked a loose shingle clear across the roof. And, *Wham!—Great disaster!*

Harry swore and cursed at the wind that had left him in misery. He also swore at himself—*you darn lightweight. If you were heavier the wind would not have rocked you that easily. Darn it, I'm in so much darn trouble now.*

The only thing came to Harry's mind then was to run to preserve his life, because he knew he was staring down the path of hell.

Mary got back from the bank about three-thirty p.m, hoping to see Harry on the roof. He was not. *Hmm. I suppose he overstated the time he'd be finished.* "It's so quiet." She went into the house. "Where's your Uncle?" she asked her children.

None of them answered her. She could tell by their manner, mute and wide-eyed as they looked at each other quickly then back at her, that something here was definitely wrong.

Finally, David, the eldest child said, without looking directly at his mother, "Mama, Uncle Harry had an awful accident."

"What awful accident?" she asked in alarm. "Did he fall off the roof?"

"No Mama, he did not. A shingle did. When I said when mama finds out what you've done to her prized flower you'll be a dead uncle, he said, 'Christ! You don't have to tell me I'm in big, big, trouble because I know already.' Mama, he left in a hurry. So much hurry that he left some of his tools behind."

Mary quickened her steps to the area where the cockscomb was, hoping Harry's accident had nothing to do with her beloved plant. When she reached the area, she was dismayed to see her prized flower lying on the ground in a bedraggled condition. "Ohmigod!" she screamed, her worst fear realized. "He killed my prized flower."

The stunned Mary, fuming with anger, stamped her feet onto the ground. She buried her face in her hands and yelled, "Murderer! Murderer! You shall suffer similar fate." Tears streamed down her face. "Why?" she begged. "Why did he do that?"

Mary dropped to her knees and looked through cloudy eyes at the flower on the ground. As if she'd get some comfort, she turned her face up towards the sky and said a prayer on her brother's behalf. "God," she prayed, "today You've witnessed what my brother did to my prized flower. Strike him down. Strike him down with thunder and lightening. Let him suffer the same fate as my flower. Because Lord, You know he broke my heart."

Mary picked up the flower gently, stood up and walked with it in her hands into the kitchen. "My poor flower!" she cried hysterically, as she laid it on the kitchen counter. "Lord, I feel like I'm about to have a heart attack."

The children heard her.

"No Mama, please don't have a heart attack," one of them pleaded while he looked at her face still wet with tears. "We don't want you to die and leave us. Please don't die because Uncle killed one of your flowers."

They had begun to cry, too.

"Hush children," Mary said through her tears. "Your mother won't die from any heart attack. It only feels that way because I'm so distressed; something I must do to ease my aching heart. I'll be right back."

Fuming with vengeance on her mind, Mary stormed out of the house in pursuit of Harry. She couldn't find him anywhere.

The disappointed Mary said, "You can run as much as you want but you can't hide for the rest of your life. I will surely find you and make you pay for your evil deed."

When James, a man of fine features who was not rattled easily and one who always had a positive outlook on life, walked into the house that evening he did not see Mary. As he hugged his children, he noticed their reddened eyes. "Were you crying?" he asked.

"Yes Papa. Because Mama said she was having a heart attack."

Mary was as healthy as could be. It was surprising to her husband to hear that she felt as though she was having a heart attack. He also thought healthy though one may be a heart attack could happen when you least expected. "A heart attack!" he said. He became afraid and anxious. "So where's your mother now? Gone to visit the doctor?"

"She said she'd be right back," David said. "I think she's gone to search for Uncle Harry. Uncle Harry did a bad thing. He destroyed her prized flower."

"Papa, I know Mama is going to kill Uncle Harry when she finds him," Robert said.

The non-judgemental James breathed a sigh of relief when he found out Mary's heart problem had nothing to do with ill health, but only had something to do with the loss of a flower. *Poor Harry, he thought, I wonder, did he finish the job? We'll find out next time it rains, probably in a month or two. Anyhow, I hope for his sake that she does not find him.* "I don't think your mother will kill her brother," James said to his children, "if she finds him. I know how upsetting it is to her to lose her prized flower. She'll calm down in due time, I hope."

Mary came back home without her mission accomplished. "Hi dear," she said, still somewhat more than a bit angry.

"How are you doing?" James said, with a straight face.

"Awful. Today my brother caused me so much heartache."

"I know," James said. "The children told me what had happened, and that you were about to have a heart attack. Sweetheart, losing a prized flower is not the end of the world."

"Not the end of the world," Mary shouted angrily. "If you knew the pain I'm enduring you wouldn't be so insensitive." She burst out crying again.

James put his arms around her and hugged her tight. "Dear," he said, "you're wrong about my being insensitive to your agony. But again, I will say, it was just a treasured flower that your brother accidentally destroyed."

"No, assassinated!"

"Yes dear, assassinated. Nevertheless, let's thank God the accident did not happen to any of our children. You know, as well as I do, a flower has a short lifespan. They bloom, we enjoy them, then before long they wilt and fade away. I know that special flower of yours gave you much pleasure, but it wouldn't last forever. Nothing does. Not even life. My dear, we should always be prepared to lose things we love."

"Don't you think I know flowers don't last forever? I'd rather watch it die naturally than to lose it at the hands of a careless carpenter. At least it wouldn't break my heart."

"I know," James said softly. "Comes tomorrow, I'm sure you'll see this unfortunate situation in a different light. I know it hurts to lose something or someone you love dearly. I'm certain you'll have another cockscomb standing majestically in your garden again—maybe sooner than you expect."

"I hope you're right with your assumption," Mary said. "But regardless of all you've said, it will take me quite a long time to overcome what happened to the most beautiful flower I've ever had in my flower garden. I'm so sorry, really sorry I accused you of being insensitive."

"It's all right. Anyhow, I'm glad you did not find Harry and happy you lashed out at me instead. No harm done."

"Well then, give me another hug you considerate, handsome man."

David, Robert and Grace watched their parents' action with smiles on their faces. Then they gathered around their parents. "Papa, Mama, we love you."

"We love you, too," their father said.

"Me too," Mary said. "I'll be all right."

Two weeks went by while Mary still searched for her brother. His disappearance was as that of a sailor washed overboard and vanished into the deep, blue sea. By then her anger towards him had waned considerably. However, a month after the disastrous event, Mary went to the area market place to purchase some produce. Ahead of her in the same queue, about six people deep, the profile of someone caught her eyes.

"Wait just a minute," Mary said. "Isn't that Harry?" She stepped around those in front of her. "Hi there Harry."

Harry, patrons in front of him with their shopping carts, the cashier's counter to his right and more patrons behind him with their shopping carts, too, recognised Mary's voice before he swung his head around to look at her. He tried to slip away, but her hands were much quicker than his feet. She grabbed his shirt and would not let go. Realizing he hadn't a chance to get away with his shirt on, Harry stood his ground and began to apologize, begging for forgiveness at the same time, too.

"Fight, fight." someone shouted.

"This is not any fight," Mary said. "I am just taking care of family matters."

"Then go right ahead ma'am and do your thing." The person said.

"Harry," she said, "it's too late for your apology, and do you think it is that easy for me to forgive you for assassinating the most majestic flower I ever had in my flower garden." And Mary knew she had began to agitate. So she closed her eyes tightly for a quick second, open them, and continued. "Harry, next time something like that happen to you, or you find yourself in similar situation, stand up and face it like a man should."

"But . . ."

"No Harry, there's no but. Had I caught up with you the afternoon you assassinated my prized flower there's no telling what might have happened, with the rage I was in. God probably was responsible for me not finding you. Since then I've had time to review the hostility I felt towards you, for destroying my pride and joy. You didn't destroy my flower intentionally—I know it was a freak accident."

Harry shook his head slowly, and "Freak accident or not . . . I still can't understand how, or why, that shingle went clear across the roof. Anyway, Sis, to be honest about it, the wind was partially responsible for the demise of your flower." He daren't tell her that he had been gambolling on the roof.

"Wait a minute, Harry. What did the wind have to do with it? The wind was not laying shingles, was it?"

"No, it wasn't. But it was the sudden gush of strong wind that nearly blew me off the roof, and when I struggled to right myself my feet kicked the loose shingle clear across the roof."

"If you had listened to my advice, to fatten yourself, maybe the wind would not have had such an easy time with you. Nevertheless, wind or not, I do believe everything that happens in life to me, you, or to any other person happens for a reason. You know, my brother, I have this strong feeling that God, through your hands, taught me a very valuable lesson that afternoon. He knew I did not only love that flower—I idolized it. And you know what . . . ?

"No, please tell me."

"Harry, I also realized God showed me that afternoon that things we love, or idolized, we could lose at any time—including me losing my beautiful flower. I hold no animosity towards you. You could say I have forgiven you. Stop by any time you want and pick up the funds I owe you. Let me know when to expect you so I can prepare something sumptuous, or otherwise, for you."

Picking up the money was the least on Harry's mind. He also knew she did not have to make any special preparation for him. Because whenever he dropped in she always find something for him to eat. Being forgiven, meant the world to him. "You really meant it. You've forgiven me?"

"Yes, Harry, you could say that but I won't forget."

Harry felt as if a heavy load had been lifted from off of his shoulders.

Mary hugged Harry tightly. Then she looked into his eyes, and said, "Harry, my brother, my love for you is much greater than any love I could have for any flower on earth. By the way, did you do a good job?"

"Thanks Sis. I love you, too. Yes, I believe I did a good job."

"Good, my brother. Very, very good," Mary said through an ambiguous smile.

Harry felt he was back in his sister's good grace once again. Beaming, he said, "God bless *The Flower Queen.*"

"Yes indeed," Mary said, as she formed a fist, and then she pounded Harry hard on his jaw.

The astonished Harry saw darkness and light as he blinked quickly several times. "You almost killed me."

"Give thanks," Mary said, "that I did not, like you killed my special flower. Now, Harry, your deathly debt is paid. You are completely forgiven."

DOVE IN BLUE

-I-

His Revelation Shocked Roxanne

AFTER DETECTIVE DAN'S STARK demise his partner detective Roxanne Green began solving cold, old and new cases at an alarming rate. Was it coincidental, or did she suddenly become a psychic detective? Was Dan helping her according to his afterlife ambition, a secret which had shocked Roxanne when he revealed it to her? Or maybe it was something else? Like someone coaching her secretly, and thus helped her to enhance her ability to solve cases at such breath taking pace? Could she explain why? Did she suddenly become a super detective after she woke up one morning?

Roxanne Green and Daniel (Dan) Stark had been working on the Shultz case for months. Chief Inspector Monty Traverse thought they could use a break from the case, so he brought to their attention the file of a Person of Interest, someone under investigation. Both detectives studied the suspect's file. They suggested to the Chief a stake out would help to make it easier to corner him. The Chief was reluctant to give permission to proceed, nevertheless he did. Both detectives were on the stake out for about two weeks. Without having any success, they abandoned the dreary mission.

"How can we face the Chief?" Roxanne said.

Dan rolled his eyes. "Partner, I am so nervous, I can hear my heart beating. No, Roxanne, not just beating heavy but also Racing."

So on the day they had abandoned the surveillance, both detectives walked into Charley's restaurant at 537 North Street, eight blocks South from Headquarters on Wilson Street, to have lunch. Some of those who worked at Headquarters frequent Charley's restaurant, but not Roxanne and Dan who happened to eat there because it was the closest eatery to their surveillance depot; however, it would be awhile before Dan or Roxanne would venture in there again. That day they sat at a table where Roxanne could look out through the huge tinted glass window (one could see clearly out the window but one had difficulty looking through it into the restaurant) from where she could see what was happening on the street. Because being the perceptive detective that she was, she always like to have the advantage of surveying her surrounding, including the patron's area of Charley's, where she could view movements and actions. Was she paranoid about her surroundings? Just a thought.

Dan had to turn his head, to his left, to have a clear view of the outside and the street.

They brushed the menus that were not in their way to one side of the table as if it had something to do with their misadventure. Then Dan sighed, picked up a menu and threw it angrily back on the table, *no good.*

Roxanne looked at him without commenting.

Furthermore, their frustration were compounded by the though that they had persuaded the Chief that a stake out was necessary. Now, not having anything positive to present to him, from their two-week long assignment, they were very anxious as to what the Chief would say. All that time stalking the villain at public expense and not one iota to show for it.

That day Roxanne heard something she was not expecting to hear from her partner. She was astonished! Because being his partner for all those years, and for him to make such a statement, made her wonder if she really knew what he was all about and, what other secret he could have locked up within."

Shortly after, both detectives sat at the table, Charley the owner—the restaurant named after him—joined them. He did not start a conversation with them as he usually did; conversation he thought would be in his interest, hoping to get juicy stories from the detectives pertaining to cases they were working on. But up to then, what he had hoped for he was yet to realize.

The four feet six inches Charley, with a boyish face, wore a suit as green as the awning above his restaurant front door. Although he was not the one to serve Roxanne and Dan, he asked through a small smile, while rubbing his palms together, "What is it for you today, the same as usual?"

For the past few days Roxanne and Dan ate burgers and fries because they did not want the Chief to think they were eating extravagantly, when they give him their reports and also receipts for foods they ate while tending to their task.

Charley's question *the same as usual,* caused Roxanne to shake her head, in a way she thought wouldn't be noticed by anyone. *Nosy, so very nosy.* "Charley, you've been keeping stock on us," Roxanne said.

"You are some of my favourite clients," Charley said to Roxanne and Dan, in his restaurant in north-west London. "Whatever some of my regular patrons eats, in this case you, whom I associate with, linger in my memory."

Favourite clients, Roxanne thought. Since when did we become favourite clients? We began coming here since last week and I doubt what we had to eat makes us clients to be in the favourite's class. Roxanne smiled. "Charley—"

"Yes, beautiful."

Roxanne clenched her teeth. God, I hate that. If we (I then) are favourite clients, why the hell doesn't he call me by my name? Or just plain detective would do. "Charley, how many of your patrons do you associate with?"

This time he did not refer to her as beautiful, as he said, "Quite a few."

Quite a few all right. I bet his nose is in everybody's plate. What's it to him anyway, what we'd been eating? "Charley," Roxanne said, "we are not in any haste to order today. To begin with, I will have some water. We will study the menu then decide what we want to eat."

"While we're scrutinizing the menu," Dan said, (Charley eyes in his boyish face zoomed on Dan and he showed him a half smile but did not say anything.) "I'll have a beer."

"Ha! A beer? That's all?"

Dan looked at Charley from the corners of his eyes, and a slight frown. "Yes man, that's all. What's wrong with that?"

Dan's demeanour probably sent an indirect message to Charley that he should serve one of his favourite clients who was not in a good mood, without belittling his order. Because Charley raised his right hand quickly, then he snaps his fingers.

Roxanne suppressed her smile. What's he up to now, she thought. He thinks he's clever. Ever since we started coming in here, and showed him the picture of the suspect, he'd been fishing indirectly from questions he'd asked. He'd got nothing and he won't get anything. Let him keep on fishing.

But what Roxanne did not realize was, someone was probably watching Charley. Because at his beckoning a tall finely shaped server in green skirt and a white short sleeve shirt, a small white cap partially covering her cropped hair, came to the table. "Yes, Charley," she said, an aura of contempt in her voice, "Do you want something?"

Charley waved a hand. "Not me, but these two beautiful people."

Roxanne gagged. There we go again. Now Dan is included. We are both beautiful people. But he won't get anything from these beautiful people.

The waitress smiled. "Well then, beautiful people, are you ready to order?"

Roxanne hesitated for a couple of seconds, while showing her captivating smile, hoping Dan would place his order first. However, during those seconds, Dan was thinking: *I can see only one beautiful person at this table, with such a captivating smile that has warmed my heart from the first day I saw her at headquarters, and she's just as beautiful as when I saw her for the first time. Such a beautiful partner.*

Charley smiled at Roxanne. She glowered at him. *Today, Buster, is the last day I hope to see that sneaky smile.*

The first day Dan saw Roxanne at Headquarters in London, he thought she was a client. He was amazed when Chief Traverse said to him, "Dan, here's your partner". Dan thought someone as beautiful as her with such heart-warming smile, a figure if put on the cover of a magazine would skyrocket sales, was suited to be a model. He wondered why she had chosen such a profession. He even thought she'd be a distraction. As he studied her he was tempted to ask her why she had chosen to be a detective. That she must have bought her way in, one way or the other. Nevertheless, she was a far cry from his previous partner who had worked for years passed his retirement year, and if it was not for the acting up of his Ulcer probably the establishment would have to force him out. He'd also learn in time that Roxanne Green was not as a slapstick, but a devoted no-nonsense detective he'd admire unequivocally. And her being his partner brought some of the zest back in his cloudy life due to his great loss.

"Just some water for me," Roxanne finally said.

"And a beer for me," Dan said, again, looking at the waitresses' curvature, then down to her eye-catching immaculate pair of legs, her feet housed in a pair of low heel black shoes.

"A glass of water for her—Sir, do you want your beer in the bottle or should I pour it in a cold glass?"

"In a glass," Dan said. "That'll be just fine for me."

The waitress repeated, "One glass of water," and added, "one beer served in a glass. Both orders are coming up in a jiffy."

Water and beer, Roxanne thought. That sums up our relationship perfectly. I have taken what our body needs seventy-two percent of the time. He chose a beer, something our body can do without. "Dan, why choose a beer and not a glass of water?"

"I just have this thirst for a beer."

Before Dan could say another word, Charley jumped in. "Beer is a man's drink. Besides, it's the first time since you've been coming in here he'd opted for a beer."

"Oh, a man's drink?" Roxanne said. "Women drink beer, too, don't they?"

Yes," Charley said, "but not nearly as much as men. Many of the beer drinkers, oh I have to go."

"Take care, Charley," Roxanne said. *And mind your own business. One has to be very careful around you.*

"Of course I will, you beautiful thing."

Roxanne was livid. "Charley, well, never mind. Go ahead!" . . . *and good riddance.* She was about to straighten him out about his use of the word 'beautiful', but changed her mind because he was leaving from their company and she hoped she might not be talking with him again before they leave the restaurant.

The waitress served Roxanne and Dan, nervously.

Why is she afraid of us, Roxanne wondered? What is she thinking? Does she have secrets in her head, if revealed could have her paying a serious price? Could she? I know she saw the picture of the suspect when we showed it to Charley. She was standing next to him. She peaked at the picture and walked away quickly. Why? I'll find out if Dan remember any of this.

When Charley left, from their table, Roxanne watched him walk towards the front door where he greeted a man carrying a briefcase. He slapped the man lightly on the shoulder, and they went through the patrons' area, pulled opened a door and they disappeared.

Now with Charley out of the way, Roxanne said to Dan, "Dan, did you noticed how nervous the waitress was? If the glass of water were any closer to the glass of beer they would've clanged."

"I did not."

Just like a man and his carnal mind. "You were having an eyeful of something else."

"Like what?"

"Well, never mind. Anyhow, the waitress who served our drinks I'm seeing for the second time. She was standing by Charley when we'd showed him the suspect's picture. As she walked away, I'd asked her if she'd seen him. She said no abruptly. Do you remember?"

"I was the one showing the picture and doing the asking. You were the one doing the observation. No, I can't remember?"

Roxanne jogged his mind back to a time while they were doing the surveillance, when she had looked out through the binocular and thought she saw someone with the resemblance of the nervous waitress who'd served them.

"Dan, she said, "do you remember when I told you I saw someone resembling her, the nervous waitress who served us now, coming out of the door a few houses from the suspect's?"

"Yes. I took the binocular from you, observed her and told you the resemblance was far fetched. She was wearing street clothes then. I guess she looks different in uniform."

"Dan, she might look differently in uniform but you know I never forget a face."

"I know you are quite observant, but we couldn't be sure."

"Should we ask her some questions now?"

"We did not when we should. Let's forget about her. Besides, she knows we are detectives and some people behave nervously around law enforcing officers than others. She could be one of them."

"Okay. So be it."

Roxanne, wearing a brown suit over a beige shirt, took sips from her glass of water. Dan, with one hand clasping the glass of beer, was yet to take a sip.

"Dan," Roxanne said, after a spell of silence, "you're sitting here with me but it's obvious your mind is somewhere else?"

"Roxanne, my mind is on the Chief and what we do not have to report to him. This is a huge let down. Isn't it, partner? Situation such as this is bad for the heart."

"I know," Roxanne said. "We were sure we could get the suspect. It did not work out as planned. We failed miserably. Drink your beer, have something to eat, and then we'll do what we have to do next."

Dan, head bowed, drummed the fingers of his right hand on the table. He was in deep thoughts. He sighed. "Roxanne, I wish there were ways we could solve cases more easily. Like having the ability to read the minds of others, you know, figure things out like a true psychic."

"Dan, if it were possible to read minds probably there would be no crimes and there would be no need for detectives. I have yet to hear of a detective who is a psychic."

"But there are psychic, aren't there?"

"Well, there are people who claim they can read the minds of others. That's a guessing game as far as I am concerned, which sometimes do have positive result, but I believe there are much more misses than hits. Also, that they are able to see into the future, another segment of their guessing game that have the same result as their claims of reading minds. Now Dan, if those who claim to be psychics were superb with the ability to do as they claim, wouldn't there be at least one of them employed by the Force, somewhere? Maybe not just one but several? Can you imagine how much money the Force could save just by employing them as consultants? Dan you've been on the force longer than I, have you ever heard of any?"

"I suppose I haven't," Dan said.

"Dan, I'm sure if there were psychics who knew what they were doing without a doubt the force would secure them in such a way that no one could get near them. Anyway," Roxanne teased, "It hasn't happen yet. Probably going forward I could become the first psychic detective. What do you think about that, Dan?" She laughed light-heartedly, "Ha, ha."

"Roxanne, you laughed as if it is impossible, but who am I to say it won't or can't happen. Isn't there a first to everything in life? Aren't all things possible, to the believer?"

"Perhaps partner, but not in this case because I am not a believer."

"Well, you might yet surprise yourself."

After that short discussion with Dan, Roxanne trained her eyes out the widow. Besides what she saw happening on the busy street was a pigeon hovering over the heads of people on the sidewalk. The bird partially closed its wings, descended a few metres, flapped its wings gently, stopped and levelled its wings with its body, as it held steady in mid-air. The bird flapped its wings again, then it manoeuvred from side to side.

It is probably looking for a suitable place to land, Roxanne thought. If it should land, isn't it afraid it might get trampled on by those hustling feet?

The bird landed softly on the sidewalk. For a moment there, it moves just like a man, like a man on a mission as all those other people are supposedly doing. But isn't everyone on some kind of a mission? Whether their missions are or were of great importance? If it could talk to me, I wonder what it'd say its mission is or was. Well, bird, we are about to get our hides kicked resulting from a failed mission. She kept eying the bird, with other aspects of the bird roving around in her thoughts. *It has no fear of people. It must be someone's pet-bird out for the afternoon.* While she was in that train of thought, she thought she heard a distant voice saying "Roxanne, Roxanne, what's up with you? What are you staring at, so blankly?"

Roxanne shook her head as if waking from a dream. "Dan," she said in a pondering voice, "I was looking out there at that bird. Did you see it?"

"If I was looking out the window," Dan said, "I believe I would."

"For a moment, while I was looking at the bird, I vision myself flying. I could go from one place to the next so easily."

She visions herself flying like a bird. Hmm, if only we could. "Roxanne, humans were not meant to fly unless they're in an airplane or if they're in the category of an angel. Are you ready to place your order? No burger and fries for me today." Dan licked his thin lips. "Partner, I don't know about you but I am going to eat a juicy steak with all the trappings that comes with it. If the Chief should refuse to reimburse me, I won't mind. I'll absorb the cost."

"Dan, a steak sounds like a good idea. I'll have the same."

A few minutes after they ordered their main course, Roxanne pushed back in her chair. "Did you see the puzzled look on the landlady's face when you gave her the key and told her you won't need the room anymore? I wonder what she thought of us. No Dan, not us, but you. Dan, you were the one who rented the room."

"You were there with me, too," Dan said. "Anyway, I don't care what she thought of us. It was not a pleasant place: small, hot, and smelly."

"Dan, it's too late to make a fuss about it. That unsavoury room on Chestnut Street is behind us now."

"Yes, it is. I am happy we're out of that place. She had her first and last months rent as she'd requested. We left the place the way we got it. Now she can rent it to someone else. She has nothing to worry about or nothing to lose."

Their meals were served in wide oval dishes, platters, patterned with multi-coloured small leaves, flowers and fruits around their edges.

"Enjoy!" the waitress said.

Dan looked the food over. "If it is as good as it looks," he said, a whiff of aroma from the food drifted across his nose, "and with such pleasing smell, then we should."

After the waitress walked away Dan said, "Chinese job," as he looked down at the meal in the oval platter. The steak meal came with steamed rice, mashed potato, crunchy asparagus, green beans, broccoli and cauliflower, similar as Roxanne's.

"Chinese job, Dan? Are you referring to the meal?"

"No Roxanne. The platters the meals are served in were made in China."

Dan, army cut hairstyle, broad face, and brown eyes, pulled up the sleeves of his Taylor-made grey pinstriped jacket, one of the two suits he had designated for work. The other, also Taylor-made, was a light-blue suit. He alternated his suits every other week for the fifty-two weeks of the year, wears a blue tie with his grey suit and, a white tie with his blue suit.

Dan tucked his blue tie, diamond patterned, in between one of the spaces between his shirt buttons. He smiled by spreading his lips. "I am going to do justice to this meal."

"Justice you say?" Roxanne said. "Eat your meal and forget about doing justice to it." By then she had taken a bite from her steak. "This is so good, mmmm, very good. Dan, the only justice you should be worrying about while you're eating is the justice awaiting us when we report to Chief Traverse."

"Right now," Dan said, "with this platter of food in front of me I have no time to think about that. At least when we go to see the Chief our tanks could still be almost full." He took a bite from his steak and rendered it as being very good, too. *Yes sir, I am ready to do justice to this sumptuous meal.*

"Now then," Roxanne said, after they were through eating their meals, "get your notebook out. We must make sure when we go to see the Chief there won't be any deviation in our reports. Or else the pleasing meal we've just had could be like floods in our stomachs."

Dan slapped his stomach lightly, a couple of times. His burp carried an echo. "Oh, excuse me," he said. "I didn't intend for my burp to come out as loudly as it did. Anyhow, that was a very satisfying meal. Let's get it together then go see the Chief."

The strapping Chief Traverse with a very deep voice, who'd put the fear in you just by looking at him, was expecting them. "Come in," he said, at the nock on his office door.

Roxanne pushed the office door open, gingerly. She and Dan walked in.

Chief Monty Traverses showed them a half smile. He waved them to sit down on the two chairs that were in front of his desk.

Roxanne's heart was beating heavily in her chest and through her ribcage. The distinct worried look on her face was a clear indication to the Chief that something was divinely wrong. And as she opened her mouth, and even before she could finish saying "Chief Traverse—", he held up his right palm, which indicated to her, *to hold on.*

"Now," the Chief said, "detectives, knowing you as I have over the years, I can't remember the last time I'd seen such despondent look on you faces. It is a dead giveaway that you have nothing positive to report. Anyway, how did it go?"

"Sir," Dan said, "at the stake out, through our binoculars, we saw several folks entered and left the premises but nobody we could positively identify as the suspect."

Chief Traverse shoved his spectacle up above his brown eyes. He rolled his eyes from side to side at Roxanne and Dan.

"If you should remember," Chief Traverse said, his voice filled the room, "in the first place, I was somewhat reluctant to go along with your idea to set up a watch."

"Yes Chief Traverse," Roxanne said, her voice soft and low, the hazel eyes in her sombre face not centred on him, "you were not—"

"Hold on, detective Roxanne" Chief Traverse said quickly, as he removed his spectacle from where it had set above his brown eyes and put it down on his desk. "Detective, when you are speaking to me please speak at a volume where I can hear you clearly, and look me straight in the eyes."

"Yes, Sir," she said humbly. "I won't let it happen again."

"All right, detective . . . Now, as I had thought in the first place, I should've listened to my heart instead of my head. Because I had feared something like this could happen. Nevertheless, I consented. The result I do not like at all. Neither do I like to waste taxpayers' money as we did in this particular case. Taxpayers are our Bosses. They pay us to look out for them. We should serve them well—without wasting a single nickel."

"Yes, Sir," Roxanne said. "It is perfectly clear and we do understand. We apologize, sir."

"Chief," Dan said, "again, sir, we are very sorry that you'd listened to us; gave us the go-ahead then it turned out to be a complete failure."

"Detective Roxanne, um—"

Roxanne realized that, because the chief was seething her surname had slipped from his thoughts, momentarily. "Um, it's Green, Sir."

"Well, detective Roxanne Green and detective Daniel Stark, I feel like benching you. You are good detectives. A situation like this had never happened before. I would be more enraged if you'd had more than one steak meal. Go out there," he paused. "Anyhow," He shook his head, meditatively. "Detectives, I am not happy with the negative result from this endeavour, not happy at all. Now get out of my office, you—"

Roxanne thought, you what? "Yes, Sir," she said.

They got up, walked out of his office without uttering another word.

In the Chief's last sentence, which he'd cut short, because he was so disgusted with the two detectives, he was about to say "You make me sick!" But although he thought of saying it, he suppressed spitting it out. Because he was not the type of a Chief to verbally, or otherwise, belittle his subordinates. He showed them respect and they respected him. "Hmmm. She's still such a fine looking detective." Roxanne always made heads turn in her direction wherever she went.

"Roxanne," Dan said shortly after they left from the Chief's office, "I—"

"Now what is it Dan?"

"Chief Traverse was very understanding. Anyway, before we'd walked into his office, I had this feeling that before we got out of there we would be shredded mentally, and left feeling as though we'd been through a tree branch shredder."

"Dan, he's the Boss we have; very understanding about the situation. He showed restraint. He was reluctant to give us permission to proceed, but he did because he trusts and respects us. Besides, it gave us a break from the Shultz case. We, up to the time of the stake out, had been doing very well with some other cases, but the Shultz case really has us out on a limb. From now on, going forward (and I dread going back to the Shultz files), we should not do anything to rattle the confidence the Chief have in us."

"Yes, we shouldn't," Dan said. "But I came out of his office feeling ashamed as a dog, an expression used by many people whenever they make a boo-boo."

"Dan, I've heard folks used that expression several times. Maybe I had used it too. So expressing your feeling by using that expression—ashamed as man's best friend—I believe is not so bad at all. I'd say it is nothing to worry about. Life goes on."

"Well, partner, I suppose indeed life does go on; on and on, and on and on."

"And even though I sympathise with you and the way you are feeling, I have my own disgusted feeling to deal with, too. However, I am glad the Chief did not rip us to shreds."

"I am happy, too, that he did not tear us apart as I had expected he would although he was angered. And that, to me, is the only bright spot in the whole episode."

Then Roxanne heard Dan say something she was not expecting to hear from him.

"Roxanne."

"What is it, Dan?"

"Honestly. I wish I were a dog. A dead dog."

Roxanne gasped. "Dan, what are you talking about? First, you felt ashamed as a dog. Now you're wishing you were a dead dog. What's up with you?"

"Roxanne, while you were sitting in Charley's restaurant and observing the pigeon, did you really want to come back as one—or any kind of bird? Well, if it's your wish, I wish to come back as a dog. In fact, I really wish I were a dog right now, but seeing that it is impossible bring me back as one in the hereafter."

Now what is he talking about here? Roxanne thought. I did not say I want to come back as a pigeon or as any other kind of bird. Why does he think if I should want to come back as a bird, which I did not say I wanted to happen, he'd want to come back as a dog? What's on his mind? All of this makes no sense to me. "Dan, what's up with you anyway? Why are you wishing you were a dog—a dead dog at that—or to come back as one in the hereafter? Anyway, what's the hereafter you're harping about?" She was also of the impression he had other troubling issues, other secrets maybe, but she wouldn't seek to find out.

"At Charley's restaurant you told me you'd like to fly like the bird you had in your sight, because it would allow you to move from one place to the next easily."

"And what's wrong with that? However, Dan, it was just a pipe-dream in the middle of the afternoon."

"Now, think of it seriously. When you come back in the hereafter—"

"But Dan I had said nothing about any hereafter. I only mentioned about flying like a bird."

"Granted. But if you could or should come back in the hereafter, wouldn't you want to come back as a bird? You could be the most beautiful bird to behold."

"Dan, come back as a bird from what hereafter?"

"The hereafter is also the afterlife. A transformation that takes place when one is called to the beyond. When life on this earth for that person is finished, like when someone dies. Roxanne, don't tell me you haven't heard of the hereafter or the afterlife."

Roxanne looked at him skeptically. "Dan, I don't believe there's an afterlife for any human after they leave from this earth. Nor do I think it can happen for any other kind of animals. I am beginning to think—Dan, do you think the steak I had, and the steak you had came from the same dead animal?" *I'm wondering. Did Charley, not able to dig any information from us, did he probably dust Dan's steak with stupid powder?*

"How should I know Roxanne?"

"Well, if the steak we had at Charley's came from the same animal I'd better be careful; keep a close watch on myself. Because I swear the steak lunch you had," a smile curled round her lips, "and maybe the narrow escape from the Chief is probably affecting you."

"Roxanne, we let the Chief down, and it affects all of us. If you think the steak lunch I had is having any adverse effect on me, then you're not thinking rationally. That I must say, is utter nonsense. Your mind is not where it should because I surprised you with this afterlife thing. Anyhow Roxanne, there are some people—"

"Dan, will you forget about some people and tell me why you wish you were a dog, alive or dead and—"

". . . why I'd want to come back as a dog in the afterlife?"

"Yes," Roxanne said. She was still not amused.

"All right. I told you while we were in the Chief's office I felt like a humbled, shameful dog."

"Yes, so you did."

"Maybe, come to think of it, that was probably my afterlife instinct occupying my mind."

"Dan, your afterlife instinct?" *Whew!*

"Yes, Roxanne. However, all a live dog has to do—as I would've done while I was in the Chief's office—is, listen and is not obligated to give an answer; bow its head, wag its tail, and the master would presume by the dog's reaction that it understands. Now a dead dog would just lay there motionless. Most people who had lived a good life always want to come back as themselves in the afterlife. Those who lived a life of depravity wish to come back as something else. Something good, so they would not have to relive their horrible past. I really don't mind coming back as a dog. To come back as a dog though, or whatever you wish to become in the afterlife, one has to die first. Then transformation would begin once you are dead."

"Just like that, Dan."

"Yes, according to what I've heard and believe."

"I see," Roxanne said. "Anyway, why would you want to come back as a dog? Are you not satisfied with your way of life? Are you living a life of depravity? Dan, will you forget about the afterlife of other people and tell me why you really want to come back as a dog? We just had a narrow escape with the Chief. I am trying to live it down. If you can't answer my question then I have no time to embellish in your afterlife stuff. Furthermore, what do you know about living a dog's life? I believe one has to live in that environment to experience how a dog feels and reacts when it is ashamed. The Chief let us down easy. That's enough afterlife stuff for me and, for you, too, Dan. Wouldn't you agree?"

"All right, I agree. But if you had noticed my manner: all tensed up, head down, despondency showing all over my face, my heart was beating so fast I felt as thought I was about to have a heart attack—"

"Leaving out the heart attack part, so was I. All tensed up because I was nervous as hell."

"Yes, but probably not as I was . . . eyes rolling, the piece of paper in my hand shaking like a leaf on a branch on a windy day, then you'd begin to realize how I felt. The only thing that was left for me to do was to get down on my hands and knees, all fours, lap my tail, which I don't have, tightly between my hind legs. A shameful dog exudes some of those characteristics. Then again, not everything that happens has a logical explanation."

"Dan, logical explanation or is it rational, for you or for a dog, per se?"

"Roxanne, things do happen to humans, also to animals for which there are no logical or rational explanation."

"Maybe so . . . Mmm, so you've been studying dogs? Can you read their minds, too?"

"Roxanne, it doesn't take a rocket scientist to observe mood swing in a dog. No, I can't read the mind of a dog."

"Dan, instead of us standing here discussing a dog, and the way it reacts when it is ashamed, and your wanting to come back as one in the afterlife, which I believe is impossible, don't you think we should go to our desk and tackle the work that's waiting there for us to do in this present life?"

"I suppose we should," Dan said.

The office Roxanne and Dan shared had grey walls and grey ceiling. Dan's desk was by one of the sidewalls. A little distance from the plate glass window that was almost as high and wide as the front wall in which it is erected. Roxanne's desk was by the rear wall, in front of her chair. Both detectives' desk was beige in colour.

Dan went to his desk and began to fiddle with the mountain of files in front of him, wishing he had someone to take the excruciating burden of sorting through those files away from him. Then he took a break from going through his files, clasped his hands around the back of his neck, looked up at the ceiling and began to daydream. He again reflected on what Roxanne had said to him at the restaurant, when she was looking out through the window at the pigeon and daydreaming about flying like the pigeon. With that thought in mind, and although Dan could speak to his partner from his desk, he got up and walked over to Roxanne's, and engaged her. He was still on his dog afterlife theory.

"Roxanne," he said. "If I was a dog I wouldn't have any of this file crap to deal with."

"No Dan, you wouldn't because I am certain you wouldn't have this job. I believe you are human. Or, perhaps, let me guess, I could be wrong because you could be a dog in disguise—in human form."

"Come on Roxanne." He raised his arms, crossed them across his chest, then moved them up under his throat and tapped both of his shoulders with his palms. "I am a man in its truest form. After working with you for all these years, if I were a dog I am sure a smart detective like you would've found out long ago."

"Maybe."

"This frame you're looking at is all human."

"Could be or perhaps."

"A man of flesh, muscles and bones, a fair amount of water, and of course blood gushing through my body—my veins."

"Well all right. Mister Flesh, muscles, bones and the other stuffs please go back to your desk and leave me to concentrate on my work."

"Ok, I will. But if I were a dog, and like you've said, I wouldn't have this job."

"For darn sure you wouldn't."

"Neither," he said, glancing at his desk, "such mountain of files to deal with. Just look at my desk. It is such a mess." He looked back at her. "And like I had said, I wouldn't answer the Chief but just sit there like a dog and say nothing, neither do anything. A dog does not answer to its master—never. Only reacts."

Roxanne rolled her hazel eyes, then brushed back couple of strands of her auburn hair that was dangling in front of her right eye. *Geese. Is he cracking up or what?* "Dan, will you please get yourself together. You are a detective and not a bloody dog. You are a human being and nobody forced you to commit yourself to doing this job. You are a detective by your own free will. It's beyond me why all of a sudden you have this afterlife thing crowding your thoughts."

"You are not thinking of the afterlife, but I am. Coming back as a dog is not such a bad idea. So what do you have to say about it?

"I have nothing to say Dan. It won't affect me one bit. It's your call."

"Mind you, I wouldn't want to come back as a dog to get kicked around, not just any ordinary dog, but one to be cherished by whoever owned me."

"Dan, I hope some day your wish comes through. Please don't waste anymore of my time."

Dan went back to his desk. He looked down at the files on his desk and sighed. "A dog or some dog's life is easier than this. I don't mind coming back as one of those easy living dogs." He shook his head, sat down, leaned back in the chair, lifted his legs and put them on top of the desk, crossed them at the ankles.

His chair was neither a recliner nor a rocker. He wished he had either of them instead of his straight-back chair. So he could recline or rock as he relaxed with his mind still on his afterlife thing.

He looked at Roxanne. "She's right," he said. "I am a detective, an occupation of my choosing. I had better get working on these files and put this afterlife thing on the backburner. This Shultz file is such a monumental headache, a modern-day dinosaur I wish I could get rid of as I speak." *Again, he thought of psychic detectives. That if there were any the Shultz case could've closed long ago.*

As Dan was about to take his feet off his desk, to put them back on the floor, he almost keel over. *Hmm, that is what you get from being in two minds simultaneously.*

Dan worked on his files for about half an hour. He stopped and went back to thinking about coming back as a dog. At that moment several things a dog could do, and be, entered his thoughts. And although Roxanne had told him he was wasting her time, he felt compelled to go back to her desk to share with her some of the qualities pertaining to a dog. Standing by her desk, he again reengaged her.

"Roxanne," Dan said.

"Now what?" she said, looking up at him through the corners of her hazel eyes.

"Roxanne, there are police dogs; detective dogs to name a couple, that are active in helping to solve crimes, and dogs that sits around doing nothing yet they get pampered by their owners. The latter was the kind of dog I'd said I would like to come back as. Come to think of it, being that kind of a dog would not make me a happy dog, either."

Roxanne crossed her legs at the thigh, leaned back in her chair and folded her arms across her chest. She'd begun to contemplate that Dan was taking this afterlife thing a bit too far. Nevertheless, she'd hear him out, then tell him it's the last time she wants to hear of it.

"There are guard dogs, too," she said in response. "And dogs that lead the blind so on and so forth. Dan, are you telling me you have changed you mind of not wanting to come back as a dog to be cherished?"

"Yes, Roxanne."

"Dan, don't you think the reason why you'd be cherished is because you'd bring happiness to whoever should own you?"

"I suppose so Roxanne, but being a detective I think I should come back as a detective dog; back in the—fighting against crime business—fighting against crimes of all sort and also to do what's necessary to save lives."

"You think that would make you a much happier dog?"

"Yes, a happy productive dog, and not one kept on a leach. But a free-wheeling dog with the capability to gather hidden information of cases old and new and present, and pass the information to detectives, through their minds—you'd get preferential treatment—so they could close those cases and also alert crime fighters about crimes that are in the making so they could nip it in the bud."

"Quite interesting," Roxanne said. "With you having such capability, or capabilities, mmm, I could imagine you being a very good detective dog."

"Not just a good detective dog," Dan said, "but a top detective dog. A super dog nobody had ever seen or heard of doing what he could to help detectives. Something, if you should really think about it . . . wouldn't it be something to take your breath away?"

"Indeed, Dan. Yes indeed. Do you think that could really happen in your afterlife; you coming back as a dog with such capabilities, and to roam freely on this earth?"

"All one has to do is wish fervently for it to happen, and you never know."

"So are you wishing to die?"

"No, I am not wishing to die but I am wishing to come back as a dog whenever I die."

"Um . . . Dan, did I plant something in your head when I told you I wish I could fly like a bird?"

Dan scratched his head, reflectively. "Perhaps, Roxanne. But although you'd said you would like to fly as a bird, because you could go from one place to the next without being obstructed, you did not say you wanted to die and come back as one. Anyway, just think of it. A bird would have clear advantage over a dog. A dog could only get around on all fours through the busy city streets, while encountering barriers and hazardous things, and get into buildings when assisted or where allowed. A bird could hop about in the city and fly over barriers and hazardous things. And as it is flying peek through windows of buildings from ground level to windows of the tallest buildings. A bird could hop about on the forest floor and dart effortlessly through trees in the forest. Scan Mountains and scan meadows, thus enabling it to accomplish things in a shot while a dog could only dream of accomplishing in similar period. Yes, wouldn't it be awesome—incomprehensible what a bird in its afterlife form could accomplish? You know what?" He paused for quite awhile.

"What Dan? Now what are you thinking of?"

"Instead of coming back as a dog, coming back as a bird isn't such a bad idea after all."

"And you know what, Dan?" She paused, raised her hand up to the side of her head and made circular motions with her index finger, meaning, I think you are going crazy.

Dan watched her. "I saw that gesture," he said. "No, I am not going crazy. Besides that, what was it you wanted to say? I am listening."

Roxanne smiled in amusement, a similar smile that always warmed Dan's heart since the first day he met her. "Now, Dan," she said, "whether you want to come back as a horse, a cow, a dog, a duck or any other kind of bird, from now on let it be the last time I hear of what you'd prefer to come back as in your hereafter—your afterlife, if there's one. Neither should you let the idea of yours get to the ears of the Chief or to the ears of any other person."

"If it should, I'd know how it got out," he said.

"Don't worry about me giving away your secret of wanting to come back as whatever you might choose. I am sure if anybody should hear anything such as that coming out of my mouth, about you wanting to come back as a dog or such in your afterlife, they'd think I am bordering on the side of crazy. That is something I do not want anybody to think of me. I am very happy with them thinking of me as being a sane detective." She laughed.

"Ha," Dan said. "Thinking about the afterlife does not make you insane."

"No, Dan, not at all as far as you are concerned. It depends with whom you engage with such conversation."

"All right," Dan said. "You don't want to come back as anything but coming back as a bird, a dove instead of a dog, will be just fine with me. Roxanne, case closed."

"Suit yourself, my friend. Again I'll say," Rosanna's eyes on the files, "whatever you wish to come back as has no bearing on me. It is getting close to going home time. I will tidy up, then be off. Not to any afterlife, but home."

"Partner, I hope you have a pleasant weekend."

"If all goes well there's no reason why I shouldn't. And don't you knock yourself out with that afterlife thing."

"Roxanne, if I should die this weekend you are the only one who'd know where my soul is gone, and it's mission."

"Partner, if I were you, I wouldn't count on that. I would have no idea. I've heard there is a place where human souls go to rest—but a dog's?"

Roxanne walked out of the office shaking her head.

-2-

A Dove in the Afterlife
Did Roxanne become a Psychic

THAT DAY, THE DAY Dan was so engrossed with his afterlife thing, was Friday, the last day of the workweek for both detectives. Sometimes during the week, or on some weekends when Roxanne was at home, Dan would call her to discuss certain matters, or for clarification on something he was working on, if he needed some pertinent information. So that Friday, Roxanne left the office hoping not to hear from Dan any time during the weekend. Because she feared, if he called her, he might bother her with his afterlife thing.

When Roxanne got home, she relaxed for about half an hour to forty-five minutes. She set her bath with essential herbs: drops of condiments, two litres of milk and a cup of honey. She placed a honey-scented candle on the edge of the bathtub. While having her bath she'd inhale the fragrances of all those refreshing ingredients. Bathing in such essentials, she maintained, made her skin smooth, soft, and velvety.

Each time after having her bath, she carried the candle to the dining room and put it on the dining room table. There the lit candle stayed until after she made and ate supper. She'd put the candle out before she went to her bedroom. Then she settled in bed to watch her favourite soap that recorded during her absence. After watching the soaps, she'd read something of interest until she felt it was time to put it aside. Because sleep was bearing down on her.

That Friday evening during the half an hour or so before she fell asleep, her thoughts wondered on what Dan had said to her about his afterlife idea. It entered her thoughts that Dan's afterlife idea could be according to the teachings of his religion. She was not sure what religion he practiced. Because, of all the years on the job not once had they ever discussed each other's religious beliefs.

According to her religious belief, she believed nobody ever came back in any afterlife as any creature or any other thing. She had heard of miracles, and so, if such a thing should or could ever happen, someone coming back as something else in any afterlife situation, then it would be nothing short of a miracle.

As she pondered, if it could happen, according to Dan—him coming back as whatever—and who endeavoured with his heart and soul to bring to justice anyone who defies the law, then what a tremendous secret weapon he'd be in his helping in the fight against crimes! "No," she said. "Not a chance of it happening." That was the last thing she remembered had occupied her thoughts after she woke up in the middle of the night.

It was Sunday afternoon and Roxanne's friend, Daisy, who was a few years older than Roxanne was (she could loose a few pounds, too,) called Roxanne. "Roxanne," she said. "What's up?"

"Oh hi, Daisy. I'm just taking it easy."

"I am thinking of going to the new mall to do some browsing. Probably I might find something affordable to purchase. Why don't we go together?"

Roxanne did not plan to leave her apartment any time during the weekend.

". . . don't know," Roxanne said. "After the hectic week I've had, a quiet weekend is what I'd planned on having. So far it's going accordingly."

"We'll only be out there for a couple of hours or so," Daisy said. "I wouldn't want to have a job as yours. I am satisfied with being the head of a department where the demand is not as taxing as yours. Come on, girl. Take a break from your weekend hibernation."

What the heck. "Daisy, you'll have to come and get me."

"Not a problem," Daisy said. "I'll call you when I am about to leave. See you then."

While they were browsing in the mall they stopped at a small store. The sign board, black letters on yellow background, read, Dan's Corner. Everything for two bucks each.

"Let's go in." Daisy said. "Two bucks per item? We shouldn't have any problem in finding something affordable."

When Roxanne saw the name Dan, her partner rushed into her thoughts. She almost told Daisy about the conversation she had with Dan concerning his afterlife affair. If she'd done so, she would be dishonouring the code of secrecy. Anyhow, she said, "Daisy, do you believe there's a hereafter or afterlife?"

"Why do you ask?"

"Do you believe there's such a thing?"

"Well, if there is such a thing I wouldn't know. Neither have I ever given it any thought. Why?" Daisy was curious why all of a sudden her friend asked her that out of the ordinary question.

"Just thought I'd ask if you believe there's such a thing; according to what someone had said to me the other day."

"Do you believe there is?"

"No Daisy, I don't."

"Neither do I. So stop thinking about such nonsense and let's go in and shop."

Daisy spent more than a couple of bucks.

"You did not buy anything," she said to Roxanne. "Didn't you see anything you could use?"

"I saw lots of things I could buy, but I am not here to shop. I came along to keep you company, to stop you from overspending."

"Daisy laughed. "I saved you that hassle, didn't I? Because I only spent six bucks plus tax."

"That's what I call smart shopping," Roxanne said.

They browsed some more but did not buy anything else. They went home.

When Roxanne walked into the office Monday morning, handbag between her left side and her left elbow, slung from her shoulder by a one-inch strap, Dan was already there.

"Good morning partner," she said. "How was your weekend?"

"It was quiet. And yours?"

"Mine, too, was relatively quiet."

Roxanne waited to hear if he'd bring up the afterlife thing, but Dan said not a word about it. Only, today is the start of another workweek.

"So it is," Roxanne said.

Although Dan said nothing concerning the afterlife matter, his strong, gravely voice resonating through Roxanne's ears, caused her to feel she had him in the dark about why she did not believe in his afterlife rhetoric. She was not the one to get involved in any discussion concerning religion, because she thought it was a very controversial subject. That it was always quite difficult to sway one from what he or she believed in. Unless Dan brought the subject up again, she'd let it rest where it had ended over the weekend. She also knew, out of mutual respect, when Dan said he'd put something to rest, he'd not resurrect it unless it was absolutely necessary.

Roxanne held the handbag, slipped its strap from off of her shoulder and dropped it on the desk. "Partner, it is such a beautiful morning."

"Indeed it is," Dan said.

"Have you been to see Chief Traverse?"

"No, partner," Dan said. "I got here just a couple of minutes before you."

"Well, partner, let's check with the Chief to find out what assignment he has for us today."

"I suppose we should," Dan said. He was almost staring at Roxanne.

"Dan, is something wrong?" Roxanne said.

"Who said anything's wrong."

"Your face, Dan. It's on your face."

"If the look on my face indicates to you something's wrong, it could be from your misinterpretation. Or probably I am worried about the way the Chief might react to us this morning, after what he said to us Friday when he said 'Now get out of my office, you—', I wonder what he was about to say next."

"We won't know now, will we? Dan, if you really want to know, ask him."

"Are you serious?"

"Dan, you are the one who's curious to know what he had on his mind. Ask him about it when we go to see him."

The door to Chief Traverse's office was ajar when the detectives went to see him. Out of courtesy, Roxanne tapped softly on the door. They went in.

"Chief, good morning," Roxanne said.

"Good morning to you, too."

Dan said the same and the Chief responded likewise.

The Chief asked how they'd spent their weekend. Both detectives gave almost similar answers. Roxanne said hers was relatively quietly. Dan said his was quiet, too.

Chief Traverse smiled. "Well, I did better than you. I went to a barbecue. I enjoyed myself because I like steak and the barbecued steak was succulent. Anyhow, I haven't any new assignment for you today. You went back to the Shultz files on Friday, didn't you? After that botched stake out?"

"Yes Sir," Dan said.

"Go over that file again and again. I don't care if you have to go over it a hundred times more. I feel there's something hidden somewhere in that file that could help us. Work on it detectives. Go back and keep working on it."

"Yes Sir," Roxanne said. "We are already giving it our best shot."

"Please give it more than your best shot," Chief Traverse said.

They parted company with the Chief and Dan said to Roxanne, "The Chief was in a very good mood. Just thinking of the succulent steak he said he had at the barbecue," Dan rubbed his palms together, "makes me salivate."

"Dan, he was in a very good mood, wasn't he? I guess you were salivating so much you did not remember to ask him what you wanted to ask. To get an answer to satisfy your, should I say, your starving curiosity."

"If I did I might've ruffled his feathers. I am not that worried to know about what he had on his mind. It's best to let a sleeping dog lie."

"What? Now the Chief is a dog?"

"No, Roxanne. I didn't mean it the way you're assuming."

"Partner, I'm just kidding."

Monday to Thursday of that week, Roxanne and Dan studied the Shultz case files just as diligently as they had always done. Corroborating with each other, to find out if either one of them missed the simplest of thing that could help their cause. But they were neither here nor there. Everything remained the same, the same for as long as they had been working on that dreary case.

Thursday afternoon Roxanne pulled out the smiling picture of Mr Shultz, from next to the bottom of the files. She gazed at the picture more intently than she had ever done before. She shook her head from side to side, wondering as to why anybody would take the life of another person, with such a heart-warming smile. Still shaking her head from the sadness she felt, she whispered—more like talking to herself, "He was a very wealthy man. But not one of those wealthy men who kept their riches only for themselves and their families, but one who gave freely to others; the ultimate charitable person whose life was snuffed out of his body. Then the body was set on fire. It was such a disgusting inhumane act. The person, or could be persons, who committed that act knew exactly what they were doing because the fire wiped out any useful evidence. Well, the way I see it, to crack this case let alone to solve it, we need more help than we've already had. Yes, much more help including help (*of a clairvoyant, according to Dan?*) or help from God who created us all." She shuffled in her chair, put her left hand to the side of her face, and she sighed. "I just cannot understand why anybody takes a life; a life, when taken can never be brought back by anyone. I am a detective and there are rules I must adhere to, if I want to stay on this job. God gives us Ten Commandments, rules to live by in our everyday dealing with others; rules such as 'thou shalt not kill; though shalt not steal; love thy neighbour as thyself, rules some humans ignores from time to time. If everyone should comply with these rules I wouldn't be here, and having this difficulty, figuring out how to find a darn murderer."

Still studying his face, Roxanne's thoughts shifted to his family—as she had done several times before—of his wife and the two young children he left behind. A detective is not supposed to get emotional, nevertheless Roxanne was. She also thought of what had happened to Mr Simpson, the man from her hometown.

"Oh how they (the Shultz family) must still be grieving," she said. "How wonderful it could be if we cared for each other as we should, and make the best with whatever the Good Lord gives to us all."

Roxanne put the picture down and walked over to Dan's desk. "Dan," she said, "something crossed my mind about this case, the Shultz case we're still working on."

"Something like what?" Dan said.

"We have been working on this case for quite a long time, including most of this week. We just keep going over these burred edges files without any success."

"Yes, we have. Don't forget last week we took a break from it."

"Might as well we did not go on that mission, because of the way it turned out. Anyway, it crossed my mind we should ask the Chief to relieve us of this case, then sometimes later approach it from a different angle, like coming back to it fresh. Maybe this time while we are away from it, who knows, something could happen to help us with our investigating, something we could use when we come back to it. Dan, we are entangled and I am getting weary of this case. It is not a good thing to be happening. What do you say?"

Dan smiled. "I say this is where a psychic detective would come in handy."

Roxanne looked at him curiously. "Yes maybe, but you know that's not possible. Dan, it was the hereafter as a dog or maybe a bird, now back to psychic detective? It's not funny. So please stop your kidding around."

"All right then. Anyway, I am getting weary of this case, too. Roxanne," he paused. He rubbed his palms together, then he made fists and tapped the knuckles of his fists together gently. He undid one fist and used the other to jab in the palm of his other hand, shifting the action from one palm to the other. "Roxanne, it's a darn good idea."

"So, tomorrow we'll ask the Chief? All right, Dan?"

"All right Roxanne. Let's try it and see what happens."

The strain of frustration, concerning the Shultz case, showed on Roxanne's face; hazard look about her eyes, yet, with all the frustration her face entailed, to Dan, she was still beautiful.

Sitting there, looking at her, Dan thought, this is one time I wish I'd gone and came back as a dove, having the ability to help folks like us, who are having difficulty in trying to solve cases such as this. And although I hope to live a long life, one never knows; because I am here this minute and before the minute is over I could be called away to the beyond. Hence it's like here today and could be gone tomorrow or the day after that. Nobody knows his or her own fate. Whenever I should leave this world, I definitely want to come back as a dove in a blue coat of fine feathers, similar to my blue suit; to have the special ability to help fight against crime and, lawbreakers beware. Because there wouldn't be any place anywhere to accommodate you where you could not be found, then brought to justice to answer to the crime you'd committed. And his case that is causing us such headache is the first case I'd help to solve.

"Dan." Roxanne said, interrupting his thoughts, "do you think I am pretty?"

Dan, with raised brows, wondered for a few second before attempting to provide her with an answer, because he was taken aback, a bit, as to the reason for her asking him such an obvious question. So without prolonging what he was juggling up in his mind to say, he said. "Do I think you are pretty?"

"Yes, Dan, do you?"

"Yes, you are not only pretty, but you are also stunningly beautiful and very smart. The first day I saw you . . ."

"Yes Dan, I knew from the first day you saw me—Dan, the first day you saw me I saw a surprised look on your face, let's say, a look of disbelief. I knew from that day the Chief introduced me, to you, as your partner, you had began to think why a pretty person like me (and she was not flattering herself, because as Dan said, she was stunningly beautiful and Charley and others thought so, too) is a detective?"

"Yes Roxanne," Dan said, with a couple of jerky nod of his head. "I had wondered and still wondering."

"Why didn't you ask me? Were you afraid of the answer you might've gotten, or that you would hurt my feelings?" *When is he going tell me about his wife?*

"Roxanne, I have been around long enough to know, or believe, everyone (and from remembering what you'd said a while ago) has a reason for choosing his or her profession. Anyway, since we are on the subject, and I won't feel as if I am probing you, why did you choose to be a detective?"

"I grew up in a farming town, or village, with a population of about three to four thousand. We had more convenience stores than traditional stores. Mr Simpson, a good friend of our family had a family of three boys and a wife. He owned and operated one of those convenience stores. His was the largest in the area. Every Christmas he held a huge Christmas party outside his store for folks of Farmers Corner."

"Roxanne I am beginning to envision your Mr Simpson as being a stalwart person in the community."

"Of course, he was. He was also loved, according to what I believed then, by just about everyone. There was not a mean bone in him. I always liked going to his store ever since I was a child—"

"When I was a child I had a place to go such as that, too."

". . . because, he always had treats for me. He was humorous, too. One day, I was about fourteen or fifteen Mama sent me to his store. I was expecting to see his face, with that flashy smile greeting me. When I did not see him I called out, Mr Simpson I am here! Where are you? He did not answer me. Someone else walked in the store, and I turned around to look at him. Then as I looked back to see if Mr Simpson would appear I heard the person say "What's that?" He was pointing in the direction he had set his eyes. I looked down and saw a pair of legs on the floor, sticking out from behind the counter. Those legs were the legs of Mr Simpson. I bent over and took a closer look at him; his head was severely bashed in."

"Wow! Roxanne, it must have been traumatic for you."

"To say how I felt could take forever. Dan, I could go on and on. Four years after his gruesome murder, I was about nineteen, investigating detectives were not any closer to find the culprit responsible for his demise. I could not understand why they were having such difficulties. It was then I decided to take up law enforcing. Because if I was a detective on that case I felt I would've done much better."

"Much better," Dan said. "Much better huh, like in finding Mr Simpson's killer? Like how quickly those concerned find killers on TV shows?"

"Yes Dan, something like that but not exactly. Those shows, as you and I know, are not the real deal. Only make believe. Anyway, up to the time when I left my town, nothing about the case concerning Mr Simpson had changed. Not even as I am speaking to you. The case became a cold case."

"Like some of those cases we've had to put aside."

"Yes, Dan, I suppose so. However, after I became a detective I realized those detectives were working their puts off with no positive results. Because with all the techniques detectives are taught to use when they go to solve cases, he or she needs some luck. Luck such as a ton of insightful help from others. A detective's work is not easy. Nothing is cut and dry as I had imagined."

Friday morning they went to the Chief with their proposal. They did not demand he allow them to set the case aside for awhile, maybe longer than for awhile, although that was what they really had intended. They showed him how they felt, being on the case for so long, without making any progress. And with all their studying of the files pertaining to the case they were no further ahead than when they'd begun. They hoped he would understand.

Chief Traverse listened carefully to what they had to say, but he did not make a decision at that particular time. He told them he'd sit on their proposals for a day or two before making any decision.

While they waited for the Chief to make a decision they stayed on the case-files, frustrated though they were.

It was Wednesday the following week, after they'd waited for three workdays, when the Chief walked into their office. He looked down at the files in front of them. "Although you'd asked to be relieved of this case I see you're still at it."

"Chief," Roxanne said, "until you say otherwise we'll just keep working on it."

"Yes, sir," Dan said. "Sir, we are just following your instruction."

"Detectives, sometimes some cases give us huge headaches. We work with what information we have but to no avail. I know what it feels like. So after listening to your request and ruminated over it several times, I came to the conclusion . . ."

Chief Traverse's pause, a pause which seemed like eternity to both detectives.

Now what? Roxanne thought. This does not look good to me. Will he leave us to torture ourselves with this case or will he let us set it aside?

Then the Chief said, he was not smiling anymore, "Pack up the file for this case and set it aside."

"Thank you Sir," Dan said. The expression on his face portrayed to the Chief that he, Dan, was happy about the Chief's s decision. Relieved. *Whew, it is such a tremendous relief.*

"Detective, there's no need for you to be happy about it. There are plenty of other cases to keep you busy. Maybe some of them, I feel, could bring us success without frustrating you, like some others had and also this case."

"Dan," Roxanne said, after the Chief left their office, "although we are tired of studying this case I wish we could've done a better job of it. For that dead man and his family, and brought the culprit to justice."

"Me, too," Dan said. "Roxanne, I have the strong feeling this is not the last we'll see of this case. This case probably reminds you of what had happened with your Mr Simpson, doesn't it?"

"Yes, it does. And when we eventually come back to it, I won't give up until I have it closed."

"You can also count on me. Because I'll be there with you each step of the way. "Roxanne—"

"Yes, Dan," she said, interrupting his long pause.

"Well, I hope I won't be overstating, but over the years, might I say, I have been enjoying the partnership of this beautiful detective and her camaraderie."

"Dan, I know."

"Furthermore, you became my partner when I was gong through a very difficult time in my life. I was still mourning my wife. It was about three years since she'd passed away. She died from leukaemia."

Whew, Roxanne blew out silently, secrets. After all these years he finally speaks of her.

"She was the best partner one cold ever had. When she died, I almost went out of my mind. I miss her so much, even to this day." He swallowed. "Even to this day I'm still missing her. I was happy then that you became my partner, because just having you around made me feel much better. Thanks for being my Partner."

"I knew about her," Roxanne said.

"You knew about her?"

"Yes. The Chief told me."

"Why didn't you say anything to me about it?"

"Although I knew about it, I told myself I'd say nothing unless you brought it up, because I figured you'd bring it up when the time was right."

"I suppose you were right," Dan said.

"Well, partner, although it has been years, my belated condolence."

"Thank you very much."

"Well, later."

Dan observed, amusingly, as Roxanne walked away with firm, even, commanding strides.

For about a year Roxanne and Dan were busy trying to solve other cases. As it always happened, they had success with a few cases and others they did not.

One day, the two detectives were on street mission. Dan reached into his jacket pocket for the piece of paper he wrote the address on, to confirm if they were just about at the right address. While he looked up at the number signs, someone rushed out of a clothing store, another in hot pursuit balling out, `Thief! . . . Thief! Somebody stop that thief."

If Dan saw the alleged thief or heard the bawling of the one doing the chase, nobody will ever know. Because the thief collided with Dan, with the same breathtaking speed, he was running at, and his momentum sent Dan flying into the path of a fast moving four-by-four Cherokee vehicle.

Realizing what had happened; the driver of the Cherokee stopped. He went back to the scene to investigate. He slapped the heel of his palm on his forehead as he looked helplessly at Dan lying on the pavement. "I did not see him," he said. "It happened so fast. Is he alive? Good Lord, I am so sorry I ran him over. Did I kill him?"

"It's not your fault," Roxanne said. She was on her knees, bending over Dan. "Partner," she said, "you'll be all right. Just hang in there."

"Roxanne, I am hurting so bad. I bet if I were a dove I could've winged myself out of his bath."

"That is, if you'd seen him coming. Sometimes the wings of a bird don't save it from certain disaster."

"Roxanne, I still wish I were a bird. I'll be all right. You'll be all right."

Those words were the last words Roxanne heard from Dan. He fell into unconsciousness.

"Somebody please call an ambulance!" Roxanne shrieked, as the crowd swelled. Just as she said that, she remembered she had a cell phone. She plucked it from its case and dialled 911. "Send ambulance to . . ." She told the dispatcher the name of the Street, the number of the building they were in front of, and the closest intersection. After she called for an ambulance she phoned the station and informed them—"Officer down."

Something strange happened while Dan lay on the pavement, as Roxanne stroked the sides of his face gently, one side and then the next.

"Oh my God!" she said. "What is this I am seeing? Is my mind playing tricks on me? Oh my God, no! What could that be?"

Roxanne was dumfounded as she saw a transparent figure oozed from Dan's body, which caused her to straighten up while still kneeling beside him. First, she thought the figure looked like a dog, then it seemed to have change and resembled a bird in flight.

Roxanne gazed in awe at the transparent figure as it ascended. "Did you see that?"

"Yes," a husky voice in the crowd provided an answer. "That thing is his soul; on its way to heaven where it will lay to rest for eternity."

"His soul," Roxanne whispered. "I am confused, because I could swear I saw more than one figure. That person must've perceived it as only one. Maybe he is right. My mind could be playing tricks on me."

By the time backup came on the scene, Roxanne and Dan were on their way to the hospital.

The paramedics were very busy administering to Dan, who was labouring to breathe even though he had had oxygen mask on.

Roxanne, fearing Dan was on the verge of losing his life, held his hand all the way to the hospital, encouraging him to hold on. Imploring Dan, the best way she could, to keep his eyes open. "Fight it, Dan." she said. "Fight it. You're strong. Fight it to stay alive. You can't leave us now. I still need a good partner. The good partner you are."

Roxanne called the station again, from the hospital's emergency. Within minutes the Chief showed up. "How is he doing?"

"I don't know. All I know he is hurt bad. Doctors are with him."

Just as the Chief said, "I hope he makes it", someone in green clothing, white mask below his chin, pushed open one-half of the double-sided door and came out. The doctor did not have to ask who is here with this patient, because Roxanne approached him and asked, nervously, "Doc, how is he? How did it go? Is he all right?"

The doctor shook his head sadly, while trying not to show any emotion.

"Doc, please? Please tell me he'll be all right."

The doctor looked away then looked back at Roxanne and the Chief. "We tried doing all we could for him," he said. "I am sorry. He did not make it."

Roxanne hung her head. A tear fell.

Chief Traverse consoled her. "He died in the line of duty. He'll be sadly missed. Let's go home. There isn't anything we can do for him. May God bless his soul?"

Not long after they had laid Dan to his final resting place, Roxanne got a new partner—William (Will) Dixon. He was a detective in his third year of duty. He, too, of course, was enamoured with Roxanne's charm: Her beauty, her work ethics, and her captivating smile that had always warmed Dan's heart.

"What was your partner like?" the robust broad face, Will, who had a habit of twitching the left side of his mouth every now and then, asked Roxanne.

"He was gentle, caring, understanding, stern, and never the one to put up with any nonsense. He was never one to frown or take his responsibilities lightly, neither was he one to quit regardless of how difficult the task might've been."

"I hope I will be able to fill his shoes," Will said.

"Don't try to fill his shoes," Roxanne said. "Just be yourself and everything should be all right. As far as I am concerned, nobody could fill Dan's shoes. He was the ultimate detective. Do you understand what I'm saying?"

"I suppose so."

"Now, he was the ultimate detective. And a word of the wise to you. I don't like people who procrastinate; neither had Dan and I ever fabricated information to deceive others or made ourselves look good no matter how difficult a situation we found ourselves in."

Hmm! I had better be careful with the way I go about doing business. "You've said, I should not try to fill his shoes but one has to try."

"Will, my advice to you is, just be yourself."

Six months after Dan's passing, Roxanne sat at her desk and the Shultz case came into her thoughts. The day before she'd had a very busy, exhausting day and also she did not have her usual hours of sleep, and even though she fought to keep her eyes open, she dosed off. When she jumped out of the short dose, she thought the dream she had was a very strange dream. What could be the meaning of her dream?

In the dream, she was at some place she did not recognise. But this place, like a dome with its dazzling beauty, left her breathless. Besides the dazzling beauty of the place, she saw several small houses with various colours. And as if a voice was speaking to her, which she perceived came from above; she looked up and saw a solitary dove in a coat of blue feathers hovering high up. The dove's voice told her to open the door of the small house in front of her.

The door, Roxanne thought, where is it? Oh, there it is.

When she reached for the door, while bending forward, instead of touching the doorknob she noticed, to her amazement, a file folder was in her hand. The open folder had burred edges of paper similar to some pages in the Shultz case file. While she contemplated the mysterious file—and she couldn't tell how it got in her hand—, she heard, echoed in her mind: *Roxanne, you are looking in the wrong place. Investigate O.P. You'll find the answer. The answer concerning Mr Shultz is within us.*

O.P.? Roxanne contemplated. Who is this O.P.? They are initials. But are they the initials of a man or a woman?

Roxanne thought the dream was nothing but a silly dream in the middle of the afternoon. That most times whenever someone had a dream the dream was always about the last thing on his or her mind before falling asleep. She felt, although she was mesmerized in the dream, she should've been left in that beautiful place a while longer so she could explore.

Although Roxanne did not put any meaning to the dream she had, for days the dream and its main points reoccurred in her thoughts: *Looking in the wrong place; investigate O.P.; the answer is within us?* "I can't understand it but something is telling me . . . there must be something to this dream. What it could be I have absolutely no idea. But I've heard it said daydreams are the truest of all dreams."

During this time, not once did Dan and his afterlife ambitions entered Roxanne's thoughts, although he'd told her he wanted to come back as a dove instead of a dog, his final request; He did not say he'd like to come back as a dove in a coat of blue feathers. Therefore, a dove in a coat of blue feathers did nothing whatsoever to cause Roxanne to think of Dan. However, something about Dan entered her thoughts vaguely, about when he'd said he wished there were psychic detectives. Now she wished there were psychic detectives she could consult, or someone to interpret her dream instead of her worrying what the dream could mean.

One day during Roxanne's lunch break, the dream she had and the Shultz case weighed heavily on mind. And, behaving as though she was driven by some unknown force, she went to the archive and took the files concerning the case. "What it is I am looking for," she said, "I'm not sure. The Chief will be mad at me but I have this feeling, according to my dream, something is in this file that'll help us." However, while scrutinizing the case files she kept thinking of the initials O.P.

Roxanne did not have enough time during her break to go through the entire file, as she wanted to. So she took it home, studied it until late into the night, then she began to fathom the dream.

The initials O.P.—Olive Presley, who detested with a passion folks whom are evasive—was mentioned only once in the files. She should've been one of the investigating officers of the case. She declined for personal reasons.

Although Olive Presley, a high ranked police officer, and Roxanne, worked from out of the same huge complex at Wilson Street, Roxanne barely knew Olive. Now, according to what her dream lead her to discover, she'd figured that somehow she'd have to find ways to get closer to Olive.

What was her personal reason? Roxanne thought, to cause her to back out from investigating the case. So now that she had the inkling, according to her dream, that Olive Presley could be involved—Roxanne was yet to speak with Olive—in one way or another in the demise of Mr Shultz, how could she go to the Chief and tell him they should investigate Olive Presley. Because a bird in a dream she had caused her to come to that conclusion. The Chief would think she was going off her rockers. Furthermore, she went back to the files without permission from the Chief. But after giving some careful thoughts to the dilemma she found herself in, she eventually went to the Chief and told him she had reason to cause her to believe they should investigate Olive Presley, concerning the Shultz case.

"Investigate Olive Presley," Chief Traverse said. "Why should we? What's your reason? Olive has been on the force for years, with an impeccable record. I need more than that to even think of starting investigative work on her, concerning the Shultz case or any other case for that matter."

"Yes Sir, I understand, but I still believe she is somehow involved. That's the reason, I believe, was the reason for her opting out from not getting involved with the investigating of the case."

Chief Traverse studied Roxanne's face. *If she did not have good reason, she wouldn't be here asking me to go after Olive.* "Are you sure," he said, "about your good reason?"

Roxanne did not say, yes, she was sure neither did she say she was unsure.

"Are you sure we should investigate Olive?" Chief Traverse said again. "Have you spoken with her?"

"No Sir," I am not altogether sure. Neither have I spoken with her." She was itching to tell him about the dream she had. But how could she? She felt he'd classify her dream as being nothing short of quite amusing.

"Detective, your good reason is neither here nor there."

"But it is worth a try. Don't you think so, Chief Traverse?"

"I know the case has been a headache for everyone concerned. I won't go after Olive because of you telling me you have good reason, with no substance. Detective, I know I would be laughed at. I am the Chief and I have to be practical, wouldn't you agree?"

Disappointment was evident in Roxanne's voice as she said, "Yes, sir, Chief. I understand."

Anyhow, with the information she had received from her dream, Roxanne was determined to press forward. Now she'd do her level best to get real acquainted with Olive instead of just a passing-glance acquaintance. Her dream had allowed her to ajar a door. She must open that door wide and see what's hidden behind it. That door was Olive Presley's.

Therefore, in her bid to get closer to Olive, Roxanne began going out of her way to accomplish the task. Every chance she got she waved to Olive when she saw her beyond speaking distance; slowed her movement to say hi, with a friendly smile, when she saw her and they were at comfortable speaking range. Then one day Roxanne began to see signs that the seeds she'd sown was nearing harvesting, when she met Olive in the long corridor on the second floor at Headquarters. She was happy the conversation went a bit further than a quick few words. However just as Olive was about to walked away, Roxanne shot an invitation at her. "I was going for a coffee," Roxanne said. "How about joining a fellow officer?"

The tall outgoing police officer, who was always conscious about her attire, pushed her hands down the side of her uniform trousers, as if trying to get rid of creases. Every stitch had to be in place whether it was for work or other activities. She was also very active in her community; admired by adults, loved by children, and well respected among her peers. So she said to Roxanne, "Um, thanks for the offer, but not today. Anyway, we could do that tomorrow. Downstairs at the cafeteria about this time, okay?"

"You're on," Roxanne said. *Now that comes tomorrow I should make my first step into the door of your mind, I have to tread softly because conversational mines could be lurking.*

On that day of their first coffee date, Roxanne was tempted to tell Olive that she, Roxanne, knew she Olive, was somehow involved in the demise of Mr shultz. Nevertheless, anxious though she was, she'd questioned Olive subtlety concerning the case. After each conversation, Roxanne logged whatever she figured was important.

After they'd had a few more, having coffee, dates, to Roxanne's delight Olive invited her to lunch.

"Where?" Roxanne asked.

"Do you have a favourite place you frequent to have lunch?" Olive asked.

'Well," she began to ponder.

"All right then, how about us going to Charley's restaurant? I frequent that place because I like the food."

"Oh, Charley's restaurant?" Roxanne said.

'You answer as if you know about that place."

"I'd gone there a long time ago, before I lost my partner. The steak dinner I had then was very good." She did not bother with any other details. Going there for lunch, she thought, would be the first time since the last time Dan and I were there.

"Well you know what I'm talking about. Why I frequent Charley's restaurant."

They set the time for their lunch date.

That day, before they went to lunch, Roxanne armed herself with a tape recorder. After they finished their meals, both women went into a lengthy conversation, but Roxanne stayed away from mentioning anything concerning Mr Shultz. But she cunningly pulled a rabbit out of the hat she hoped would lead up to her getting positive feedback, concerning what she was hoping to hear. She began talking about men, and the reason why she kept them at arm's length because of what they had done to her. *Truth or not truth was anybody's guess.* She could tell Olive was intrigued. Bit by bit Olive responded with interesting comments, until the conversation got to a point where Olive was revealing to Roxanne almost everything about what men had done to her, too.

Aha, Roxanne thought, harvest time.

Olive mentioned Mr Shultz, but stopped immediately after she said how she'd met him. Because she felt anything said about him could implicate her. However she finished by saying, "Men promise you the world, but once they got what they wanted they treat you like garbage. I have tried trusting in them, but I will never trust another man again."

During this time, Olive did not know Roxanne was recording the conversation on tape. Roxanne wanted the conversation to continue.

"Mr Shultz was such a charitable man," Roxanne said.

"Of course he was," Olive continued. "He gave a lot to those who needed his help, but he made promises to someone such as me that he was very reluctant to keep."

"So you were involved with him in one way or another?"

"I did not say I was, so don't go putting words in my mouth. He was my friend and I am sorry about what happened to him. As I sit here, his death is still haunting me. Although I was asked I could not investigate who or what led to his demise. Every time I thought of what they say led to his demise, I suffered some more."

"All right," Roxanne said. "He was your friend, wasn't he? Don't you think we should do all we can to bring to justice whoever is responsible for taking his life? Why do you say his death is haunting you?"

"Rich men and their money," Olive said softly. "They used and abused you. I am a law-abiding person, and one whose job it is to make sure others abide by the law. But there are times when enough is enough. You know, whenever someone has been mistreated, or manipulated, by someone who believes he could do no wrong because of his money power discontent develops followed by serious consequences. And more often than not, the person who was on the receiving end counters irrationally only to regret his or her action." She paused then said under her breath, "May Stanley Shultz, that Manipulator, rest in peace."

"Olive, what was it you just said regarding Mr Shultz?"

"I said may that Manipulator rest in peace." *Nobody knows the hurt that man put on me. God knows nobody but me.* "Anyway Roxanne, enough about men for today, agree?"

Roxanne shrugged. "I suppose so."

"Well, shall we go? I have a little mater to tend to before the day is done."

Roxanne did not mind. She already got what she wanted from Olive.

The next day Olive sat in her cruiser, her police car, and something regarding the conversation she had with Roxanne at lunch the previous day entered her thoughts. She began to wonder. "I know she's a clever detective. Hey! Was she cunningly interrogating me yesterday? Did I let my emotion cause me to say more than I should've said? God, I hope I did not say anything that could implicate me. Was she fishing? If she were, why would she? Oh God, now to think of it, I hope she wasn't. Did I talk myself into a trap, an ambush? Comes to think of it, and I never thought of it during our conversation yesterday, hadn't she been fishing according to some indirect questions she'd asked me on those coffee dates concerning Mr Shultz? Yes, I wonder."

That Olive would find out sometimes later, if she did or did not give ammunition to Roxanne, to use against her.

Several times Roxanne went over the taped conversation, between herself and Olive.

"Why did she," Roxanne said, "find it convenient to separate herself from the investigation, and according to what she'd said, why did she say he was a manipulator—a Manipulator? What does she know about Mr Shultz's demise that she could be hiding? What will the Chief say when I go back to him with this new information? I know I taped the information I have. If he ask me, if

Olive knew I was taping her, should I say yes or no? Only if he asks to hear the tape will I present it."

Roxanne went back to the Chief. She told him she secured new information on the Shultz case. Would he give a listening ear to what she had gathered?

"If it's about Olive," he said abruptly, with a wave of the hand, "I don't want to hear it."

"Strangely enough, Chief, it's about Olive. We were at lunch and she said things to me concerning Mr Shultz that made me wonder."

"She did, did she?"

"Yes, Chief. She did" Roxanne could tell the Chief was contemplating.

"Detective Green, I know you're still concerned about the Shultz case. Even though I told you months before Dan had passed away to give the case a rest. In recent weeks, however, without me sending you back to study that file, you came to me and told me you have reason to believe Olive is involved. Nevertheless, this time I am prepared to give you the benefit of the doubt. So what new information do you have to disclose to me concerning the case, and Olive's involvement?"

Yes! Yes! YES! "I was not probing her," Roxanne said. *But she was.* "We talked about different things, then, when the Shultz case came up, she said something about him that caused me to believe that, where she's concerned, something is amiss."

"Something amiss like what, detective?"

Roxanne told the Chief what she and Olive talked about concerning the Shultz case, and that she could not understand why Olive referred to him as a 'manipulator.'"

"You have to have something more concrete. Something more than just a simple, innocent conversation—merely chitchats—between a detective and a police. A detective who believes the police is involved, but the police is not telling all she knows. Roxanne, you are a good detective but you have to give me more than just a conversation between you and Olive. If you can't, then I won't listen."

Roxanne had the tape of the conversation in her pocket. She contemplated that by revealing the taped conversation that she'd taped without Olive's knowledge, was entrapment. However, she would play it for the Chief to prove her point, and wait to hear what he'd say about it.

The Chief swivelled in his chair, slowly, one way then the next, while he reluctantly listened to the taped conversation. Then he ceased swivelling before the tape stopped. He pushed back in his chair. He did not look directly at Roxanne, as he said, "You have enough information here we could use to go after her. Did you tell her you were taping the conversation?"

Roxanne formed a fist, *oh no!* She hit her right thigh softly with her fist, because she knew she'd done something unethical; she must declare it. "Sir, she was not aware."

"Well, detective, it's no good."

Roxanne's heart sank. "Chief, the information we have on this tape indicates to us she is somehow involved." *Oh gawd what more car I do?*

"Detective, you taped the conversation without her knowledge. It is no good. You should've known better."

"Chief, I know I should've known better. Nevertheless, we, or you could call her in and prod her discretely. Pretend you know more about her and her involvement with the deceased Mr Shultz than she led us to believe, and observe her behaviour while she's being questioned. Or when you talk with her?"

"I suppose we could chance it, but I don't believe I should. Leave the situation with me. I'll think what to do next."

Several weeks went by since Roxanne left the situation with the Chief to think about it. And during that wait she and Olive still had coffee dates. Now and then, the subject concerning Mr Shultz was sparse.

Not getting a feedback from the Chief, Roxanne wondered what was going on. Burning with the desire to know whether he'd use the information she had given him, she braved herself and confronted him. His answer did not satisfy her anticipation. She left his office still wondering. She was bewildered.

Another week went by and Chief Traverse called Roxanne to his office. "Detective . . . ." His long pause worried her.

"Yes Sir, she said, and she waited with nervous anticipation for him to go on.

"Detective Green . . . ." He paused again, not as long as before. "Detective Green, I've sat long enough on the taped information you gave me concerning Olive. If she's involved any at all, I am the first who'd like to know. Although it would please me to know she's not involved, I am very reluctant to use the information you gave me. The information I heard in the taped conversation between you and her . . ."

"Chief . . ."

"Please hear me out, detective. Now, to use the information, given the way you obtained it, makes me as unethical as you. Although my head could be on the chopping block, reluctant though I am, I am willing to chance it."

That was good news to Roxanne. A rush went through her body. She was so excited she felt as if she could jump out of her chair to give him a hug and a kiss.

"Detective, I know you are delighted over my decision. So you must swear this decision I've made today won't go beyond the grey walls of this office. Whichever way it turns out, not a word should come out of your mouth about it for as long as you live or until you and I are dead. Do you understand detective Green?"

"Yes sir, I understand clearly! Clearly, sir. Very, very clearly."

"Very well, I hope it's not lip service. I will speak with Olive, soon."

Roxanne would wait, impatiently, yet anxiously to hear the result.

Chief Traverse, not knowing what to expect from Olive, summoned her to his office. He asked her how she was doing, if she'd taken her vacation as yet. He touched on other topics he thought might interest her, while edging his way to the Shultz case.

Meantime, Olive was contemplating why she was in his office. Because to her recollection she'd done nothing to give him cause to call her in. She wondered where he was going as he touched on some cases she dealt with in the past. She was also hoping he would not mention the Shultz case.

To Olive's dismay, the Chief brought up the Shultz case but he did not mention conversations he had with Roxanne. Only that from revisiting and studying the case files he believed the reason for her opting out of the investigating process was not because of personal reason as she'd stated, and he was of the impression she was withholding information pertinent to the case. If it was so, he wondered what it could be and if she was in anyway involved.

Olive became jittery when the Chief mentioned about Mr Shultz. *Chrise, he's getting to me.* Olive began to bite into her nails; first the nail of her index finger on her right hand, then switched the action to the one on her left hand.

Chief Traverse could tell she was uncomfortable, nervous, by her chewing on her nails, and the pushing forward and backward of her upper body, in her chair. He saw pimples of perspiration on her forehead when she removed her cap, and he felt something was tormenting her on the inside.

"Olive, are you all right?"

"Why do you ask that of me?"

"You are uncomfortable, aren't you?"

"I need some fresh air."

"Olive you've been in this office more times than I can remember. Never once had I seen you behaving the way you are behaving now. Is anything wrong?"

Olive stood up. She used one hand to spin her cap around the fingers of her other hand. She thought of Roxanne. *Am I in here because of that detective? He cannot say I personally gave him reason to call me in this office so he could quiz me as if I am a suspect. I refuse to put up with anymore of this crap any longer.* "Chief may I go?"

He could not detain her any longer, but he'd let her leave with something to think about.

"Olive," Chief Traverse said, "every living human has a conscience, and that inner voice has a way to torment each soul until they own up to the wrong, or good, they'd done. Yes, you may go."

After the meeting with the Chief, Olive began to have difficulty in concentrating the way she should on her everyday task. Each time someone asked her if everything was all right, and she looked the person in the eyes, she felt as if the person knew she was hiding something. So then, was something happening to her according to Chief Traverse's reminder about 'that inner voice thing'? That invisible tormentor? Could it be that her conscience had begun to slowly eating away at her?

Regardless of what it was that made Olive feel uncomfortable, she kept assuring herself that no one has anything on her. The Chief is only speculating. Because if anyone had, including the Chief, why only now after all this time the Chief takes it up on himself to question her concerning the case? As long as I keep my mouth shut, nobody will be able to corner me. *Olive, keep your mouth shut and everything will be all right. Life goes on.*

Olive did as she told herself to do—kept her mouth shut. In the meantime, something else was bothering her on the inside. Something mercilessly churning about in her, like mighty waves of floodwaters. However, with all that deluge taking place in her mind she was determined to hold steadfast.

Also, since Olive had had the meeting with the Chief, she kept wondering if the conversation she had with Roxanne the day of their lunch had anything to do with it. Other than that, she hadn't a clue why the Chief called her to his office and questioned her. Yet, because of the length of time that had passed, between the time they had lunch, and when she went into the Chief's office, she thought it was just coincidental. Coincidental though she thought her visit to the Chief's office could've been, she had the strong urge she should confront Roxanne:

to find out from her if she was the one who dropped a dime on her. Then, too, she also contemplated a fellow officer would not or should not snitch on the other. That furthermore, that day, they'd had only a simple conversation about men and some of their selfish habits, and how those habits had affected them (women). And since she did not want Roxanne to know she'd been to see the chief and he'd questioned her about the Shultz's affair, she further contemplated if it was a good or necessary thing to do.

About a week after Olive had gone to see the Chief, from then on coffee dates with Roxanne were next to none. She avoided Roxanne (like the plague) because she was of two minds where Roxanne was concerned: to trust or not to trust her. As well, was she avoiding Roxanne because her conscience was gathering momentum?

Regardless of all her good qualities, Olive was also tough, a very tough cookie indeed. Some people were of the opinion, when she was tough with them, that she was also very mean-spirited. Nevertheless, tuff though she was, one day she parked her cruiser, got out of it for no apparent reason, even though Mr Shultz was on her mind. She took a few steps away from the cruiser, and the floodgate on her inside broke wide open. So what would the tough Olive do? Would she clear her conscience, by revealing what she kept hidden all these years?

Olive broke down and began to cry, no not cry but weep. While she wept, she tore at her uniform as if she was a demented person. She grabbed her cap and sent it crashing against the ground, tore on her long brown hair as if she wanted to rip it off—A very uncharacteristic behaviour. Realizing what she was doing she stopped. "What am I doing?" she asked. "Am I going crazy?" So was she really going crazy? Or maybe her conscience had reached its zenith, and it was eating away at her like maggots given a task; to clean unmanageable disgusting sores?

Olive was not a Christian but, at that tumultuous time, she called on the Lord. "Lord," she said, staring ahead as if she was staring at the Lord and speaking to Him in person, "I can't hold out any longer. I cannot go on this way any longer. I have to face up to it. It was an unfortunate accident but I broke the law. I have to suffer the consequence because I took someone else's life." She reflected on a verse in the Bible where it says, 'He that taketh a life shall surely lose his'. *In this case, hers.* That was not a comforting thought for Olive, because she knew by confessing her life could swing either way, like a pendulum in a grandfather's clock.

Was Olive about to reap what she'd sowed? Was her expectation too high? What was it Mr Shultz had done to her, that was so unbearable, that her only revenge was the act of murder? Then in addition, did Mr Shultz lose his life due to what he had also sowed?

Nevertheless, on her own accord, about a month after Olive went to see the Chief she went back to his office. With tears streaming down her face, she began opening up to him. The chief warned her to get a lawyer. She refused. The Chief called someone into his office, as a witness, as he, the Chief, taped her entire confession.

The arrest of Olive Presley, the high ranked police officer, sent shockwaves throughout the force.

Also, the solving of the Shultz case was the first of many that Roxanne and Dan had been working on before Dan's demise that Roxanne helped bring to closure. Of course, there were many other cases new and old that she helped to solved. She even gave hints about crimes she thought were in the making. When asked how comes all of a sudden she had the capability to help in solving those cases, she did not have any explanation as to why. As time went by Roxanne became known as—the psychic detective.

Roxanne took leave of absent, went back to her hometown and had the satisfaction of solving the case concerning Mr Simpson. When she found out who the murderer was, she was astounded.

One day Roxanne came out of a building where she helped in apprehending the suspect she and Dan had tried to apprehend, the time of the botched stake out before his demise. She saw a dove perched on the roof of her car, looking straight at her.

"Mmm! Such a beautiful bird," Roxanne said, "a beautiful blue dove." She remembered the dove she saw in her dream. "Such a coincidence, well, be on your way you beautiful blue bird with that white ring of feathers around your neck." She leaned her head to one side, and she saw a white line of feathers that went down from the white ring of feathers around the dove's neck, down its breast to between its legs, as she felt for the handle of the driver's door of the car to open it; her eyes still centred on the dove.

The dove bobbed its head, and within seconds after it had begun to coo it stopped; flapped its wings vigorously, which startled Roxanne. Then she watched as it flew straight up towards the sky, and vanished. Up to then, she still did not think of Dan and his afterlife ambitions. She only saw a dove in a coat of blue feathers, similar to the one she had seen in her dream.

The dove meant nothing to Roxanne, who did not believe in afterlife. Furthermore, although Dan told her he wanted to come back as a bird, he did not tell her he wanted to come back as a blue dove.

However, was the dove in blue really Dan's reincarnation? Was it a sure sign of his coming back in the afterlife, not as a dog but as a dove? And was he helping Roxanne in that form as he'd promised? Was it just coincidence?

Or, did detective Roxanne Green, who joked about being the first psychic detective, suddenly garnered the capability and thus became a true psychic detective?

BEFORE THE LAST SUNSET

Three Words He Longed to Hear

O NLY A MIRACLE COULD stave off the inevitable death of Mr King. So, would his last sunset occur and thereby leave his son in a lifetime of misery? Or would he of his own accord, if he realized his mistake, tell his son what he longed to hear? And if he didn't, and he was nudged, would he, due to his stubbornness according to his son, resist? Or would he, before he kicked the bucket, admit to his mistake and do what's necessary to rectify the situation, and relieve his son, Luke, from his nauseating mental anguish?

For several months, almost every weekend, Luke King travelled the highway for several hours from Toronto to Thunder Bay in his red Honda Civic to visit his dad in the hospital. Each time he pushed open the hospital's front door (and it was no different that weekend), and the familiar fresh scent of pine sol greeted him, he'd say, "Yes, I'm here again. And I'm wondering, could it happen today or some time during this weekend visit?"

And so, not a sound came from Luke's rubber sole black shoes as he strolled along the corridor and then entered his father's room, hoping to find his father in better condition than he did on his last visit. But Luke, the assiduous architect, who would rather be working on his project that was nearing its time for delivery, was hoping against hope because only a act of God could save his father. Of late, he visited his father every weekend because there was no other family member to do so. His mother had passed away and although Alvin was alive, it was not possible for him to visit.

"Hi dad." Luke said to his father lying in the hospital bed in a pair of grey cotton pyjamas, with his face to the wall.

His dad did not answer. Luke thought he was asleep. Dead, maybe?

Luke's heart thumped heavily. "He couldn't be dead, could he? Without telling me what I longed to hear? Could he?"

As Luke leaned forward to tap his dad on the shoulder, to find out if he was asleep—or dead, he noticed something uncharacteristic of his dad. Because his dad, an ardent fan of the Blue Jays, never left an open daily on his bed when he was through reading the sport pages. Or when he expected his son to visit. He always folded the paper and put it away. Now Luke's anxiety heightened, and he rushed his hand to touch his dad and he hit the target a little harder than he had intended.

"Hi dad." Luke said again, his voice a little louder. "Dad, are you asleep? Can you hear me? It's me, Luke."

To Luke's greatest relief, his dad mumbled something.

"What, dad?" He waited.

His dad turned onto his back, laboured to sit up, then timely swung his feet to the side of the bed and they touched the floor.

Luke gave his chest a light slap, over his heart. *Whew!*

His father, afternoon sleep in his eyes, looked at Luke. "Hi son. I said you don't have to tell me it's you." His dad's voice was low.

But low though his dad's voice was at that particular time it did not matter to Luke who was relieved his father was still alive, because he felt as long as his father stayed alive he, Luke, hoped he would eventually hear from his dad what he wanted to hear from him.

"I have two sons," his dad continued, "only one visits me. The other one I don't care about."

There were long bouts when Mr King said nothing about his other son. And there were times when Luke's ears were barraged with the same old thing, and Luke, as he usually did, would do one of three things; sigh, raised his brows, or gave a slight shrug. This time he sighed, closed his eyes, tapped the side of his face lightly with his hand, and said in a soft whisper, "*Oh no. Here we go again.*" However, although Luke was tired of hearing the same old thing, he would never tell his father how he felt about it. Nevertheless, he looked at his father, showed him a soft smile, and said, "Dad, of course you do care about Alvin. Otherwise you wouldn't have him on you mind."

"I don't care about him. He brought shame on this family; scarred the family name forever. He is a worm, a dirty rotten worm. Why he did not stay in University is beyond me."

Oh gosh. "Dad, haven't we been through this over and over again? Why can't you accept it? Isn't it due to your illness why Alvin dropped out of University, to lessen the burden of you keeping him there?"

Luke's father turned his head away because he was not too pleased, as always, with what Luke was saying to him, even though it was the truth.

"Dad, please look at me."

His father obliged.

"Dad, Alvin thought he was doing something legit. It did not work out for him as planned. Hadn't we, and others, came to the same conclusion that what happened to him could've happened to anyone?"

Legit my eyes. His dad undertone, just as he'd done over and over again. "Now he's sent away for years, and I still have money. I may never see him again."

Not much money. If Alvin was around you wouldn't have any. I doubt there's enough to bury you.

Consequently, Alvin knew, given the situation with his father, that as long as his father kept spending on him it would be just a matter of time before his father's funds would dry up and he did not want that to happen. So he dropped out of university. But the robust Alvin could not see himself achieving much from the job he was in to afford him what he wanted to do. He would've done almost anything, except stealing, to make some good money. So during his endeavour to find a better paying job, a friend introduced him to some young entrepreneurs.

The entrepreneurs outlined the concept of the moneymaking business to Alvin. He thought it was quite promising. Alvin did his homework; researched the young business and its owners, but young though the business was there was already a troubling dark side to it that was unknown to Alvin. Within six months, after he joined the company, the law busted the company. Now the hustling Alvin who had planned to make some quick bucks to go back to university for the next couple of years when he'd graduate, was in just as much trouble as the unscrupulous owners of the company.

"Dad, you've said you don't care about Alvin, so what does it matter if you don't ever see him again? Anyway, dad, I am still trying." *I wish he'd let it rest and let me do what I am trying to do. Or maybe I should just forget about it.*

Luke was trying to get authorities to cut Alvin some slack so he could visit his father, who had a short while to live. Medical experts had even given up on him.

"Maybe," Luke said, "when you least expect it he could be at your bedside."

Luke's father looked at him with his eyes moving around in it's sockets like eggs rolling around in a saucer as if he was searching his mind to find the right words to say. "Son, do you think I am a fool?" he said finally. "Alvin may never see me again before my eyes are closed forever. Neither after I suppose."

"Dad, don't think so negative. Look at it from the positive side. The possibility exists that he might get some time to visit you."

"Say whatever you want to say, but what happened to him is killing me. He should've stayed in University. Although I was not doing as good as I wanted, I would've struggled to my last ounce of breath, and with my last dollar, to help him stay there. Do you hear what I am saying?"

Of course. I'm not deaf. I hear it all the time. "I know you would," Luke said, "but all that is behind you now. Dad, instead of worrying about Alvin, you should be worrying about yourself. The stress of worrying about him is not good for you. Anyway, how are you feeling today?"

"The same as the last time you were here.

Although Luke knew his father was about to cross the threshold to a place from where he'd never return, this time and as he always did, he was hoping to hear a bit of good news. News that would make him feel somewhat better about his father's condition. But as always he heard nothing new.

Luke and his father started a conversation. Now and then, Luke said something that brought smiles to his father's face. A face that had seen better days, a face that now looked like a shrivelled prune. They also reflected to times when his dad was in his heyday, and they chuckled. Especially about, his left hook and he would not chuckle but laughed as strongly as he could amidst coughing until he puked. Anyway, that was one story he did not mind them talking about. It always brought out the best laughter in him. But as Luke looked at his father lying on that hospital bed, he saw someone who was a mere shadow of the man his father used to be. The hand that delivered that punishing left hook now looked like a hanging dead branch. As they conversed, nothing else was said about Alvin. In the meantime, though, Luke thought, if he were around, he, Luke, would not have to travel for hours on weekends to do visiting chores.

It became time for Luke to leave. He hugged his father and said, "Dad, take care. I love you. See you soon."

His dad only said "uh huh. Bye for now until we meet next time."

Neither Luke nor his father could be certain there would be a next time.

Luke shook his head in dismay as he walked out of the room "Why is it so difficult for him to say—son, I—" He swallowed to clear the lump in his throat. "Is it because he is so stubborn? If he weren't so stubborn probably he would not be in here. He refused to get his annual check-ups although Mom beseeched him; God bless her soul. What a terrible mistake he'd made. Probably his cancer could've been discovered in its early stages and that could have made a huge difference. Stubborn . . . Stubborn . . . Stubborn! He's as stubborn as a darn mule."

"As far as I can remember," Luke said, "I have never heard him say it to my mother whom he married. Didn't he love her? Neither, comes to think of it, have I heard him say it to my brother." He shook his head sadly. "Why? Aren't we his sons? And wouldn't you think (I think most people have a special love for their first child), wouldn't you think, being his first child, he'd have express his love? I am worried . . . so very worried that after all these years he could die without ever saying those three little words I longed to hear him say *All My Life*. Gosh! he's such a stubborn man."

But, was Bryce King as stubborn as Luke thought he was? Or, in Luke's sight, he saw his dad as being stubborn because he was yet to hear from him what he wanted to hear? As well, Bryce King who had envisioned life as a one-way journey; in which no human knew what fate has in store for him or her, was now at the end of his life's journey, since fate had dished out one last unmanageable obstacle to him, had other aspects of his life where one could not say he was stubborn. Because in the sight of many, he was also acclaimed as being a caring and compassionate person.

Caring and compassionate though Bryce King was, he did not take crap from anyone. He was a fighter who fought for what he thought was best for him and his family. He'd also fought for others voluntarily or otherwise. He'd try to win every argument (was that shades of stubbornness) and, when he could not get his point across he'd walk away, called his opponents some king of unpleasant names. Sometimes when he was caught in any unsavoury act, he'd try to writhe his way out. Of course, he would do so at someone else's expense when the opportunity presented itself. But even though he had overcome many obstacles fate threw at him along the way, he was now at a dead end. He was battling the last curve fate threw at him, of which there was no way out but death.

One day Luke was thinking heavily about his dad, and he felt pimples of sweats invading his body. He shook his head sadly. "When someone dies it's so final. Death is so final. Also given time that someone who'd passed away becomes nothing more than a fading memory, almost forgotten. Yes, no matter who you are, such fate lies ahead for everyone."

That day, too, Luke reflected on the day he saw his dad delivered his devastating left hook (the left hook happening that always intrigued them) that knocked a man senseless. The man had called his dad a liar. And when he insisted that the man apologize, the man laughed. That action of the man was like throwing gasoline on a raging fire. Again, he further insisted that the man apologize. The man would not. Luke remembered how he noticed rage building up in his dad. So he told his dad to forget about it because it was only words.

'Words?' his dad said.

Before Luke could say *Yes* dad it's only words, his dad's lightening, devastating left hook demolished the man; dropped him to the floor like a water soaked log. Luke though that that day his dad was also stubborn. As well, due to his stubbornness, he nearly got himself into serious trouble. But his dad said after he decked the man, 'I won't allow any one who call me a liar then laughs at me to get away with it. Never let anyone do such a thing to you. Always be ready to fight for your honour. Fight for your rights.'

Just then, Luke also thought, with the predicament concerning his dad like a millstone around his neck, he should share the way it's affecting him with someone and maybe he'd feel somewhat better about it. But who? Yes, he settled on his friend, David. "Would he," he pondered, "see me as being a wimp? Would he say I am making a mountain out of a molehill? That I am acting like a sissy, and that, isn't worrying about such a thing by a grown man a complete waste of time?"

Anyhow, one Tuesday Luke and David—a Civil Engineer—met for lunch at a restaurant downtown Toronto (they usually had lunch Tuesdays and Fridays) and Luke had on a pair of dark glasses, something David could not remember him doing while indoors. Nevertheless, while they waited for the Server to fill their orders, Luke took off his dark glasses. David noticed a haggard look about his eyes.

"My friend," David said, "you look so tired. Is it because you are staying up all hours to make that deadline? Consulting the spirit, maybe; using it to keep you company?"

"No. Not exactly," Luke said.

"No."

Luke, who frets about the simplest of things, and that was everything no matter how small the detail, and who had taken coupe of mouthfuls of his meal, looked down at his plate and stabbed at his grilled steak, meditatively, with the steak knife. On one of those stabs, his last that was vicious, the knife made a gritting sound as it went through the steak and crashed against the plate. He sighed, pushed the plate aside and said, "David would you beli—" he paused, tugged on his shirt collar nervously. *Should I?* ". . . David, anyone would be feeling the after effect after driving so many hours to visit his sick dad in the hospital. I left home early Saturday morning (David knew that), visited him twice, and got back home late Sunday night."

On one hand, that was not what Luke had intended to say. He switched to that passage to finish saying something and hoped David would not question him on what he was about to say at the beginning, when he'd paused. Then on the other hand, for someone who was not a professional driver, driving those long hours on the busy Highway weekend after weekend, wouldn't you agree it was possible for him to be showing some after effect less than two days after making that trip?

Twice David had taken trips with Luke to visit Luke's dad. He could not remember suffering any after-effect from the long journey, even though he'd done some of the driving.

"Luke, it's not the first time you've done that. You should be used to it by now. Anyhow, you've never look as tired as you're looking now. Neither did it bother me when I went with you."

Wait a minute. What's he talking about here? "David, those weekends you went with me was so far apart, which seemed like from one August to the next. I have to do it every weekend. So do you think, with all honesty, when you took those trips it should've affected you, as it is affecting me?"

"Well, I suppose not."

"David too much of anything, good or bad, eventually wears you down."

Too much of anything wears you down? David thought, with raised brows. He was beginning to think the too much of anything had to do with Luke's visiting his father every weekend. "Luke, is the too much of anything have anything to do with visiting your father?"

Luke looked at David contemplatively. "I am not saying or implying that."

"Then what is this too much of anything about?"

"Just forget I said that, all right! However, you being my bosom friend know I only drink occasionally. Again, I must emphasize—No! I did not have a drop. Furthermore, consulting the spirit solves nothing. I might look tired but I am not, really. I am very worried."

By this time, David had the fork close to his mouth but the food on it did not touch his lips. "Very worried, about what, Luke?"

Luke pushed the plate a little further away and said, "Could we . . . talk about what is bothering me another time?" He looked at the clock. "I've lost my appetite. Lunchtime is over for me, for today."

Luke was still in limbo; to tell David about what it was that was worrying him. He was also still in trepidation about the answer or answers David might give. He looked at David without saying another word.

David noticed his long pause. Then he said, "Maybe we could talk later, on the phone, about whatever it is that is worrying you, or at lunch on Friday."

"Maybe," Luke said with a less cheery voice.

Luke pushed his chair back and stood up. So did David, who wiped his mouth with the serviette he held in his hand and threw it in the plate. "Luke, I'll call you later?"

"I'll be at the office working on my project. When I am working late, as you know, my phone is set at mute."

"Okay, I won't call you. You can call me when it is convenient, anytime before Friday and let's talk. Or, if you want to wait until we meet Friday that's OK with me, but I am hoping we'll talk soon. Because being your friend, telling me you are worried bothers me."

David went back to work, puzzled about what it was that was worrying Luke. It was more troubling to him that Luke had refused to talk about it. And instead of eating he only stabbed at his steak, which was something uncommon for Luke who was a healthy eater, had David thinking deeply. Nevertheless, despite of what was ailing Luke, besides his father's illness and his brother being in jail, David hoped his friend would do what was necessary to meet his deadline of the project he was working on. He'd also wait, and if he did not hear from him, to see how it would go on Friday.

Came Friday, Luke was late for lunch. Just as David pulled out his cell phone to call him, he walked into the restaurant.

"I was held up on the way here," Luke said. He did not tell David what it was that held him up. "What do they have for soup today?"

"It is listed on the menu board—mushroom soup," David said.

"That my favourite soup. I'll have a bowl."

"We should order two bowls," David said.

As they eat their soups, while they wait for their main course orders to be filled, David said, "Luke, you don't look so worried today."

"I might not look it, but I am still very worried."

"It is only natural to be worried about you father's condition, and your brother's incarceration, but I have never seen you—"

"Never seen me look as worried as I was the other day?"

"Yes. Never."

"David I have no choice but to accept the condition of my father. He is destined to die. When it comes to Alvin, that's another story—" He looked up and said thanks to the person who'd served their main course meals. "David, this fish and chips looks good. Let's eat before it gets cold. We'll talk afterwards. Okay?"

"Okay. That's all right with me."

In the meantime, though, Luke still feared as to how David would react when he would tell him what was worrying him. He eyed David as they ate. The decisive test, as to how David would react when he'd tell David what was worrying him, came after they finished their meals, when he'd remind David of events that happened when they were in their teens.

Luke sighed, a small sigh then said, "David, do you remember what happened after the race in which we'd competed years ago, the one hundred metre dash?"

David looked away from Luke, thinking, why is he bringing up that now? Well, I imagine in time I'll find out eventually. "Now to think of it, we have never talked about it much. If I can remember, you won the race and I congratulated you. Or something similar to that."

"No. Not that," Luke said.

"Well then Luke, what? The race happened when we were in our late teens, and looking back, I cannot remember all that had happened that day. However, this I will never forget; since that day we became friends—and that's a very memorable occasion for me."

"Yes indeed, that was a good thing which happened because we are still good friends to this day. But that's not really it. Yes, you congratulated me and said, *One Love.* But your father did something else, which left a lasting impression on me. An impression I'll never forget as long as I shall live."

"Oh, something . . . like what, Luke? Please refresh my memory."

"My father said," with a broad smile, "boy you ran a good race. Just as I expected of you. Your father said, with a broad smile, too, which had the attribute of deep satisfaction, you came second but I know you did your best. He hugged you, slapped you on your shoulder gently and your face lit up like a thousand watt light bulb when he said, son, I love you. To me those three little words, *I love you,* was such a powerful statement."

"My father saying that was nothing new to me," David said. "It happens all the time? My father always hugged us, me my brother and sister, and expressed his love for us."

"And when I visited your home for the first time," Luke said, "also on subsequent visits, I was further impressed from activities undertaken in your home."

"Activities such as . . . ?"

"In the mornings, your family had rituals. I will always remember the first song I heard sung in your home. *'There is beauty all around, when there's love at home; There's joy in every sound, when there's love at home. Pease and plenty here abide, smiling face on every side; time does softly, sweetly glide, when there's love at home,'* and so forth. Upon the completion of the singing, one or two of you read verses from the bible. After that, your dad or someone else in the family prayed. When that person had finished praying, everyone hugged each other and said I love you. Have a good day. I was not treated any differently. You also say prayers before eating meals, at your home and individually. A prayer like you'd just said, and every time we had lunch."

Luke, those activities were not rituals. They were morning worships. Something we did every morning when I was at home. Yes, we prayed at worships and say grace, a prayer, before we eat. Cared not how small what we had to eat could be. Oh now I remember you'd asked me if we were Christians the first time you visited us, but I cannot quite remember what my answer was at that time. I was also surprised when I visited your home, for the first time, too, and I did not see similar activities that happened in my home, happening in yours. I observed it thoughtfully and concluded that it was odd, but I said nothing about it. Because I'd thought, your family-custom was different from mine. Yes, the rituals you thought we had each mornings at our home were not rituals. They were happy family morning worships."

"David, I saw so much love radiating in your family." Now, he got the courage to tell David, to share with him what it is that was haunting him regarding his father. "David, would you believe my father never once said, son, I love you." His hands went up in a gesture of surrender. He looked at David with speculation in his eyes.

That's a terrible thing, David thought. "Not once," he said, "did your father ever say he loves you?"

Luke's fear of being ridiculed was not a factor in David's response. And so now he felt he could speak openly and freely. "He had never said it to me as far as I can remember. Neither have I heard him say it to my mother nor my brother. I am worried, very worried he may pass away without ever saying it to me. David, I'm going to pieces over it."

Wow! goodness gracious. "Did you ever tell him you love him?"

"More times than I can remember to a father who's set in his own ways. Yes, I have tried many times to trick him into saying he loves me, by saying, dad, it's such a wonderful feeling when someone hugs you and say he loves you."

"And?"

"He always answered with, uh huh, okay, or it's all right. I know you do. Not—I know you love me—but I know you do. So on and so forth. Now then, is that anyway for someone to say he loves you? If he meant it, how should I know it if it's not spoken?

David was not about to slam-dunk anyone. He was careful with his response. "Luke, although he never told you he loves you, he showed it in other ways, didn't he?"

"I suppose he did, but when someone hugs you and say I love you, it is such a wonder feeling; a feeling I have experienced from my brother. Also from my Mom when she was alive."

The considerate David leaned his head to one side. *Wow! I feel so sorry for him, because he is starving for what I take for granted. Should I bother to tell him it's an ongoing thing with my dad and I whenever we meet?* "Have you told anyone else about this? How you feel about it, and how it's affecting you?"

"I don't think I did. Maybe I'd said it to my brother. Now . . . you."

"Did you tell your mother about it, before she'd passed away?"

"No, my friend. I suppose it did not matter much to me while she was alive. She, if you recall, died six years after we met. Even to this day, this day and to this precise moment as we speak, I yearn for her warm loving hugs, accompanied by a motherly kiss most of the times and her *I love you*. I know, no I shouldn't say I know because it never happened, and I should say, even though I don't think my dad's hugging would feel as my mom's, I still wanted my father to hug me even once, and tell me he loves me, similar to what my mother used to do. And just like your father did the day after the race and many more times that I'd observed."

Now David wasted no time to advise his friend. "Then tell him you want to hear him say it before he dies."

"David," he sighed despondently, "I won't beg for it."

Beg, you say? David thought, while you are suffering such mental anguish. There's nothing to beg for.

"He should say so on his own accord. A father should remember. A father should know."

"Right now your father is probably thinking about his waiting to die, and not about what he'd said or did not say to you or anyone else. So tell him."

"David, I won't." Luke said defiantly. "If he dies without telling me he loves me, so be it. Oh by the way, I met my deadline."

Just Fine. "Good for you, my friend. Luke, keep heart. It is not too late. Your father may yet surprise you."

"Perhaps! Or, maybe if he's nudged by a compassionate Angel? Well so much for that."

The conversation had soured their appetite. Neither man finished lunch.

They went back to their respective place of work.

"Someone should speak to Luke's father," David said, "on Luke's behalf, but I can't think of anyone. Alvin is serving time (the poor Guy got trapped by those others whom had labelled themselves as being legit businessmen), and perhaps except for him, I could be the only other person who knows about what is causing Luke such great worry." He threw his hands to the air. "What can I do?"

David then figured the surest way he could do something was to get next to Luke's father, and that he could only do by visiting him. But he surmised, if he should tell Luke he wanted to go with him in the morning when he'd be going to visit his dad, and from knowing what he knew then, wouldn't Luke be suspicious?

Just as David stopped ruminating, the phone rang.

"Hi, it's me, Luke. How about accompanying me next weekend when I go back again to visit my dad?"

David was glad for the invite. So he went into a quick thinking mode. Because he figured if Luke's father should die without him jumping to the first opportunity he got, to do what he thought he could do on Luke's behalf, he'd feel awfully guilty. He could not afford to wait until the next weekend.

"I couldn't go with you next weekend. I have plans." A red herring of an excuse.

"Never mind. It's okay."

David detected disappointment in Luke's voice, but he thought what he'd say next would somehow make him feel better.

"Although I can't go with you next weekend I could go with you tomorrow. I'm free this weekend."

"Sure 'bout that?"

"Of course I'm sure."

"Well okay. See you in the morning."

David enquired if the time for departure would be the same time as always.

'Yep, same time, same time as always."

After they hung up (the phone), David penned a note. "Yes," he said, "this should do it. I hope."

After work, when David went home, he put the note in a pocket of the trousers he'd wear next morning. He patted the pocket. "Yes, I am hoping this ingenuity of mine might do the trick."

Next morning while they travelled to the hospital, they talked about several things but they said not a word about Mr King. And so, when they reached their destination they went straight to Mr King's room.

"Hi dad." Luke said, "David's here to visit you today."

David greeted Mr King. He asked him how he was doing.

"Not so good," Mr King said, however, I am still alive, though barely, but I am still on the land of the living."

David shook his head as he looked at the man while remembering the story about the left hook. As he remised, while looking at him, the man who once had that powerful, venomous punch, he thought what a disease had done to have one looking so much like a skeleton. That with all the fighting he'd done, for himself and others, it had gotten to the point where he had to give up fighting for his own life and just wait to die. It's so sad, isn't it?

All three men, Luke, Mr King and David conversed for awhile. During their conversing, David kept watch on the time. About fifteen minutes before visiting time would end David left the room. He engaged the nurse at the nursing station, to while away the time. But he kept a watchful eye on the time while looking towards the door of Mr King's room. He pretended not to see Luke make his exit.

"Hey David," Luke said. "The time for visiting is over. It's now time for us to leave."

"Okay. I must say goodbye to your father. It will only take a minute."

David went back into the room. "Hi Mr King, I'm leaving now." He went close to Mr King, leaned forward, as he, David glanced quickly from side to side over his shoulders. *Fine, no eyes are watching us.* "Mr King," he said, softly. "Sir, I am leaving you a note concerning something that is worrying your son—Greatly!"

"A note." Mr King said apprehensively. "A note concerning my son, what is it about? Besides, he has all right to be worried because I'm dying."

"Sir, yes and no. However, sir, it's not a disturbing note, I hope."

Mr King was somewhat reluctant to take the note, so David tucked it in his hand.

"When you are through reading it, please get rid of it. Promise me," he paused, because he thought he should make a direct statement. "Sir, don't whisper a word about it to anyone, especially not to your son. I hope you won't be mad at me."

"Okay," Mr King said, without showing an ounce of enthusiasm, "okay."

David straightened up and raised the decimal of his voice just a little louder, "Sir, take care. I am hoping to see you again."

"Perhaps," Mr King said.

Although David told Mr King he hoped to see him again, he did not tell him he'd come back the next day.

"Why did he leave me a note concerning Luke?" Mr King said, after they'd left. "I am curious to find out what it's all about."

Mr King gasped as if his lungs were about to go on empty, from his alarm when he read the note. Alarmed to know that not once did he ever told Luke, who expressed his love for him in action and words, that he loves him. And, if a nurse were in the room, she'd swear Mr King was gulping his last ounce of breath, thus surrendering his soul to its maker.

Mr King felt deep disgust towards himself, because he realized the pain his son was going through from him not defining his love for him verbally, when his son had hugged him and expressed, verbally, that he loves him. It was also disturbing to him to know that all these years Luke was waiting to hear him say he loves him; and that

Luke was very worried he'd die without telling him he did.

Luke's dad heaved a sigh. "Thank God," he said, while he destroyed the note. "Thank God someone brought it to my attention. I hope I won't die before I see him tomorrow—when I will hug him and tell him in words that I love him. I really love him. God, I truly love him."

Luke and David booked in the hotel closest to the hospital, had something to eat, watched a few programs on TV and then they retired for the night. Next morning, after they had breakfast, they went back to the hospital to visit Mr King. After that visit ended, they'd head home.

"Luke, I see you *true* friend is still with you."

"Dad, we did not come in separate vehicles. I am the chauffeur and he can't go and leave me behind."

Their routine was similar to yesterday's—talked to each other. After they'd chatted for about forty minutes or so David, who did not have much to say, said he felt peckish; a sandwich would suit him fine. He left the room to search for the hospital's cafeteria.

When Luke was ready to leave—David had not returned to the room because he deliberately stayed away. Anyhow, Luke hugged his dad and said, "Bye dad. See you on the weekend. Stay as good as you can until we see each other again. Dad, I love you."

"Son, I . . ."

"Yes dad! Yes!" Luke said excitedly, in anticipation.

"You all right, son?"

A disappointed Luke said, "Yes dad." *Oh God how much longer must I wait? Do I have to break my own code of silence?*

And his dad finished with, "I'll do my best to hang on until we see each other again, but who knows. Don't be surprised if you—"

". . . if I should," Luke interrupted, "get a call from someone from this establishment telling me you're not breathing anymore."

Statement similar as that Luke had heard many times. Of course, he would not be surprised, only saddened. Because there was no if; only when? Only his dad's maker knew when that time would occur. He would not tell his father he wouldn't be surprised, but he'd only be saddened when it should happen.

However, a revelation was about to happen.

As the frustrated Luke was about to leave the room, the man he'd classified as being stubborn, said, "Son, please come back here."

"What does he want now?" Luke said.

Luke walked listlessly back to his dad's bedside.

"Son," his Dad said, "um, son, will you please hug me again?"

"This is strange," Luke whispered. "Strange to know my dad wants me to give him a second hug? Something he'd never done before."

With reluctance, Luke did as his dad asked.

Mr King wrapped his weak arms around his son's neck, in surprising strength, squeezed him as tightly as he possibly could. Then he said passionately, "Son, I love you. I love you more than you could, or would ever know."

Luke, wide-eyed, whispered from his being surprised, although he was hearing for the first what he longed to hear, Chrise! Yes. At last." His hug tightened around his dad in a jerky manner.

His dad uttered a soft, "*UH.*"

Luke slackened his tenacious hug. "Sorry dad." *I'd better prepare . . .* "Dad, do you know what you are saying. Can you hear yourself, telling me, you love me?"

Mr King had just delivered his son a verbal left hook that almost brought him, Luke, to his knees.

"Yes, my son. Yes. I truly love you."

"Dad, I've been waiting all my life to hear you say you love me."

"Son, are you telling me I never did say I love you?"

"That I can't remember."

"Maybe your memory is like running water?"

"My memory is fine. Dad, if you had said it to me, you might have done so before my senses were developed. I was so worried you would've died without telling me you love me. Now that you have said it, it makes me feel so good. Dad, I love you, too. Hang in there. Have to go. See you next weekend."

"Yes, you have to go, but remember I truly love you."

"Thanks dad. See you soon."

Luke, his heart filled with exceedingly great joy, felt as light as a feather as he bounced out of his father's room into the corridor. He pumped his fist in the air from his elation. He was so excited he forgot about David, and only remembered him when he saw him through the panes of the revolving exit door.

"Oh high David." Luke said, beaming, his face as bright as the rising sun. "Got your sandwich?"

David did not supply an answer. *Oh my, he looks so happy!* "What happened to allow you such radiance?"

"David, I'm so very happy! Can you believe it? My . . . ."

"Luke, let me rush inside and say bye to you father."

"Okay."

"Mr King, I'm leaving. Is everything okay?"

Mr King showed David a small smile. His slight nod assured David everything was—just fine.

Luke was almost by the car when David caught up with him.

"Now, Luke, what was it you wanted to tell me?"

"My friend, it is over. It has happened."

"What is over? What happened?"

"Let's get in the car. We'll talk about it as we drive along."

"Won't you be distracted?"

"Nothing could distract me now. I'm so darn happy."

They hit the freeway and Luke said, his voice animated, "My friend," and then he laughed loudly, as he took one hand off the steering wheel and then slapped that hand back onto the steering wheel. "David, I still can't believe it. Would you believe my dad hugged me and told me he loves me!?"

"I am so very happy for you, my friend." *And very satisfied from knowing I did something that brought happiness to you.*

"Yes indeed. An angel must've touched his ailing soul." Tears of joy rolled down Luke's cheeks.

"Luke, isn't it wonderful that wonders never ceased?"

"David, overwhelmingly wonderful!"

"Watch your speed now," David said, "with all that happiness bubbling up in you, you're likely to exceed the speed limit." *Now I should sit back, relax and let him savour his happiness.*

"I will, my friend." Luke began humming a tune, something like, *Do you love me.*

While they travelled back to Toronto, David fell asleep.

That long journey home was the most pleasurable Luke has ever had, because he finally heard from his dad what he'd been yearning for over all those years.

Luke dropped off David, and went home. He poured himself a small brandy, walked to the sofa and sat down. The phone was close by. He checked his voice mail. He got to the third message, the last that said, "Mr King, please call the hospital. It's concerning your father." Fearing the worst, his heart throbbed.

The hospital personnel confirmed his dad had passed away.

Luke thought of Alvin. "Dad was so right," he whispered. "Now he's gone to the beyond without blessing his eyes on Alvin one last time. Will they grant Alvin time to come to the funeral? I'll have to try."

Luke called David. "Well, my friend, the angel of death claimed another victim. My dad is gone."

"Oh no! So sorry to hear that. My condolence."

"David, I will miss him. God bless his soul."

Whew, we made it just in the nick of time. "My friend, it's a road we all have to travel."

"David, so true. Just before his last sunset I got what I wanted, but, I've lost the father I had."

I WILL NEVER LEAVE YOU

-I-

Mark, please don't go

On a bright, calm day in June, when birds, bees, butterflies etc feasted on sweet nectar from flowers of all verities in full bloom, Jennifer and Mark stood in a chapel in front of a Pastor, witnesses, and made a vow: To have and to hold until death do us part. As they vowed to each other they had glint in their eyes, radiant smiles on their faces in anticipation of a blissful life awaiting them in the future. In the meantime Mark was thinking, *Oh what a night.* Because it would be the first night, he and Jennifer would begin to share each other's human nectar that was much sweeter than honey and sweeter than any nectar flowers and the likes could ever produce.

Probably Jennifer, with auburn hair about two inches below her shoulders, brown eyes, would still be unmarried, or married to someone else instead of the muscular Mark who had a passion for skiing. He had been skiing since he was about four years old. In his adult years, he usually took time-off from work to go on long skiing trips, and he'd visit several ski resorts.

Hadn't Mark made a firm commitment to Jennifer, who had no interest in skiing; she wouldn't touch snow skies with a ten-foot pole or go on snow skies even if she was paid, because she felt skiing was a dangerous sport, probably the union wouldn't have happened even though she loved Mark passionately. Jennifer feared, although Mark did not have any accident during the years he'd been skiing, as long as he kept on skiing he is open to a potentially deadly accident that could happen at any time, similar to the deadly fate of one of his skiing friends he had been skiing with for years. She also imagined him on a pair of runaway skis and he could meet the same fate as some other skiers, too.

Jennifer feared that if she married Mark and he met similar deadly fate, she would become an early widow, something she was not planning on happening to her. But when Mark had committed himself, she was of the opinion that by the end of two years away from the ski slope, and with the death of his skiing buddy constantly on his mid, probably he'd not go back to skiing, and he'd find other sporting activities to compensate for skiing. Upon committing himself, that he would lay off his skies for the first two winters of their mirage, a delight to Jennifer, they planned their weeding date and soon afterwards became man and wife.

Mark even hinted that after his moratorium— his promise to stay away from skiing for two winters after their marriage—maybe he'd give up skiing, depending on the way he felt. He did not bother with skiing the year following his friend's tragic death. Anyway, he could not ski because the snow, which fell that winter, was not enough to entice him to go skiing.

One morning in December, not long after they had pledged their vows, Jennifer found out the promise made by Mark was just what it was. A promise in words that sounded like the wind that passed by. Words from a mouth which spoke soothing, loving words; a mouth which once sang as beautifully as a nightingale sings—Mark used to sing on his church's youth choir—, and even spoke words of anger, made a promise only to break it when it was in his interest.

That Jennifer found out was the case when twenty-eight year old Mark got out of bed, walked to the bedroom window of their home on Big Red Avenue in Scarborough, and parted the curtains and saw the first heavy snowfall that December day, about six months and few days since they got married.

The sight Mark beheld filled his heart with joy. He couldn't help but exclaimed how excited he felt, sounding like a child who had gotten its Christmas wish list fulfilled. "Oh my!" he declared, staring out the window in awe, "what a beautiful Morning?" He had something else on his mind, something more than what he thought was just a beautiful Morning.

His wife rolled onto her side. "Mark, what is so beautiful about this Morning? It's winter, and even when the sun shines in winter months, it is still cold outside. Last night before we went to bed, the person who had forecasted the weather said we should expect a monster snowstorm overnight. When that happens, you know as well as I, everything comes to an abrupt halt. Is there any snow out there?"

"The Forecaster was exactly right, did not miss a beat. Sweetheart, there's tons and tons of the white stuff everywhere I cast my eyes. It is such a beautiful sight."

Immediately Mark thought of Northern Ontario where there's always an abundant of snow: the region of several ski resorts, where some residents of Southern Ontario goes to ski.

"So what's so beautiful about that?"

"I am just thinking of all the fun those who love to ski could be having. This is the time of winter I enjoy the most."

"I know why he's so excited," Jennifer whispered. "He'd like to go to the ski resort to have fun in the snow like other skiers could be having. Lord, I hope he doesn't have it on his mind."

Shortly after Jennifer was through ruminating, she heard him say, `I would love to be out there with my skies. They are waxed and ready to glide me down the ski slope.'

Jennifer pretended not to hear him.

Mark waited for her response. But while he waited, the promise he made to her before they got married was on her mind.

Then Jennifer heard him say, "There's nothing more in the world I like more than skiing, besides loving you of course. Skiing gives me such a high. Skiing was my first love but now it's become my second love. I can't find words to explain the pleasure I get from skiing. Sweetheart, I always kept my skies waxed and ready for a time such as this."

Jennifer was not in the mood to listen to whatever he was saying concerning his waxed skies. So she said, "Please don't harbour the though of going out to play in the snow. Come back to bed. I want you here more than I want for you to go out in that white stuff."

Mark ignored her plea. So she walked over to him, hugged him and said, "Isn't it a wonderful feeling to know you can snug with someone you love, in a warm place, than going out in the cold when you really don't have to do so?"

"Going out to ski was only in the back of my mind, but now that you've mentioned it I get the sudden urge, a sudden heart throbbing urge to get into my four-by-four and head slowly to the nearest ski resort, strap my skies on, go on the slope and frolic and have the time of my life."

Jennifer thought she would get his mind off skiing, by proposing something else. *I'll go to the kitchen and fix him his favourite breakfast of poached eggs, steamed mushroom, asparagus, sweet red pepper and green string beans.* She backed away from him and put on her blue-and-white silk robe. She pulled the strap of the robe and knotted it. "Darling, I'm going down to the kitchen to fix your favourite breakfast."

"Good idea." Mark said. "I am quite hungry. After that workout last night, anyone would—let's just say, need something good to replenish his strength. Sweetheart, don't you think—" He did not finish that sentence.

"Think what?" Jennifer asked.

"Never mind," he said. "Go on down and fix breakfast as you say you intend to do."

Jennifer glanced back at him, over her shoulder, as she walked out the bedroom door. As she made her way down the stairway, something entered her thought. *I should put something in his meal to knock him out, but that would not be a nice thing to do. Why did I think of it anyway? Besides, I haven't anything to do the job.*

Meantime, while Jennifer was fixing breakfast, Mark was in the bedroom contemplating the promise he had made to her. "I wonder if she'd remember the promise I made," he said, lying across the queen-size bed. "Hm, of course she would. Hadn't I made such promise she wouldn't have married me."

While he was contemplating, Jennifer called out, "Mark, come on down. I am just about ready to put breakfast on the table."

"I'll be right down," he said.

Mark went downstairs, in his light-blue and beige silk robe. He sat at the table.

The first serving was cornflakes, slices of pineapple and some blueberries.

"The rest of the breakfast," Jennifer said to him, "is keeping warm on the stove. As soon as you're through eating this portion, I will serve the main course."

Mark took a few spoonfuls from his bowl. And like a child would, one who hates to eat vegetables, twirl his spoon in his plate in discontent, so did Mark as he twirled his spoon in the bowl, without looking at Jennifer. He stopped twirling his spoon, laid it in the bowl with its handle resting on the side of the bowl. He rubbed his palms together slowly. His behaviour was unusual.

Jennifer noticed his action. She said nothing then. But after she observed him for awhile, she thought to ask what was wrong with him. She knew her man. So she said, "Mark, what's on your mind? Why aren't you eating?

"I know I made a promise to you, not to go skiing anytime during the first two winters of our marriage. But—"

"Yes. You did. But what," Jennifer said.

"Sweetheart, never mind about it," he said again.

"Mark, it's the second time you've said it. I am hoping with all the snow on the ground you'll stick to your promise." She also reminded him that he'd said he probably might give up skiing, because the death of his skiing buddy was still troubling to him.

"Yes," Mark said, "he's gone but I am sure he wouldn't want me to give up skiing because of what happened to him."

"How sure are you about that?" Jennifer said. She got out of her chair, walked over to Mark and tried to sit on his lap. The space between him and the table was tight. Jennifer couldn't make it.

"Please wait a minute," Mark said, to the petite Jennifer. He readjusted the position of his chair to make more room between him and the table to accommodate her.

While she sat comfortably in his lap, Jennifer said, "Mark, are you sure your buddy would want you to go skiing? In so doing leave yourself open to potential danger, as you always did. Him, too! It's the reason why he's dead. I am sure if he could live his life over, he'd have second thoughts about engaging himself in such a dangerous sport. Maybe he would turn to the sport of ice hockey; played in a more controlled relatively safe environment, figure skating or other less dangerous sports people play on the ice. You know I like hockey games and figure skating."

"Who knows," Mark said. "Maybe he would and maybe he would not. We knew every time we put on our skies and went on that ski slope we flirted with danger. But we liked that white fluffy stuff and the way it trailed behind us as we glided along. I miss him so much."

"And as a friend, given what he'd been through, again I say probably he'd tell you to get involved in other less dangerous sport."

"Perhaps," Mark said.

Jennifer rubbed her hand gently from his forehead, over his head and down the nape of his neck. "Mark," she said, "I love you so much. We have nothing else to do after we finish breakfast but to take it easy for the rest of the day. How about," and she pushed her hand through an opening in his robe and rubbed his chest softly, "we go back upstairs to where we'll launch ourselves into each other's bliss?"

Mark hugged her tightly and kissed her. "Sweetheart, it's such a good idea, why not?"

When the lovemaking was over, Jennifer felt Mark's behaviour was not something like she'd experienced before. He was restless, and his action was as if he was disappointed with what he got.

"What's the matter dear?" Jennifer asked Mark, who was lying on his back, "why are you sulking. Wasn't it good this time for you?"

"Yes, it was. As good as making love to you have always been. My darling, sweetheart, it couldn't be any nicer."

"So you say. But given you behaviour it makes me feel otherwise."

"Don't worry about it," Mark said, still lying on his back. He pulled up his knees and almost pull the cover off Jennifer.

Jennifer heard him make a small sigh, which made her wonder what was bothering him this time? Still she said nothing to him.

Mark stretched, and following that, he clasped his hands on the top of his head and his elbow almost hit Jennifer in the face. He undid his clasp, brought his hands to his side, and then turned onto his left side—Jennifer to his back. He sighed again.

Jennifer had enough of his restless manner. "Mark," she said, "I can tell something is really bothering you and don't tell me you're all right. Let's talk about it."

Mark turned onto his right side. *How can I?* He laid his hand across her bosom. "So lovely!" he said. "I could lie here and caress them forever."

Such a statement was like music to Jennifer's ears.

"Forever is a very long time," Jennifer said. She wriggled her body from the excitement she felt. "We could do this all weekend, until we have to go to work on Monday. Although they are mine, they also belong to you. Short of abusing them, you know you can do whatever you want to do with them whenever they're in your hands or wherever else. When you play with them, it gives me so much pleasure. Just like you, I also wish we could keep on doing this forever, but there are times when we have to take breaks. Now, besides playing with my bosom . . . stop for awhile you're making me hot." She held onto his hand, "Now what else is on your mind?"

Should I? Maybe I should forget about it. It feels so good lying here next to her. Even so, I'd still like to go skiing. She said she knows something is bothering me. Better get it over and done with. "Sweetheart . . ."

"Yes my love," she said, as she squeezed her body tightly against his, under the blue quilt cover, "what is it?"

"While I am lying here next to you," Mark said, "the promise I'd made to you not to go skiing anytime during the first two winters of our mirage is on my mind."

"So what about it?" Jennifer said.

"You know I love to ski."

"Yes, my darling. I know you have a passion for skiing." She waited to hear what he'd say next. She also knew he was somewhat nervous. "Darling, don't be timid with what you want to say. Just let it flow and see what happens."

Although she can't read my mind, I guess she is prepared for what I might say next. So here I go. "If I should tell you I really want to go skiing, would you be mad at me?"

"Of course I would," Jennifer said. "You are not thinking of it, are you?"

"At first when I saw the snow, the urge to go skiing entered my thought to some degree, but the urge only got much greater when you brought it up. Skiing is in my blood. Although I am lying next to you I also vision myself gliding down the ski slope."

"Mark you made a promise to me. I am bent on holding you to it. Don't think I will sever you from it, because I expect you to keep it." *You take a pig from the mud, but it's a tough job to keep it from going back to the mud.*

Mark was in turmoil. He thought the only thing to do, which might please her so she'd let him off the hook, was to bribe her but with what? Several bribery ideas ran through Mark's thoughts. He smiled as he settled on taking Jennifer on a Caribbean cruise the following year. *Aha! This should do it.* "Sweetheart, if you'd agree for me to go skiing this time, I promise to take you on a Caribbean cruse next year and I won't go skiing for the rest of this winter or the next as I had promised."

Jennifer thought the idea of a Caribbean cruise sounded quite appealing. It was something she'd love to do. Then she thought he came up with such a scheme because he wanted her to let him off the hook so he could go skiing. So still holding onto that thought, she looked at him belligerently and said, harshly, "Mark, you were not supposed to go skiing this winter. Now you want to break the promise you made by making me another, to take me on a Caribbean cruise—well, isn't it bribery? How should I believe you? I can see you breaking this Caribbean cruise promise when the time comes. Now it is clear to me you'd made a promise, a promise with no substance."

"But sweetheart the promise I'd made was not a hollow promise . . ."

"It was, Mark. It was!" She wriggled away from him. "What if I hold steadfast, could I still look forward to going on the cruise?"

"To go on the cruise," he said, "is the trade-off. Anyway, whichever way it goes, I won't break the promise I'm making to you now."

Jennifer sat up it the bed, the upper part of her body completely exposed. "Look at me Mark. Look at me! Isn't this landscape much better looking than where you're pining to go?"

Mark looked at her, but it was obvious to Jennifer Mark's heart was not where he centred his eyes.

"Are you telling me you'd rather leave this beautiful, warm body to go out in the cold, to go and play in the snow and leave this behind? Do you love skiing more than me?"

Mark said nothing, only lay there and stared at her.

"Look at you. Now you have turned into a stature and a mute. Gee. You're really killing me. You know, although I am your wife who loves you very much, and even though I had said I am bent on holding you to the promise you want to break, come to think of it, I have no intention to control you. Today, only six months after being married to you, you have planted a seed of mistrust in my mind. Mistrust a Caribbean cruise may never erase. I did not ask you to give up skiing forever, only for a while. Now you make me feel like a bloody fool. Besides, who knows, you could have an accident in this bad weather on you way to the ski resort, or if not, while you glide down the ski slope. A very serious life changing accident or maybe one like your friend had that took his life."

Mark, the Auto body Technician, said, "Sweetheart, for years I've driven in weather conditions such as this to get to ski resorts, and I have never had a whisker of an accident. I have no intention to let an accident happen to me this time on my way to the resort. Neither can I imagine one happening to me on the slope."

"Neither did your friend. I suppose he did not plan to have an accident either, but it happened when he least expected it. A very tragic accident. Mark, no one plans an accident, it just happens."

"If he didn't lose his goggles on that windy day during the heavy snowfall, and if the snow did not blind his vision and made it impossible for him to see where he was going, I am sure he would not have skied into that tree. Sweetheart, what makes you think this time I could get involved in an accident of any sort. Furthermore, I'll take care more than ever, because now I have a loving, beautiful wife who is waiting at home for me. So what do you say my dear wife? And no, Sweetheart, I am not taking you for a fool. I love you too much. I'll get to the ski resort and come back as whole as when I should leave from here."

Regardless of what Jennifer may have done or what she might have said, she realized it was not enough to sway Mark from his obsession. He wanted to go skiing.

"All right, all right!" she snapped, almost to the point of loosing her cool, "seeing you're bent on going, your dear wife says it's up to you. If you want to go out there and get your high, Mark, it's really up to you."

"You don't have to remind me it's only for this one time, sweetheart. From now on I will keep my promise—and any other I should make to you."

"When the next heavy snowfall comes you'll be burning with the desire to do the same."

"I won't," Mark said. "Sweetheart, I won't. Trust me on this. So you don't mind if I go, do you?"

"Mark, like I'd said before and I really meant it. It is up to you. It seems to me the only thing I could do to prevent you from going is to tie, or nail you down. That I am not prepared to do."

She'd need help to accomplish that task.

Jennifer watched Mark gathered his skiing gears. He went to the garage and loaded his skiing gears, his waxed, polished skies into his white four-by-four SUV. He went back into the house, hugged Jennifer, kissed her and said, "Sweetheart, I am on my way to Horseshoe Valley."

Horseshoe Valley is located in the skiing belt about an hour drive north of Toronto, one of Mark's favourite places to ski.

"While you are having fun on the ski slope, my darling, who knows, I could be having some fun of my own."

"What fun, my dear wife?"

"Don't you worry? I might take it upon myself to venture out in the snow, as you are about to do. Although I have nothing planned at the moment I am sure I could find something to do."

"Something like what?"

"There are lots of things I could do, especially something pleasurable during your absence." Jennifer pushed him gently towards the door. "You can never ever say your wife prevented you from enjoying your favourite sport."

"Whatever you may do," Mark said, "don't do anything silly."

"Mark, I have no intention of doing anything, as you say, silly. May God go with you? God the unseen pilot, your invisible company, the One who's always there for us, the One who have our lives in His hands."

Highway 400 leading north towards the ski resort was slushy but not overly dangerous for driving. Also, the sun was shinning. But shortly after Mark turned off the major highway onto the road leading to the ski resort, the sun suddenly disappeared and it became gloomy and snow began to fall. The snowflakes were like nothing Mark had ever seen before. They seemed weighty, too.

"Good grief," he said. "It's as if I can hear those snowflakes crashing against the windshield."

The windshield wiper blades had difficulty keeping those flakes off the windshield. Tire tracks made in the snow, from wheels of vehicles, were covered quickly by the snow.

"I have never seen snow coming down like this before," Mark said. "It is coming down as if it is angry, with a vengeance. This is not good for driving at all."

Mark had about another thirty-five kilometres to go before he reached the ski resort. He thought the road was desolate for that time of day, because up to then, only one vehicle went by in the opposite direction. He was coming to a bend in the road, precipice on both sides, and just about at that particular time, his conscience began to bother him. His conscience was telling him he was doing wrong to his wife. He also thought they would not be man and wife, had he not told her he'd forget about skiing for the first couple of winters of their marriage, and he should not have broken his promise so soon after they'd gotten married, if at all.

"I'll call her," he whispered. "I'll call her to tell her I am coming back home. I am being unfair to her. If she had made a promise to me, and broke it as I have done, I'm certain I wouldn't have liked it at all."

Mark took his eyes off the road to locate his cell phone that was in the passenger seat, so he could call Jennifer. He undid his seatbelt so he could have easier access to the phone. He glanced at the phone again as he reached for it, and that was not a good thing . . . a huge mistake. He found out days afterwards how costly his mistake was. Because, with his mind off his driving for a split second, whatever he did to cause the vehicle to change course, was enough to send it into a slight skid.

In Mark's endeavour to bring the vehicle under control, by engaging the brake pedal gently, Mark inadvertently pushed on the gas pedal. Realizing what he'd done he shifted his foot from the gas pedal and jammed it onto the brake pedal. The vehicle went into a huge skid. It skidded off the road, rolled several times, bounced off and over obstacles while going down the embankment and into the precipice on the left hand side of the road. Mark bounced around in the vehicle as a ragdoll would. When the white vehicle settled at the bottom of the precipice, it was almost buried completely in the soft snow, and could barely be seen because of its blending with the snow in the gloomy weather. The snow, raining down from the sky, quickly covered tracks made by his vehicle, too.

Mark was trapped in his vehicle. He was badly hurt. He called out for help as loudly as he possibly could from the bottom of the precipice in the enclosure of his vehicle, but with no pedestrian traffic in the area, his weak cries for help were useless.

Mark drifted into unconsciousness.

Would he die in the vehicle or would someone rescue him?

-2-

He Suffered Greatly because of His Insubordination

BEFORE MARK HAD LEFT the house for the ski resort, he told Jennifer he'd come back home around eight to nine o'clock p.m that night. When he did not show within the time he'd specified, and beyond, Jennifer began to worry. Many things that could've gone wrong with him entered her troubled thoughts.

Mark had also left her the phone number for the ski resort. She called the resort. Mark did not book in.

If he did not make it to the resort, she wondered, where could he be?

Jennifer called Mark's parents and a friend of his. They knew nothing about his whereabouts. She called her close friend, Dona. "Dona, today Mark left here to go skiing. He did not make it to the ski resort. I am very frightened. I don't know what to do. He should've been home hours ago. Nobody, not even anybody at the ski resort, could give me a satisfactory answer about him."

"That's strange." Dona said. "If he hadn't called you and you don't know where he is or could be you should call the police?"

"Dona, call the police? What for?"

"Since nobody had heard from him . . . nobody knows where he is, the police might know. Probably his vehicle was disabled along the way."

"He has a cell phone. If he'd gotten into any difficulty, I'd have known about it."

"What if he was involved in an accident and he was unable to use the phone."

"An accident!" Jennifer said with a frightened voice.

"Calm down Jennifer, calm down." Dona said. "I did not say he was involved in an accident, I only made reference to an accident. Sometimes when somebody is in a bad accident, even though a cell phone is in his or her position that person is unable to use it. Since nobody knows where Mark is, if he was involved in an accident the police should know or might know. Call them and see if they know anything."

"Dona, an accident? I told him. I told him." Jennifer said her voice racing. "I told him not to leave the comfort of his warm house to go skiing because by doing so he was breaking a promise he'd made to me."

"I understand, Jennifer," Dona said. "It's no point in getting hysterical. Hang up and call the police, all right?"

"All right, I'll do as you've suggested—call the police."

"Call me back after you speak with the police."

"I will," Jennifer promised. She hung up.

Instead of calling the police station in the area closest to the ski resort, Jennifer called the police station closest to her home. She explained the reason for her call.

"We are unable to help you from this station," someone said to her. "You need to call the station in the area closest to the ski resort."

"Do you have the number for that station?" she asked.

"Please wait just a minute." He came back and gave Jennifer the number for the police station in that area.

Jennifer hurried her call to that station, gave her name to the person who answered, and told him why she was calling.

"Please stay on the line," the person said to her. It'll only take a minute."

Jennifer waited. The wait seemed like forever. She was fidgety. "What's taking you so long? Will you please hurry up?"

The person came back on the line. "Mrs. Dawes, I'm afraid we can't help you. We cannot connect the name you've given to us with anyone bearing that name who was involved in any auto accident in our jurisdiction any time during the day, even up to now as we speak."

"What do you mean by, you can't help me? My husband is missing, I believe, somewhere in the area under your jurisdiction and you can't help me?"

"Mrs. Dawes, I am sorry about you husband, but we can't help you. Oh, by the way, what's his plate number?"

"His plate number?"

"Yes, his plate number. Can you give us the licence plate number of his vehicle?"

Jennifer rocked her brains quickly. "Licence plate number? I can't remember it. I don't know his licence plate number. That was something I never thought of memorizing."

"If you had the plate number to give to us maybe it would help us to help you. I know you've seen his vehicle's plate number many times. Please try your hardest to remember it, and when you do call us back."

"I've already told you I don't know the plate number of my husband's vehicle."

"Mrs. Dawes, I heard you. Anyway, settle down and try your best. Sometimes when we are not thinking straight we tend to forget. I'm so sorry we are unable to help. I/we wish it were possible to help you."

The distraught Jennifer reluctantly hung up the phone. She called Dona back, as she'd promised.

"Dona, the police can't help me. Where is my husband? What has happened to him? Good Lord, what happened to him? Where is he?"

"Don't worry yourself too much," Dona said. "If the police have nothing on him, let's presume wherever he is he's okay. It's late, and the weather outside is nasty but I'm coming over. See you in a bit."

Dona could walk from her home on Dragoon Crescent to Jennifer's home on Big Red Avenue. Instead, she took her car out of the garage and drove over to Jennifer's.

Dona hugged Jennifer. "I know how you're felling, but you should not worry yourself unnecessarily."

"Dona, I can't help but worry."

"I know," Dona said. "It's human tendency to worry over something that's bothering them. Again I must say, wherever Mark is, let's hope he's all right."

Both women chatted for awhile. Sometimes whatever they say to each other brought smiles to their faces, and small laughter, too.

Dona thought of something. "Am . . . the police did not help you. Did you ask them to list him as a missing person?"

"Report him as being a missing person? No, I did not. What good would that do? They asked me for the licence plate number of his vehicle. I could not give it to them. They said it would help them to locate Mark. Oh how I wish I knew or remember his licence plate number."

"All is not lost," Dona said. "Although you don't have the plate number to give to them call them back and list Mark as a missing person. That could get you some action, where they are concerned."

"Dona, are you sure about this. Do you really think it'll help?"

"At a time like this, we can't wait for the sure thing. We have to act on a hunch. A hunch that more often than we realize brings result in ways we did not expect."

Upon Dona's suggestion, Jennifer called the police station for the second time that night. And even before she stated who she was, the person who answered the phone recognized her voice.

Mrs. Dawes," the person said, "do you have the plate number for us?"

"I have already told you I can't remember the plate number. The answer is no, no, no! How many times do I have to tell you? It is *NO* for the very last time."

"Mrs. Dawes, please tell me this. Why are you calling us back?" he said with a calm voice.

"To put my husband on the missing person's list."

"According to my recollection, Mrs. Dawes, you haven't heard from your husband in a few hours. Am I right?"

"Yes, you're right."

"Well, Mrs. Dawes, according to the law, a person cannot be reported missing until after he went missing for twenty-four hours or more. Do you understand?"

"Yes I understand but what kind of a law is that? What does it matter if a person is missing for an hour, twelve hours or more? Anyway you cut it he is missing, isn't he?"

"You say your husband is missing, that's your prerogative. If we devote time to calls such as yours, and there weren't any guideline as to how to handle those calls, we would be on a forever wild goose chase. Sometimes folks call in, as you are doing now, and later we find out their calls were of the mischievous kind. That is the reason for guidelines, standard for everyone. Call us back later if you haven't heard from or see you husband within that period. Again I'll stress, without knowing his plate number there's nothing we can do to help."

"Okay," she said almost at a whisper. And very dejected. "What else can I do?" She hung up. Then she turned to Dona and sad, "It's no good. Dona, it's no good. We can't report Mark as a missing person before he's missing for at least twenty-four hours."

"Well, my fried," Dona said, "there isn't anything else we can do, but wait. Wait, wait and hope he'll eventually come home the way he'd left."

"I hope so. Dona, I hope to God he does, with a very good explanation."

Dona, the owner of a convenient store, spent the rest of the night with Jennifer. In the early morning hours, she called her subordinate, gave her instructions and told her that she, Dona, probably won't come into the store anytime during the day.

The sun shone brightly on the day after Mark and his vehicle got buried in the snow. And although the warmth of the sun was felt through window panes, outside it did not make too much of a difference, because it was just as cold as it was the day before. However, although the sun did not do much to warm humans while they were outdoors, it was enough to warm some materials to a degree. It melted snow from the roofs of some buildings and from roofs of some vehicles.

So, near noon that day, someone on her way to the ski resort thought she saw something like the roof of a vehicle at the bottom of the precipice. She stopped, viewed the object, and sure enough the object was the roof of a white vehicle.

She dialled 911 and reported what she thought she'd seen. The police were on the scene shortly after she reported her find. And it took rescuers quite awhile to get the unconscious Mark—cold as ice—from the badly damaged vehicle, and they were amazed that with all the damage the vehicle sustained not a single window was broken. They took him to the area hospital.

They also found out, from the information they gathered from his driver's licence, who he was and where he lived. And they obtained his home telephone number from a receptionist at the telephone exchange.

It was well passed midday, the day they found Mark, when Jennifer's phone rang. She grabbed it impatiently and said "Hello! Hello!" with a frightened voice.

"May I ask you?" the officer said, after he'd identified himself, "what's your connection with a person by the name of Mark Dawes?"

From her anxiousness to hear of her husband's whereabouts, without giving much though to questions asked, she readily gave information.

"I am Jennifer Dawes. Mark Dawes is my husband. I don't know where he is. Yesterday he left from here to go skiing. I have not seen or herd from him since then. Why are you asking?"

"Yes, we know you haven't seen him since yesterday, because you phoned here last night enquiring if we knew anything about his whereabouts. We know he did not come back to his home last night."

"Oh yes! Yes I did phone in about him." Jennifer gave some thought to the last part of what he'd said. "Why did you say you know he did not come home?"

"Mrs. Dawes," he said. He paused; pulled in a couple ounces of fresh air into his lung before he delivered the message he anticipated would cause her great worry. "Mrs. Dawes, we should send someone to talk to you but seeing you are so far away we'll have to do so over the phone."

". . . send someone to talk to me, about what?"

"About your husband, Mrs. Dawes."

"What . . . my husband? You found Mark? What happened to him? Where is he? Is he all right?"

"We found your husband shortly before noon today—"

"Is he all right? Is he all right?" Jennifer asked hurriedly, while feeling emptiness in the pit of her stomach.

"No Mrs. Dawes. Your husband is not all right."

"What happened to him? Oh God . . . what happened to him? Please tell me!"

Dona was listening while Jennifer was on the phone.

"Mrs. Dawes, well, your husband had an accident."

"Oh no, an accident? Oh no please God Almighty. An accident? Mark, Mark!" Jennifer shouted, stamping her feet on the plush, beige carpet. She dropped the phone and buried her face in her hands. She began to sob.

Dona jumped up. "Jennifer what's wrong . . . what accident?"

"Mark had an accident," She said with a weak voice.

"How bad is it?" Dona asked, wrapping her arms quickly around Jennifer.

"Dona, I don't know."

At that moment, both Jennifer and Dona had forgotten someone was still on the line.

"Oh, the phone!" Dona said. She picked it up and said, "Hello!"

"Is that you, Mrs. Dawes?"

"No. I am her friend, Dona Sanghster. Tell me what else you want to say to her."

"Will you please ask Mrs. Dawes to come back to the phone?"

"Can't you tell me what else you want to say to her?"

"I'll only speak with you if Mrs. Dawes is unable to come back to the phone."

"Wait just a minute, please?" Dona said. She covered the mouthpiece of the phone. "Jennifer, he won't talk to me." *It must be some top secret why he insists to talk to her.*

"All right," Jennifer said, "give me the phone. Officer, what else do you want to say to me . . . How bad an accident was it?"

"Mrs. Dawes, we found your husband's vehicle at the bottom of a precipice. He was in it. Ma'am, your husband is badly hurt. He is in the hospital, in a coma. I am sorry to give you such bad news."

Jennifer wailed. She squeezed the phone tightly. "Good Lord!" she said, "I can't take it! This is too much for me to bear."

"I am sorry, Mrs. Dawes," the officer said. "I'm so sorry. Let me give you the address of the hospital where he is."

Jennifer told the officer she was shaking, and was unable to write, that he should give the information to her friend. She gave the phone to Dona. "Take the address of the hospital." She dropped limply into the sofa and lie down, her hands cupping her face.

During her taking of the information from the officer, Dona heard Jennifer's mournful whimper of, "Lord what am I going to do? Will he live? If he'd listened to me, he wouldn't have end up having an accident. Why did he have to leave the comfort of this home to go skiing? Lord, please help me? Please help him, too. If he did not break his promise to me none of this would've happened."

After Dona finished taking the information, about the hospital, she hung up the phone. She sat beside Jennifer.

"Jennifer," she said, "come here."

Jennifer sat up.

Dona hugged Jennifer. "My dear," she said, "in life whatever must be; must be. Mark could have been in this house and still could've had an accident of some sort."

"But how? That would not be possible."

"Not possible. Jennifer, accidents do happen is homes, accident where even lives are lost. Have you heard the story of the man who said he's not leaving his home, because he wanted to stay out of trouble?"

"Yes. The story of the coconut husk the man threw out the window when he was through eating the meat of the coconut."

"Exactly. He was sitting in his home, yet he was involved in an accident."

"But there is no similarity," Jennifer said, "between that man's accident and Mark's. Mark left the comfort of this home to go skiing, something he did not have to do. If he'd stayed home, I am positive he would not have had an accident."

"Yes, I understand," Dona said, "but . . . so you see, accident do happen when you least expect it. Let's hope he gets out of that coma and get well."

"Dona, there isn't anything else we can do but hope. I must go to see him, but I'm in no shape to drive myself."

"What are friends for?" Dona said. "I don't like to drive in this type of weather but I'll take you to the hospital."

"You will?

"Yes. We'll leave whenever you're ready."

Jennifer thought of Mark's parents, whom she told she feared for his safety, and up to then none of them had bothered to call her to find out if she'd found Mark or if he was OK. Nevertheless, she'd let them know she was aware of his whereabouts and the condition he was in.

Upon informing her, Mark's mother, his father was not at home, she was alarmed, said she feared for her son's life. She also wanted to know which hospital he was in because she wanted to go and visit him, or maybe go to the hospital with Jennifer. But Jennifer told her she was going to the hospital with her friend. She'll keep her informed.

Jennifer said a silent prayer before they began their journey to the hospital. And except for whiteouts here and there, their journey went smoothly, even though Dona had feared they could encounter problems along the way. Upon reaching the hospital, they went in and Jennifer went to the information desk. She told the receptionist who she was.

"Mrs. Dawes, your husband is on the second floor."

When Jennifer got to the second floor, Dona behind her, she again said who she was.

"Mrs. Dawes," the nurse said, "such a pity about your husband. I hope you are not taking it too hard. He is in . . . give me a minute, please. I'll take you to him. When we get to his room please be as quiet as you can. We shouldn't do anything to disturb him."

Jennifer and Dona looked at Mark lying motionless in the bed with his eyes closed, small tubes attached to his nose and one arm, a leg in a sling. Jennifer held his hand, sighed deeply and said softly, "Mark, Mark, it's me Jennifer. I am here for you. And Dona is here with me."

Mark did not move a muscle.

Jennifer bent over him, gave him a semi hug and kissed him. She held his hand again and said, "Mark, darling, if you can hear me please open your eyes. Squeeze my hand, darling, that way I'll know you know I am here."

The result was the same as before.

Jennifer broke down and began to weep, not loudly, so as not to cause any noticeable noise, or disturbance, to anyone but Dona, whose shoulder she wept on.

Dona hugged Jennifer and tried to console her. Jennifer kept on weeping. However, she managed to say softly, "He's so much out of it, Dona. He's really out of it. Am I going to lose him? Dona, I am so scared for him."

"All we have to do is wait," Dona said. "Wait and see what happens."

Dona's emotion was about to overcome her. "Jennifer, she said, "I share your grief. Do you mind if I go outside for a minute?"

"Why, Dona, and leave me all alone?"

"I don't really want to leave you by yourself. If I should start crying, as you are doing, we could get swept away by our emotions, and without realizing it cause uproar. We're supposed to keep it as quiet as we can."

"I know, but I can't help expressing the way I am feeling. Go ahead," Jennifer said. She released Dona from her embrace. Jennifer wiped away the tears from her eyes.

Dona calmed her own emotion while she was away from Jennifer. She went back into the room and as she was about to speak to Jennifer, the nurse walked in. The nurse saw the sorry look on Jennifer's face.

"Mrs. Dawes," the nurse said, "I know how you are feeling. This may not be any consolation to you, but we are doing all we can for him. Over the years, I have seen a multitude of accident victims come into this hospital: Some of them with their limbs dangling; some with very bad lacerations, stab wounds, and some of them with situation similar to or worse than your husband's. Sometimes we wonder how some of those with limbs dangling ever made it, and why some of those in similar or better state than your husband's did not make it. Nevertheless, according to signs we observed from your husband, we believe he'll recover. When he comes out of his unconscious state, we hope soon, we'll send him to another hospital in the big city (Toronto was the big city), probably at a hospital close to where you live."

"I'll like that very much," Jennifer said. "Could I stay with him for the night?"

The nurse thought for a while. She knew visiting hours were over, but with the understanding Jennifer came a long way to see her husband, she was not about to push her out.

"Mrs. Dawes," the nurse said, "you have exceeded visiting time. I am here until eleven o'clock p.m and I can't assure you the next nurse coming on duty will let you stay for the night. I know you want to stay with your husband, but may I suggest you go to a hotel or a hostel, rest up for the night and come back tomorrow to see how he's doing? If you wish, I'll call some place closest to here for you. It's a service we provide for someone like you, who's experiencing a difficult time."

"Thanks nurse, but there's no need for you to bother," Dona said. "Just tell us how to get to any of those places. We'll go there and make our own arrangements."

During the night, Jennifer said to Dona, "From our haste to get to the hospital we did not think about change of clothes."

"We were not thinking straight," Dona said. "Probably deep down in our minds, without saying it to each other, we thought we could visit Mark and make it back home in good time."

"I suppose it did not occur to us," Jennifer said, "because two many other things were going through our minds all at once. Anyway, change of clothing is the least among the things worrying me. I must call Mark's parents."

Mother Dawes was relieved to hear from Jennifer. She also felt, according to Jennifer's report as to what the nurse had said, her son had a good chance to pull through. In addition, again according to the nurse, he might come to a hospital in the city soon, one she hoped was close to her home so she could visit Mark at will.

When Jennifer was through talking to mother Dawes, she said to Dona, "There must be somewhere close around here where we could go in the morning and do what's necessary to rectify the clothes situation."

"I suppose so," Dona said.

"Also in the morning," Jennifer, a teacher, replied, "before we go out, I have to call the principal to let her know I won't be coming in; maybe not for the rest of the week, either."

"I have to do likewise," Dona said. "Call my helper again and tell her not to expect me, either."

Jennifer called the principal and explained the reason why she'd be absent. The principal said she understood. She sympathised with Jennifer and told her she wished the best for her husband.

Jennifer and Dona went to the hospital in new clothes.

"Mrs. Dawes," the nurse said, 'your husband was asking for you. I told him you and your friend were here last night and that you'll be back today. I hope he fully understood." She did not tell Jennifer he'd drifted back to sleep without replying.

Jennifer opened her eyes wide. She stabbed the index finger of her right hand at her chest, "Me!" she said excitedly. "Really? Was he really asking for me? Dona, did you hear that? Mark was asking for me. That means he's conscious then."

They rushed to his room.

"Darling," Jennifer said, as she hugged Mark who was still groggy, "how are you feeling? Yesterday I was here and you did not know I existed. You are back with us and I am so very happy. You'll be all right from now on. Hold me darling. Please hold me. I thought I was about to lose you forever but you're back with us. It is such a wonderful feeling. I love you darling. I really love you."

Although Mark was still highly sedated, the look in his groggy, brown eyes told its own story, when he saw Jennifer. He tried lifting his arms to hug Jennifer. They were weak, so he was unable to lift them. In fact, his whole body was very weak. He was yet to sit up since they brought him to the hospital.

Nevertheless, he spoke slowly with a weak voice, through an apparent smile. "Sweetheart, I love you too. It's good to see you. I am not feeling good at all. My whole body is numb." He closed his eyes and said nothing more.

Jennifer hung her head out the door. "Nurse, nurse!" she called out. She'd forgotten to keep it as quiet as she could.

The nurse, from hearing the urgency in Jennifer's voice, was alarmed because she thought something had gone dreadfully wrong. She rushed to the room.

"Nurse, I was talking to my husband and he flaked out."

"Don't worry," the nurse said. "Your husband is still sedated. It takes awhile when someone was heavily sedated, as you husband was, and mind you, he's just coming out of a coma, to be totally coherent. Your husband is making progress in the right direction. Don't worry about him not having long conversation with you now. He'll be okay. As planned, we will relocate him later today or early tomorrow. We will let you know which hospital will accommodate him, preferably one close to your home where you'll be able to visit him regularly. Mrs. Dawes, when visiting time is over you may go home. We shall inform you while your husband is in transition."

Early the next day, and luckily for Jennifer, they transferred Mark from that hospital to another hospital in Scarborough, only blocks from their home. She visited him, and she was very happy to see a much-improved almost fully coherent Mark. He was also very happy to see her. Now they were able to converse with each other. Mark also felt a surge of strength, a surge of strength that came only from within his mind. He tried sitting up but had difficulty doing so.

Jennifer noticed his struggling. She assisted him, in using pillows to prop him up.

"Darling, you are looking much better than when we left you yesterday."

"We?" Mark said.

"Yes. Dona and I. You spoke to us for a brief moment and then you drifted away. The day before we were there and it seemed to me you were not aware of our presence. I had said something to you as I held your hand, hugged and kissed you. You did not respond."

"Probably I heard you and was unable to respond," Mark said. "Because—maybe it was the day before yesterday, maybe the day before that, or whichever day it was I'm not sure—I felt as though I was having a very bad dream. A dream in which danger lurked, a dream in which I was trapped; a dream in which I called out for help but nobody came to assist me; a dream in which I thought I herd wee, faraway voices. Probably those wee voices I heard in the faraway were that of yours, a nurse or somebody's. I struggled desperately to respond to the voice. I could not. I felt trapped in that dream, helplessly trapped. Nevertheless, though I spoke with you briefly yesterday, I knew you were there. Today I am feeling much better than I did yesterday. Now I know I was not dreaming during the time I thought I was hearing wee faraway voices, but that I had a very bad accident."

"So how are you feeling now?"

"From my waist down I have no feeling in one leg, very little in the other; otherwise, not that bad."

That's a sign he could be partially paralysed, Jennifer thought. Although within her heart she thought, given time, she hoped he'll recover fully.

"For now, darling, don't worry about it. Give yourself time to heal."

"I asked the doctor if he thinks I am paralysed. He said it's too soon to tell. More tests are needed before he could come to that conclusion, but time and good medication could help me to recover fully."

"We have to wait and see what happens," Jennifer said. "In the meantime while we're waiting, you must do whatever you can to help yourself to get well. God is on our side. He will help in the healing process."

Mark sighed heavily. "If I did not break the promise I'd made to you I wouldn't find myself in this situation, sitting here in this hospital bed feeling less than a man. You begged me not to leave the comfort of our home, to go skiing. Why, oh why, I did not listen. Just look at you, so radiant and so beautiful, and I am in this hospital bed practically useless. Yes indeed, I made a huge mistake. I should've kept my promise. "Sweetheart—"

"Yes darling."

"I owe you a huge apology. I also want to explain . . ."

From perceiving what he was about to say, Jennifer said quickly, "Mark," while putting her finger over his lips, "Darling, don't say it. This is not the time for any apology or for any explanation. We can talk about it some other time. You must rest and don't do anything to excite yourself. I am happy you are still alive. Regardless of what you may do or say now won't change the situation. We just have to accept it, take it one step at a time, adjust our lives and learn to live with it. Regardless of the bad shape you're in I hope you're happy you did not lose your life."

"Yes, sweetheart," Mark said with a low voice. "Happy I am. I am also very, very grateful, too, to be alive."

Jennifer visited Mark as often as she could for the rest of that week. She went back to work the following week, therefore she could only visit him during evenings of each workday, but did so on weekends as often as she were allowed, according to hospital rules. But Mark was not short of visitors, because his parents visited him often, also friends were always dropping in.

Although Mark had agreed to wait until the time was right to apologize to Jennifer, to explain what caused him to have had the accident, he felt as if he was muzzled. After waiting for more than a week, he decided to cast off the muzzle. Since he felt the delay was doing him more harm than good. He wanted to get it over and done with, to relieve himself of the stress of having what he wanted to say to her off his mind. Several times, he reflected to what his father had said to him, hours before he got married, as he stood in front of his father and his mother, his mother nodding her head in approval to what his father was telling him.

'Son,' his farther had said, 'you are about to take the biggest oath in your life, by taking an oath to become the husband to a woman. Listen to yourself carefully as you repeat the vow after the Pastor. It is a very serious vow like no other. You must abide by the vow, and as you go along add your own attachments to it. We have, and that is why your mother and I are still having a wonderful life together. Mark, any negative deviation and you may live to regret it.' Mark sighed, *Dad you were so right.*

Therefore, on one of Jennifer's evening visits, he said, "Jenny, sweetheart, I'd like you to hear me out."

"About what, darling?"

"The apology I owe you and what caused the accident. If only I had listened to you. Sweetheart," he squeezed her hand gently, "I do apologize to you from the bottom of my heart. I should not have done what I did. I will never break another promise to you. I am so sorry I did."

"Darling, I accept your apology wholeheartedly. I was not worried about not getting one, anyway. My concern is for you to get well."

"I understand, but I owed it to you."

Mark explained to her how the accident happened. *Wow, It's such a relief.*

"You should've just turn around and come back home," she said, "instead of reaching for your phone to inform me. Besides, and you should've kept your seatbelt fastened, you know it is not advisable to use the phone while you are driving, let alone in such terrible weather condition. Because of that, you have learned a very painful lesson. Thank God, you did not lose your life. We could also look at it from this point of view that, the accident happened because of your insubordination. Then again, maybe not, because it could be that you were meant to suffer this fate. Mark, nobody, but only the Good Lord, the Good Lord who's the author and dictator of each person's fate, knows why the accident happened."

"I am so sorry, sweetheart, I'm so sorry," Mark said sadly. "Why, oh why did I break my promise to you?"

"Mark, you did so because of your passion for skiing, and that's the bottom line."

"Yes, I know . . . but just look at me. I am now less than the man you vowed to spend the rest of your life with. My life, where I am concerned, is now worthless."

"Mark, don't ever let me hear you say that again. Please don't harbour those thoughts. I know you are in a bad way. I know you're saying these things because you're worried, and scared, wondering if you'll have to rely on a wheelchair or crutches to get around. By now, you should realize you won't heal in a hurry, or overnight, so you have to give your body time to heal. Nevertheless, no matter what, you are my husband. I love you. We made a vow, which says, for better or for worst. I will take care of you; this I promise. Whether you have to rely on a wheelchair or crutches to get from one place to the other, *I will never leave you.* Under no circumstance will I ever leave you. I love you too much."

"But sweetheart, my dear wife . . ."

"Mark, there's absolutely no but."

In due time, Mark was discharged from the hospital, fearing out much better than he had imagined. He was able to get around with the full use of one leg.

Jennifer did not have to worry about him strapping a pair of snow skies on his feet any time soon, nor maybe not for the rest of his life.

In took some time, but Mark made good on his Caribbean cruise promise.

Sometimes, due to accidents, changes for better or for worse do occur. And whether it was Mark's fate or not, would he ever forget that near fatal day in his life?

LUCKY CHILD

-I-

Money Worries

Circumstances forced him to join the Work Force, but the disadvantaged Johnny Price vowed he would become a millionaire.

It was Friday evening and Johnny Price (JP), in worn out jeans and thick plaid shirt with several pencil-size holes, had just been paid. He strolled to his red and white jalopy while squeezing stolidly the pay cheque in his hand, wondering from where he'd get his next pay cheque. He sighed deeply, then got into his jalopy and drove home slowly, and thoughtfully, to his badly repaired house in Williamsfield Road, the province of Wellington.

He leaned against his car, looked to the blue shy, and shook his head sadly. "Lord," he said, "another one of those Fridays—I don't need you any more. When a situation such as this will end?" Then he turned to his left and walked casually to the front door of the house to the aroma of fried chicken, the meat that he often had for dinner. The door was ajar. He pushed it open, walked in and said "Hi" to his mother—Miriam. And to his siblings, David, Alvin and Rachael.

Miriam—Mom or Mama—, in her housecoat, hair in curlers, a huge, long silver fork in her right hand, noticed JP's unusual frown. "Is everything all right?"

Jp did not answer. He pulled his pay cheque out of his pocket, glared at it but did not give it to his mother as he usually did. Instead, he slammed it hard on the kitchen counter.

His mother jumped. A couple of her curlers dislodged. "What's that all about?" she said.

"No more to come from where this usually comes from. This is the end of it. And it hurts badly." Cry lines formed on his face.

"We had talk about it, didn't we?" his mama, Miriam, said.

"So does that change anything?"

"This is not the first time. And no, it does not. But we always make out, don't we?"

"Make out? Just barely, and I am sick of how often it happens."

They stared at him in alarm.

The weary JP with fingers almost like prongs of a pitchfork, whose hands could almost spawn a basketball, dragged himself to his shabby room. He pulled off his brown leather boots, and took off his plaid shirt with its sleeves amputated halfway up thus giving it the appearance of a short sleeve shirt. He lay in his bed. He clasped a pillow on his chest.

While JP stared blankly at the ceiling, that would need more than a pale of paint to give it an eye-catching appearance, his thought flashed to his deceased father who'd died months after the last addition to the family. "If only we had money, and furthermore, if dad was not working as a labourer," he said, "he'd probably be alive today and I feel things would be much better. I miss him so much." JP sighed again. He sat up, and the pillow almost came apart as he sunk his huge fist savagely into it. Then he sprang to his feet as if he was a cannon ball shot from a Cannon, and he said with the tone of the lowest male singing voice, "Why are we so disadvantaged?" He grabbed a white piece of paper about eighteen inches long by about six inches wide.

What was JP up to? What, if anything, did the white piece of paper have to do with him being disadvantage? Would he simply crush the piece of paper; take his anger out on it?

Jp found a pen, and with that pen, he wrote on the white piece of paper in very large letters in red ink—I AM GOING TO BE A MILLIONAIRE! He fastened the piece of paper above his dilapidated dresser, stepped back, stared at what he wrote and said emphatically, **"Money is out there! I am going to get my share! I will be a millionaire!"**

JP's mother, and David, heard his raised voice, which did not alarm David. But his mother wondered what was going on with him, because she knew he was fuming with anger. "JP," she called out, "what's bothering you now? Are you all right?"

"Yes, Mom, I am all right. But why are we so disadvantaged? I was telling myself I am going to be a millionaire."

Due to a pregnancy, in her teens, Miriam got married at the age of sixteen. She kept herself well. She could pass for JP's elder sister. Besides being his mother, she and he had something else in common: forced into the workforce because of circumstances, caused by the untimely passing of Joseph the head of the family. Therefore at the time of his outburst, of this millionaire thing, she had begun to think the pressure on him helping her to take care of the family, since he turned seventeen, was getting to him. "JP," she said, *Oh God I wish Joseph was alive, oh how my heart still bleeds for him,* "JP, I know its been hard on you helping me to take care of this family since I lost my full-time job." She paused and waited for a response.

Miriam did not get as much as a whisper from him, so she continued by saying, "JP, we are, were, because now he doesn't have a job, barely seeing us through from your odd pay cheques and my two days pay each week, which I hope will continue. Where your next pay cheque will come from, and we also know, only God knows. So what makes you think, under these unsavoury circumstances, you can become a millionaire? Yes, we are disadvantaged because we have no money. Well yes, we have no money."

Now JP said, "Mom, it is awfully troubling we are so disadvantaged because we have no money. Money is out there. I am going to get my share, and we won't be disadvantaged anymore."

"How can you make it happen? Did you fall asleep and dreamt about becoming a millionaire?"

"No Mom, nothing like that. I just know I will be a millionaire," he said with much conviction.

"Huh! A millionaire? That is such an unattainable wishful thinking."

"Yea, right Mom," David said. "I say puff to that."

JP did not hear David's comment. He heard what his mother had said, and he responded with, "Mom, I heard that. That comment of yours tells me you are thinking that, what I'd said about becoming a millionaire is pure foolishness, but you'll see."

"JP, my son, if it'll make you feel any better, good luck to you and that way, way-out dream of yours."

"Mom, please don't think so negative. Many times the poorest of the poorest people become millionaires. I am confident I will be one of those poor people who become a millionaire."

His mother who was still making dinner chuckled. "Ha! I hope I'll be around if or when that happens. A millionaire, huh!"

About forty-five minutes after JP and his mother had their short conversation; she called out, "Come JP." (By then his siblings were already gathering at the dinner table.) "Come JP and let's have dinner."

"Yes Mom, I'm coming." *Darn chicken again. Before long, I may grow wings, chicken, chicken and more chicken. Whatever happens to a steak now and then? Yes, I know, steak dinner is unavailable to disadvantaged people like us. Right now, some people cannot even afford chicken. Better go and eat the darn thing, and give thanks.*

Before the strong willed JP went to the dinner table he breathed in deeply and exhaled slowly, upon remembering those times, though not often, when his father took the family out to dinner. Those times were happy times, which he knew would never ever happen again.

The next day, Saturday, JP woke up. Still lying in his bed, he rolled onto his back and stretched his muscular body. He yawned, a long lazy yawn, rubbed the sleep out of his eyes gently, and then looked out through the windowpanes of the partially draped window. "Yep," he said. "It's blue sky all right. Yep, I can see nothing but blue sky."

By then everyone was already up and about, doing one thing or the other. So, JP dragged himself to the kitchen to see what was there for his breakfast. He was not surprised to find, covered in a frying pan without a handle, half of fried egg and two strips of beacon with more fat than lean. "Well," he said, "another one of my typical breakfast. This morning I was expecting some porridge, but one has to ask for whatever he wants and it might be granted." He dunked couple of slices of brown bread in the toaster and waited for it to pop.

Halfway through eating his breakfast, his mother walked in the kitchen in a pair of wellington boots. She had taken a break from tending to chickens that in a few weeks would be on the dinner table. Her rearing of chickens was the main source of the family's meat.

"Find your breakfast?" his mom said. "Of course you have because you're making a feast of it."

"Yea, you're so right mom. I was expecting some cornmeal porridge. Anyway, I should've asked for it, but I wonder if it would've been possible."

"JP we have to go to the store. You could have oatmeal porridge tomorrow instead of cornmeal, how 'bout that?"

"Mom, whichever is just fine with me." *If we can afford it.*

Taking his mother to the store was one of JP'S weekend projects. He also had to take her to go and service Sister Joyce, an older woman of his mother's church members who lived by herself. She did not mind having chicken whenever Marian visited her because it was always a welcome meal.

JP and his mother were driving along on Radcliff Road, on their way to Sister Joyce. Just as they passed the Library, the pedestrian crossing at the stoplight about four car-lengths ahead of them, JP's mother cried out, "JP watch out!" while covering her eyes with her hands. She did not want to witness the impact, which she thought would have occurred.

"Mom, these days you seem to be a bit edgy. I would not have run him over. Even though he shouldn't have darted across the road like that. Why he had to do that when he's so close to the pedestrian crossing makes you wonder. Old faithful," and he tapped on the dashboard of the car, "when I get back home I'll take care of you."

"JP, I have quite a lot to worry about that could put me in the category of edginess. Nevertheless, I am not. You are the one behaving more than edgy with all the strange things on your mind of late. So, do me a huge favour, please?"

"Like what Mom?"

"Please keep your mind on your driving. This car," she said facetiously, "could not withstand an impact with a fast moving human or worse, another moving or stationary vehicle. Every time I open this door, and she pulled on the strap used to pull the door closed, probably for reassurance that the car door was still closed, I keep praying not to have an accident. And also hope I don't accidently leave any of my clothing when I'm getting out." She leaned forward, looked out the windshield. "JP, a bit cloudy but I'm hoping it doesn't rain." She knew if it rains, the chances of her getting wet was a sure bet.

JP's mother had never said such unsavoury things about his car before. So he felt like responding to her according to the way he felt. Instead, he said in a tone in which he hoped she'd not detect his annoyance, "Mom, this car has been and is still taking us wherever we wanted to go. And you could be pleasantly surprised, regarding what you'd said about it, that it could, I feel, come out the better should it encounter a collision with either of the subjects you'd mentioned. Anyhow, I was not actually driving absentmindedly. Do you smell that overpowering chocolate aroma, more like you're tasting it?"

"Yes, such a pleasant smell."

"It's enough to make you salivate, doesn't it mom? Well I was just turning my nose, and of course, you have to turn your head to the direction you want to point your nose, to zero in on the direction where such sweet smell is coming from. Now, we'll do whatever you want to do and get back home safely, then, I'll pamper this old beauty. My old, mama you know, my aged faithful."

To take care of his jalopy, either on a Saturday or on a Sunday, when he had a job, was one of JP's weekend activities, too. He'd put his coverall on, a piece of rag sticking out of its hip pocket, couple pieces of wrenches in his hands; he was not a mechanic but he'd do some light mechanical maintenance. Then he'd give his jalopy a bath, sometimes with the help of David. Or, with the help of his best friend Toby who worked part time at a neighbourhood gas station. Toby lived One Street north of JP's and they hang out together quite a lot.

Sunday, about noon, the athletic David, also the clown in the family, bounced into JP's room. His hands wrapped around a brown basketball with black stripes. JP, in a pensive mood, was sitting at the foot of his bed facing the door. He greeted JP as they did sometimes—with this brother thing.

"Hi, big brother," David said, bouncing the ball on the wooden floor a couple of times. He settled the ball and threw it at JP. JP punched it back at him. He caught the ball. "Hey! You're quite alert in your moment of contemplating. He looked at JP's sign hanging above his dresser. "Contemplating about becoming a millionaire?"

"Something like that, my little brother." His lips barely curl a small contemplative smile. "Now, what's up?"

"JP, you heard what mama had said about this millionaire thing, don't you? She'd said that this millionaire thing won't happen; that you are dreaming an impossible dream. Of which I have to agree. So—if I were you—I would take that banner of yours *I will be a millionaire* thing down, and forget all about it."

JP clenched his teeth. His brother did not understand how disgusted, he, JP was about their lowly life.

"David, hmmm," he breathed out, "they say when you want something badly or want to accomplish something you should make a note of it and put the note at a place where you can look at it as often as you can; centre your thoughts on it and sooner or later whatever you hoped for will eventually happen."

'JP, the way I see it, before that happen you could go mad concentrating on it. I am going out to have fun while exercising at the same time as I concentrate on throwing a few hoops or kick a few balls."

Having fun, that's all he can thing about.

David bounced the ball on the floor again, but he could not gather it cleanly. The ball bounced off his hands and hit JP softly on the side of his head.

And JP barked. "What do you think you're doing? That thing almost hit me in the eye. Get the hell out of here to where you are going."

"All right my big bro. I'm sorry. I am leaving."

Then JP, who felt he was too harsh with his words, said, with a softer voice, "Be careful. We can tend to bruises but we can't afford to pay hospital bills. Be back in time for supper."

David looked back over his shoulder at his brother as he stepped out the door. "Sure you don't want to join us?"

"Not today, little bro.,—just don't have the energy."

"Well, don't worry. I'll take great care and I won't miss super."

After supper that Sunday evening David, Alvin and Rachael excused themselves from the dinner table. They wanted to watch a program on the black and white, snowy TV screen. During their absence JP and his mother began to dialogue, which was nothing new between them. But when she again mentioned about funds paid out by the insurance company after his father's passing, JP stopped her.

"Mom," JP said, "You don't have to go over it anymore. So far since dad's passing you've done whatever you could to take care of us, without depleting the insurance fund. I am only twenty-two, but I am old enough to know, and he did not say a thing about his meagre earnings, it has not been easy for you neither is it an easy road ahead for us. One of these days, by the help of God, or my Guardian Angel, things will get better. Um, Mom," he rolled his eyes as he looked up to the ceiling, then back at her with a soft gaze. A gaze that suggested he was about to reveal an important message, "Mom, I've read about the lottery in some countries. Where, by choosing a set of numbers, one could become an instant millionaire. Not hard work at all, is it. I wish I could go to one of those countries."

The lingering aroma from the curried chicken they had for dinner was still prevalent in the room, as his caring mother, and who was always hopeful that somehow the future could get better but being a millionaire was not something she ever hoped for, reached across the table and held JP's hands gently. She smiled at him. "JP, for you to move to one of those countries is only wishful thinking."

"Mom, wishful thinking or not, I was also thinking if something like that should ever happen, me leaving to go to another country, it would be somewhat painful for me to leave this family. But if it should happen, I would have to give it some careful consideration."

"JP, that separation pain I'm certain you won't experience. So my son, you can forget about it. Anyway, I can only hope and pray that things will eventually get better. Thank God, David is in his last year at technical college. I hope when he graduates he'll find a job in his chosen field. Alvin is in his second year in high school. It's Rachael's turn next. There is barely enough funds left, from the insurance disbursement, to see Alvin through his last year. What we'll do when it is Rachael's turn, only God knows. And just look at this house, it is still falling apart slowly.

"Furthermore, and like I have always maintained, instead of you being here thinking about being a millionaire or to go away to another country, you should still be in school working towards a degree."

"Mom, why are you still so hang-up on this school thing? Haven't I told you over and over again not to worry about it. You know why I haven't stayed in school, which I don't mind, because helping to take care of this family is more important to me than staying in school. Besides, not everyone was born to be a bookworm, or to attain higher education. I am satisfied with what I have, which I know will work well for me. So stop worrying about it. In other words, please forget about it."

"Don't you think a good education is worthwhile?"

"I have a good education," JP said, "but not one in the magnitude of higher learning, which I don't yearn for; neither do I think that you have to have to be a millionaire."

"JP, why is it that this weekend you are so taken up with this millionaire thing?"

"Mom, millionaires are rich people. They have tons and tons of money."

"Well, the way I see it, one does not have to have tons of money but just enough, just enough to bring them happiness in life—JP, just enough."

JP looked at his mother, sadness in his eyes. *Why are we so disadvantaged?* "Anyhow, Mom," he said, "as long as I am alive I'll make sure none of us will have to worry about a thing. We won't even count on David finding a job to help us, because of Job uncertainty. Soon we'll get this house back in good shape."

"JP," his mother shook her head, "we hope."

"Ok mom. Anyway, I haven't anything to do tomorrow but I feel, with the help of God and my Guardian Angel, I will find something to do."

"Son," She sensed how sad he was, "these days it seem to be getting much more difficult for you to find something to do but, I am keeping my fingers crossed, along with some prayers, on your behalf."

"Yes mom, please do. I know God is standing by."

He has such a good heart, she thought. "I love you JP. I really do."

"And I love you, too, Mom."

His mother sighed deeply. "Well," she said as she stood up. "Better get on with it, finish my chores for the evening." She meant doing some cleaning up.

JP stood up, walked over to her and wrapped his arms around her. He kissed her on the cheek.

"Oh," she leaned her head back, "that feels so good, as always."

"Mom," JP said, while he still hugged her, his thoughts drifting. "Mom, somehow we'll manage. Need some help with your chores?"

"No," she said. "I'll be all right."

"Well then . . ." He let go of her and turned around. "Seeing that you don't need any help, I'm going to my room."

With his back to her, she watched him walked away, and it was as if she was looking at Joseph walking away from her. She sighed again, "Just like his father, he really has such a good, big heart. No wonder I love him so much. Then too, something I cannot explain, and I really don't know why it is so, but I can't explain why lately every time he gives me those tender hugs, and kissed me I get those mixed-up feelings. Well, I had better get on with it and occupy my mind with something else."

Miriam stopped ruminating and gathered the few dishes that were left on the table. She walked into the kitchen and put those dishes in the kitchen sink. Then, while resting her palms on the edge of sink, she leaned forward. "Joseph." she said, "I am still missing you so much." And as she began to relive the cause of his death, she went into that tantrum—the vigorous shaking of her body, which was not as severe now as it used to be. She had also overcome the grabbing and throwing of objects. "Joseph," she said again while shaking her head sadly, "you were such a caring person; the love of my life. I can never forget you. Oh how my heart still yearns for you.

"Ouch!" she said, as if she felt the thrust of a small pointed object deep into her body as she thought of the way they told her Joseph met his death, something she'd been trying hard to forget which did not show any signs of going away, "that was such a horrible way to die. That concrete slab flattened him as flat as a pancake. They had to use shovels to scrape up whatever was left of him, from off the concrete pavement. Probably if he had died of natural causes and I had gotten one last look at his face, it might not be hurting as much as it does. However, I would still be missing him."

In an effort to compose herself, Miriam sat on a chair she had in the kitchen. After awhile, she said a little prayer and then began humming a tune as she went back to finish doing her chores. Then she stopped humming, because she felt someone had entered the kitchen. But when she turned and looked no one was there.

Again, she thought of her husband. And she said, in a voice that was more like a whisper, "Joseph, I know that you are gone forever but I still have your legacy: out three beautiful children and this house, which needs considerable repairs. Also those beautiful memories of the good times, mixed with the bad times that we had spent together."

That weekend too, besides doing his chores, JP had also spent some time focusing on things he thought he could do to help himself to get rich. But as he'd always hope to do, he needed money to start a cartage company that he thought would be the first step in his quest to becoming a millionaire. For now though, he was staring at other immediate pressing issues.

Came Monday morning JP studied the newspaper as he always did, even when he was on a job, hoping to see offerings of fulltime employment. That morning he saw in a page of the classified pages, labourers wanted for a Construction Company, the location where one should go to apply for the job. So, the six-foot-four JP, who could use a haircut, spit on the ground as he usual did when he is somewhat nervous, before he got in his jalopy that was on life support. He hurried to the office of the construction company. His heart sunk as he joined the line that was approximately sixty people deep with people of all ages: a line that only grew longer each minute.

"Oh my gawd," JP whispered, running his hands over his hair from his mild frustration. "With all these people here, I haven't a chance. Anyway, I have nothing else to do for today, neither tomorrow nor the day after. I'll wait and see what happens."

When it was JP's turn, to speak with the interviewer, he went in the office. And the interviewer; straight face under a brown bill cap, said, "Good morning!" and, "have a seat."

JP returned same. As he sat in a metal chair to seat one, a grey metal desk between him and the interviewer, he thought, *Garlic. He must've had something for breakfast with garlic in it. Anyway, I don't mind the aroma of garlic because it's one of my favourite vegetables.* And while that thought ran through JP's mind, the man stood up and formed fists with both hands. His strange action alarmed JP.

Now what? JP thought. What's he up to?

But the man only pushed this fists up as far as he possible could. In the meantime, his brown work Jacket open wide, and JP noticed a pair of white tennis rackets emblazoned on the man's mauve shirt pocket, joined in the formation of an X at their handles. The man sat down. "I hope you don't mind," he said. "Tension."

"No. Not at all," JP said. "Indeed a stretch now and then does help to alleviate tension."

After that little exchange, the man said his name. He asked JP his. When JP said his name, the interview's brows flicked slightly, in a manner that was not noticeable to JP. He shook JP's hand, something he did not do to any other he'd interviewed before JP, and said, with an animated smile, "Oh hi Mr price!" Because Mr Allan Price, no relation to JP, immediately took a liking to the burly, somewhat buoyant, six-foot-four JP who was in his best manner, doing his best to show his captivating smile. At that time though, JP felt he was not a shoe-in because the person interviewing him had the same surname as his.

Mr Price, his eyes on JP's plaid shirt with those pencil size holes, stated the terms, condition of the job. He waited for JP's response.

"When do I start?" said the elated JP, knowing he'd be employed for the next eighteen months. The longest time he'd hoped to spend in any one job since he'd been forced to go out to work for a living. Or should it be more appropriately said, go out to work in aid of helping his family to survive.

"Well—"

"Sir, I could start right away. I mean, today."

"Well, young man," said the former soccer player who now play tennis for recreation, "next Monday, God's willing." He gave JP the address of the job site. "I hope to see you there." He stretched his hand to JP again as he said "Goodbye for now. Have yourself a great week."

"Sir, I will. I'll be the first one at the job site," he said, shacking Mr Price's hand vigorously—the first handshake was nothing in comparison—but a vigorous, powerful handshake that almost lifted Mr Price from out of his chair. "Thanks for choosing me. You won't regret hiring me." *And thanks for telling me to have a great week, which, you bet, has already began the moment you hired me.*

Mr Price waited until JP left the room before he took a good look at his hand. "My word," he said, "such a powerful handshake. Oh my gosh! It was so powerful."

Getting that job was a delight to JP and his mother.

As agreed, Monday morning JP showed up for work in his plaid shirt. Instead of him lumbering with bricks for bricklayers, the boss gave him chores of running errands for the company, also doing things to cater for other labourers and bricklayers. Doing those kinds of chores did not bother JP at all, because he had a job. The smile on his face, the day he received his first pay cheque from that company, was probably the widest smile his face had ever experienced. Never in his life had he ever received such a hefty first pay cheque.

JP was on the job for about six months, when Allan Price said to him, "JP, have you ever thought of getting a better car?"

"No," JP said, "I have all intention on keeping my car until it quits."

"I see," said Allan Price who had no children of his own. "JP, go get my car for me."

JP brought the five-year old burgundy Cadillac to the front of the office.

"There's no need for you to get out," Allan said.

JP thought for a moment. "Why?"

Allan Price smiled. "JP, this car could be yours for five hundred bucks."

"Sir, it's a very nice car all right. I would be delighted to own it but my budget cannot stretch that far. I am sure it is worth more than five hundred bucks."

"Yes, it does, but for you the offer stays open." Mr Price was also contemplating something else, in the back of his mind. But the playing of Tennis wasn't the dominant thing he really had on his mind; however, he asked, "JP, do you play tennis?"

"Ha," JP said, "I have never taken up a tennis racket let alone playing a game of tennis."

"If you did, I could just imagine your opponent having a difficult time keeping up with you. So do you think you'd try it? I am a good teacher, and while I'm teaching you, you could also be my new partner."

"That doesn't sound like a bad idea." JP said. "As of right now I have to keep that in the back of my mind."

That evening on his way home, JP—and by then he was able to afford more than one change of work clothes each week but his plaid shirt was always called to duty on Thursdays and Fridays—did not have on his mind what Allan Price had said to him about playing tennis. Only, he kept thinking, "If I had money that beautiful car could be mine." He shook his head in annoyance because of his spartan way of life. "I will be a millionaire, and nicer car than that and host of other beautiful things I could afford, and I, my mom and siblings, too, could have whatever we want to make us very comfortable and very happy."

Although JP could not afford five hundred bucks to purchase Mr Price's five-year old car, it did not mattered much to Mr Price. Because he'd perceived—when JP told him, he could not afford to purchase the car for the small sum of five hundred bucks—that every penny JP made was already spent before he had it in his hands. He knew what families in the area were going through because of the scarcity of jobs for breadwinners and for heads of families. Let alone young people who were willing to work but could not find worthwhile employment. And that that such condition was happening because the country was enduring it's harshest recession in recent memory. Or as from far back as one could remember.

As if he knew the high regards JP had for him, and because of his fondness for JP, Mr Price extended an invitation to JP to come to his home for dinner, which JP accepted.

Therefore, to fill his dinner engagement, JP had to go to Valley glen Crescent in the district of Epsom, about ten miles from his home. When he got into the district, he thought it was a quiet neighbourhood. From his observing of vehicles, he saw parked on driveways and on the streets, he was beginning to think that his jalopy was not a vehicle folks would appreciate seeing in the area. Nevertheless, he continued on to the intended address and drove up the long driveway to the huge house that was in front of a community park. He parked his jalopy, got out, and started his journey towards the front door of the house. As he passed a parked car, a current year silver Mercedes Benz, before he'd step onto a cobblestone pathway that would take him directly to the front door of the house, he stopped momentarily, looked at his car then looked back at the Benz. "Well," he said, with a slight shrug, "my car; their car. Well, that's all I can . . . mmmm . . . barely afford. So what does it matter? Not to worry."

When JP pressed the button for the doorbell of the house, Allan Price, who was expecting him, opened the door within seconds.

"Hi, JP," Allan greeted him, "come on in." As he closed the door he called out, "Sofia! It's JP. He's here."

As soon as JP raised his eyes from observing the sparkling ceramic tiles, Sofia appeared from around the corner, wiping her hands on her apron. She stretched a hand to JP as she said, "Welcome to our humble dwelling."

JP shook her hand. "Thank you." *I swear her hand had never encountered a rough day's work.*

"Come on in!" she said. "Come in and make yourself at home. I am a little busy right now so we'll get better acquainted later. Right JP?"

"I suppose we shall," JP said, observing her and thought how pretty she was.

"Come JP," Allan said, as they went into the direction Sofia went after she had greeted him.

JP saw an opening to his right, as they made their way to the family room. He realized the kitchen was located in that area. As he entered the room and stepped onto the beige carpet, he felt as if his feet were sinking.

"Sit down JP," Allan said.

JP, whose eyes were surveying the room, contemplating that the decor of the room reminded him of decors he'd seen in home decor showrooms and in home and living magazines, did not sit down. Probably his sense of sight was interfering with his sense of hearing. He eventually sat down when, for the second time, Allan told him to have a seat.

Allan asked JP if he'd like a drink, but JP, who only drank water and soft drinks, said some Ginger Ale would suit him fine.

While Allan went to the kitchen to fix JP's drink, JP thought, she said this place is her humble dwelling, but I swear this place is nothing short of being aristocratic.

"What are you going to do with that?" Sofia asked Allan, when she saw him pulled the Ginger Ale bottle from the giant white fridge.

"It's for JP. He wants a drink."

"Allan," she said, "put that thing back." She stepped out to where she could see JP. "JP, dinner is almost ready. I don't want you to fill your stomach with that cheap stuff and I hope you're really hungry." She casts her eyes to JP's feet. "JP, I know it matter not to Allan; however, if you don't mind, could you please take your shoes off and put them out front?"

"OK ma'am. Mr Price," he called out, "don't bother with it." *Cheap stuff, huh? I wonder if she'd believe straight Ginger Ale is premium at my house. Cheap stuff, huh?* He took his pair of dull looking black loafers off, exposing one of his big toes from a hole in one of his sock, and did as Sofia had asked.

"Please do me a favour?" Sofia said to Allan, "while you're in here."

"A favour, like what?"

"Please put these containers with the food on the table, while I rush upstairs and change my dress." She came back downstairs in a short while, looked the table over. "Good," she said. "JP, please wash your hands. We're ready to have dinner."

Wow, JP thought, she's dressed even more elegantly now. He also thought of his mother. After dinner, Sofia and JP spent some time being more acquainted. On couple of occasions, she commented on his physique. He thought she had a funny way of laughing, which made him laugh even more. He referred to her as Miss Sofia, who gave him a parting gift, the first of many to come. That first dinner date, too, was only the first of several to follow.

The small parcel Sofia gave to JP, contained four pairs of socks, each of a different colour.

From the first time JP saw Sofia, and she had dazzled him with her eye-catching attire and at every dinner engagement since then, also whenever he saw her at other times, he believed if they did not have money there was no way she could always be dressing so elegantly. That made JP more determined to have money, because he envisioned his mother looking as elegant as Sofia was, and he'd lavish his mother with similar exquisite clothing. His mother did not drive, but she'd be driven around in the most expensive car there was.

Often times, on those dinner dates, JP thought of his siblings with almost every bite he took of the sumptuous foods. He even thought of asking Allan or Sofia, if he, JP, could bring along his siblings even just once. However, unless any of them offered, he would not bring up the subject. He even thought of doggy bags. But even if he could ignore his ego he knew he had his mother to deal with. Because that was something he knew his mother would not allow. Anyhow, sometimes later, JP's siblings and his mother feasted on mouth-watering foods at couple of Allan's barbecues.

On one of those dinner engagements Allan Price said to JP, "JP, I'd offered you my car for five hundred bucks. You told me that price was too high."

"I did not say it was too expensive, remember? I had said I could not afford it or something like that. I could not afford it then, and neither can I afford it now."

"What would you say if I give it to you for free?"

"For free? Mr Price."

"Yes JP. I do mean for free."

"Why would you want to do such a thing?"

"Your car is on life support and could die at any time. Besides, I don't really need this car."

Life support? You're wrong because it had died and I resurrected it. I am still riding on my twenty five bucks. "Anyhow, JP said, "don't you?"

"I have access to all kinds of vehicles: Company vehicles to start with and even car dealers are waiting for me to come in and select a vehicle of my choice. The company will pay the cost for the vehicle, of course."

Oh gosh! I wish I were in his position. Free vehicles and all? Man, that's awesome!"

". . . here's the key JP."

"So where is the car?"

"Follow me."

They went to the garage.

"Here it is, JP. Drive it home and see how you like it."

JP could not believe his good fortune. "Why Mr Price? Why are you giving me you car? What did I do to deserve this?"

"Just say it's a gift from me to you. The signed ownership is in the glove box. If you accept it, tomorrow before you come in to work change it into your name."

JP, weak knees and in disbelief, looked at Mr Price with dropped jaws. He sat in the car, and the new car scent he had experienced the first time he was in the car was still prevalent. He scrutinized the burgundy and white leather interior of the car some more. "Nice!" his voice hummed excitedly, "this car is soooo Nice. Thanks Mr Price. From the day you employed me I knew my luck had begun to change."

JP started the car. As he drove off, a rippling smile on his face, he waved goodbye to the man who gave him something he could only dream of possessing.

The overly excited JP reached home without any incident. Still in disbelief, he sat in the car for a while. He sighed contentedly. Then he got out of the car, and within a split-second, his spit crashed onto the ground. As he walked towards the house, his steps as light as that of a cat's, he realized his palms were sweating. A condition he had developed because he was so overjoyed. He rubbed his sweaty palms together vigorously in an attempt to dry them. Yet still overwhelmed with happiness that engulfed his being, from the incredulous gift he had just received, he exclaimed, "Wow! Isn't it incredible awesome!" He pushed open the entrance door of the house, and yelled joyfully, "Mom, David, Alvin and Rachael come take a look at my new car."

Although they heard JP, no one moved a muscle because they thought he was joking.

"Hm, what's happening here? They couldn't have gone to bed. It isn't dark yet. Mom, David, Alvin and Rachael I have a new car. Come take a look at it."

Rachael's name he called last both times. She was the first to respond. She looked up at JP. "So where's this new car you are wailing about? You aren't kidding us, are you?"

JP, rubbing his palms together, jerked his head slightly towards the door.

Rachael went closer towards the door. She peeked. Her eyes landed on JP's new acquisition. "WOW JP, where did you get this car?" She did not wait for him to answer as she turned and yelled with that *wow* in her voice, which echoed throughout the house, "Everybody, it's no joke, JP's got a brand new car. Come take a look at it."

"No kidding," David said. "Alvin, you heard Rachael, didn't you. JP's got a new car. Let's take a look."

They cantered to the front door, looked out, then at each other in uncanny amazement at what they saw. They did not take the time to walk down the short flight of steps, but instead jumped from the veranda to the ground. Their mother, who had also heard JP's excited voice, was wondering as she trailed slowly behind his siblings to the point of excitement, this is not possible. I can't remember him saying anything about getting another car.

While JP's siblings milled over the car, he stood with arms folded across his chest with a smile that could light up the neighbourhood, if it were dark, as the prints of their palms smudged the beautiful paint job. His mother, observing how excited they were, nodded her head in agreement, that indeed it was a beautiful looking car.

"Hmmm." his mother said, after awhile, "it's a fancy looking car all right. JP, from where did you get money to purchase a new car? Have you been holding out on us? Were you concealing portion of your pay cheque to achieve this?"

"Mom, I did not purchase this car. The boss gave it to me."

"Let's go for a ride," one of JP's siblings interrupted.

"Not tonight," JP said. "There's plenty of time for that. Oh, maybe we can. I have to go back to his place to get my other car. David, my old car is now yours."

"JP," his mother said, while she thought of the close relationship that had developed between her son and his boss, "it's really a beautiful car. You said you boss gave it to you."

"Yes mom."

"He gave this car to you for nothing?"

"Yes mom."

"For . . . free?"

"Yes Mom. He said it's a gift from him to me."

His mother, still in a pensive mood, said, "I don't like it one bit," while rubbing a palm across her forehead meditatively.

"What's the matter, Mom?"

"JP," *I don't mind you having dinner with him, but now this?* "JP, in this place, nobody gives you something for nothing. I am thinking if I should let you keep this car."

"Mom there's nothing to worry about. Mr Price and I hit it off from the first time we met. At the interview for the job, he made me feel as if I was talking to someone I've known for a very long time. Mom, don't worry yourself over him. Mr Price is not only my boss; he's also my pal, my good friend, too. Besides, mom," JP opened a door of the four-door car and slammed it shut, "when you enter and leave this car you won't have to worry about having an accident. You know, like your fear of the door falling off, nor getting wet if it rains, or loose any of your clothing when you are getting out."

"Well, he gave this car to you and I suppose he has his good reasons. Although I have my doubts I must admit it is really beautiful. A welcome sight from . . ."

"Mom, a welcome sight from my old jalopy?"

"Yes, and I might just—"

"Just enjoy riding around in it?"

"Maybe. Maybe or something like that." A small smile curled on her lips, and JP knew her ambivalence concerning his gift had begun to wane.

"Mom, my old red and white isn't yet dead. It will still stay around because I'm sure you heard me give it to David."

"Then we'll see how much longer it will stay alive." *Allan Price, she said under her breath.*

One day at work, the benevolent Allan saw JP standing beside an object, which he thought could cause an accident to somebody. He shook his head, walked over to JP and said sternly, "JP, you should know better than that. Why do you have that thing in the way? Aren't you aware someone could get hurt?"

The surprised JP explained it was not of his doing, and he'd take it away.

Allan, feeling a bit foolish, apologized.

Although JP had another twelve months to stay in that job, Allan Price was already looking to the day when he'd have to give him his walking paper. That was something that did not sit well with Allan Price who'd formed a bond with JP. If JP had a trade, he thought—maybe he could learn to become a bricklayer, which is not too late even though it takes time to learn the skill—his chance of securing another job after he leaves here would be much greater. "But given that he's only a labourer," he said, "I know he'll have a difficult time in finding another job.

I'd hate like hell to let him go when it becomes necessary, but what choice would I have. Anyway, I'd really like to do something more for him, but what can I do?"

Nevertheless, eight months after he gave JP his car, he said to JP after they'd had dinner, "JP, in five month's time I have to give you your walking paper and it is worrying to me."

"Sir," JP said, "If I were you, I would not worry myself about it. Because I know if it were up to you I could be employed with this company for much longer than eighteen months. However when that day comes, for me to walk, I'll walk and I'll keep on walking until I find another job. Besides, I have a better car now."

"JP, before you got this job, you were used to walking out of one odd job to another, that was, whenever you found it. However, when you leave this job, looking forward, what do you hope to do with your life?"

JP did not hesitate with his answer. "Sir, whatever it takes, I want to be a millionaire. Ever since you gave me a job I've started to save towards making that move."

Allan Price almost laugh at JP's idea. "It doesn't sound like a bad idea," he said. "But have you given much thought as to how you could become a millionaire in this country?"

"I know my chance to become a millionaire in this country is limited. I have my mind set on going to one of those heavily industrialised prosperous countries, especially one where I could play the lottery. I feel my chances of becoming a millionaire could be much greater, but lottery games or not, I am not particular."

"Many people, I've heard," Allan Price said, "played lotteries for years and dreams they've had, such as yours, have yet to be realized or never realized at all. Your chance might not be any better than theirs."

"Perhaps," JP said. "Anyhow, if I were at a place where I had steady employment I could save my money, and when I save enough start my own trucking company as I want to do, a start towards my dream. I don't mind working my butt off towards achieving that."

Hmmm, Mr Price thought, such an ambitious young man. "JP, do you have anyone who could help you to go to one of those countries?"

"No. But in time God will help me to find somebody."

"Well, you never know. Anyway, we'll see."

At JP's mentioning of going to another country, instantly Allan Price thought of his brother Charles Price, a retired man who lived in Canada. His children had left the nest and they were doing quite nicely for themselves. So, he thought if JP could get to go to Canada, with his mannerism and work ethics he could definitely make something of himself, as his nephew and niece were doing for themselves. He was certain JP would have steady employment and in time even become the millionaire he yearned to be. He did not tell JP about what he was thinking; that he'd speak with his brother on JP's behalf. "This young man could pass for our nephew," he whispered with his gaze fixed on JP. "He's like family, so why not?"

With five months to go before he gave JP his walking paper, Allan Price began to dialogue with his brother. He gave his brother reasons why he wanted to help the young man. However, three months had passed and his brother was yet to make his mind up, whether or not he'd go along with what Allan was asking of him. But with less than six weeks to go before he would have to lay off JP, Allan received the news he was waiting for and it was positive. He felt relieved because JP's wish to leave the country could become reality.

So Allan Price said to JP, "JP, I didn't tell you this, but I've been talking to my brother who lives in Canada on your behalf. His name is Charles. Now I can tell you he has agree to help you to leave this country. What do you say?"

JP, overjoyed by the news, looked at Mr Price in amazement. "What, Mr Price? Are you telling me I have a chance to leave this country? Is it for real, Mr Price?"

"Yes, it's for real. You can start making plans to leave soon; if you really want to leave."

"Are you kidding me, sir? Soon would not be soon enough!"

"The lottery is not played in Canada, you know."

"I won't worry about it," JP said quickly. Then he thought why this man is doing all this for me. "Mr Price, you gave me a job, then your car and now this. Why?"

"JP, from the first day I saw you I took a liking to you. Since then, in my heart, I adapted you and I told myself I'd do anything to help you to succeed."

"You did, did you?"

"Yes JP, I did."

"I could tell you had a liking for me but not enough to be doing all these things for me."

"JP, someone had to give you a break and I'm happy it's me, and my brother, of course."

"Thank you," JP said. "I thank you from the bottom of my heart."

Now, nothing besides leaving the country mattered much to JP. Already he had begun to plan in ways he had not dreamt of before, because he was about to turn a monumental corner in his life. Even though it being a blind corner that would not reveal what it had hidden within its parameter until he was actually in its confines.

The elated JP couldn't wait to get home to impart the overwhelming news to his mother and siblings. "How will they react," he said. "When I tell them I have this opportunity to leave, for what I feel, to chart a different and a better path in life?

That evening JP waited until after they'd finished supper. When he interrupted a conversation, the family was having at the dinner table, by stating, "I am going to Canada!"

For a few seconds a hush filled the room, and David was the first to break the silent barrier by saying, "What are you saying bro? Did I hear you say, you're going to Canada?"

"JP," his mother said, "I thought I heard you say you're going to Canada."

"Man," David butted in, "few months back it was, I'm going to be a millionaire. Now, and it sounds like nonsense to me, I am going to Canada. My bro, if I didn't know you better I'd swear you were drinking."

You can forget about that nonsense," JP said. "But seriously, I have a chance to go to Canada. Mr Price . . ."

"Here we go again," his mother said. "That so-an-so Mr Price—"

"Yes mom, that so-an-so Mr Price. It is because of Mr Price why I have a chance to go to Canada. He knew I wanted to go to a prosperous country, and he and his brother, his brother lives in Canada, are willing to assist me."

"So with all this Mr Price has done for you . . . JP he is never satisfied until he had the chance to pluck you away from this family."

"Mom, you shouldn't say that because, since the day Mr Price came into my life everything seems to get better and better."

"You're right about that, bro." David said.

"But son, you are too young to be going so far away from home, to live on your own. I am afraid, if you should leave, we may never see you again. Now I am the one who's beginning to feel the pain of separation slowly but surely creeping in on me, and it makes me feel a bit nervous."

JP looked away from his mother because it became difficult for him to keep his eyes on her saddened face. In the meantime, though, he was somewhat ambivalent about leaving. However, as he turned his face back towards his mother, he said, "Mom," and he paused.

"What is it now JP?"

"I have never met anyone but people my age or younger immigrated to distant places from their homelands and, they've done nicely for themselves—as I hope to do. Or even do better."

"Yes, that might be so," his mother said. "Anyhow, I don't feel comfortable about your wanting to leave us. What do you know about this Mr Price's brother? Will he be kind to you? Will he treat you fairly? Will he provide for you until you can hold your own? And what if things do not work out for you, would you be able to buy your way back home?"

"Mom, I have no intention of not making it work out for me. So—we can forget about that."

While JP and his mother conversed, his siblings listened on, wondering among themselves what it would be like when their elder brother is no longer with them.

"I can only hope," JP continued, "given the way Mr Price treats me, let's hope, if his brother's mannerism is anything close to his, Mr Price's, that will be OK with me. Mama, please look at the situation from the positive side. When I reach Canada and settle in, life should become increasing better for all of us as long as I stay healthy."

And Alvin, who did more listening than talking, who drew objects such as landscapes, houses, automobiles, planes and trains or whatever entered his mind, stopped chewing on his nails. "JP," he said, "when you go to Canada where will you live?"

"Like I'd said, I hope to stay with Mr Price's brother, but only for a while."

Then Rachael who's always arranging and rearranging things with those nimble fingers of hers, even when things seemed perfectly in place, said, "All I know is that I'm gona miss you."

"And I will surely miss everybody, too. So Mama, David Alvin and you Rachael, I've been given a chance of a lifetime, which I will accept. I want everyone to promise me not a word of this will go beyond the walls of this room. In other words: say nothing of this to anyone. And please, Mom, not to anyone at your church."

"But they'd pray for you, JP."

"Mom, that's a good idea, but don't. Let's keep this among ourselves, please? Comes next week, if Mr Price grants me some time off, or soon, I will begin to get my stuff together. You know, document and such which will enable me to make this transition to what I hope, a place where I could have a better future."

Next day, JP told Allan he was very serious about wanting to leave as soon as possible, and if it were possible for him to have some time off to start making plans. Allan, who sensed it coming, agreed to JP's request. He even stated that, with JP's term of employment nearing its end, he had another five weeks to go, it made him happy to know he won't have to worry about finding another dead end job. He also told JP he should terminate his ties with the company the first week of the following month. And he should take the other three weeks in that month as his vacation time. Then his week's pay and his vacation pay he'd get the end of the month, thus completing his tenure with the company.

Of course, JP knew that day was sure to become a reality. Now that it was neigh, he had an unpleasant feeling about giving up the job (although it was inevitable) thus separating him from working with the man, and not the company, who had done so much for him. The man whom he's grown to love and respect; even though he and Allan would still be in contact until the day he leaves Wellington—even beyond.

Although JP's mother, and his siblings, promised to do as he'd requested, as time passed while he prepared, to leave, he noticed there were change of moods within the family. Also rumbling as to why they think he should not leave, especially to go to a country so far away.

From sensing the discord, one day he said to his mother, "Mom, something is wrong and I don't like it one bit."

"Something like what JP?"

"I have noticed a lack of harmony within the family, which I believe is caused by my announcement to go to a foreign country. It has me feeling as if I am traitor."

"Well, JP, what do you expect? Your unexpected announcement shocked us. You know we don't want you to leave, don't you?"

"Yes mom, but—"

"JP you're like the head of the family. Your leaving is troubling to us."

"Um, I can . . . and do understand. So Mom, maybe, if we should get together and have a frank discussion why it is necessary for me to leave, probably we could be on the same page. What do you think?"

His mother shrugged. "Maybe that'll help. Who knows?"

JP did not try to air it out with the family then. He'd do so when he thought the time was right.

One evening after dinner with Mr and Mrs. Price, JP said, "Mr Price, your brother . . ."

"Oh JP," Mr Price said. "There's something I have to show you." He went into his room and came back with a faded picture of his brother.

JP took the picture and looked it over. He looked at Alan then back at the picture. He did so a couple of times. "Mr Price I was about to ask you if you had any picture of your brother for me to look at, to observe the other Mr Price's profile. It seemed to me you've read my mind. Looking at this picture, though it's not recent, I can see there's some resemblance, close resemblance I might add."

At the time when Charles took that picture he was in a sitting position, therefore it was difficult for JP to guess Charles' height.

"Anyway, JP said, "which of your parents do you and your brother resemble, your mom or your dad?"

Alan's face brightened. "Our mother!"

"She was a beautiful woman, wasn't she?"

"Very attractive JP"

"So that's where you and your brother, if you don't mind me saying, inherited your handsomeness."

"JP," Alan said, "I won't knock you over the head for saying that."

"Well, if your brother's feature hasn't changed much, I shouldn't have much difficulty in recognising him when I get to Canada."

"If you don't, I'm sure he will recognise you."

"How is it possible?"

"He has a pretty good profile of you."

"A good profile of me, how?"

"To be honest, I was a private photographer, you know? When I was speaking to my brother on your behalf I secretly took your picture. I sent it to him so that he could see what you look like."

"Oh, I see," JP said. "Why didn't you tell me?"

"I deliberately kept the whole thing a secret because if it did not work out you would be none the wiser. Therefore, if you did not know about it there was no way you could feel disappointed."

"Uh huh! It worked out just fine and I am very happy about it."

"I am happy, too. Anyway, let me have a copy of the picture you used to obtain your passport so that I can send it to my brother."

"Tonight when I go home I'll be sure to stick one in my pocket, then give it to you tomorrow."

That evening when JP got home, he thought the time was right for his discussion with the family.

During their discussion, he pointed out the overwhelmingly reason for his wanting to leave. "As we are speaking," JP said, "I don't have a job, and you know the best paying job I've ever had was the one Mr Price gave me. Now, thanks to him, I do not have to go in search of another job in a place where it has been and is still touch and go. Now I have a chance to go to a prosperous place where, I believe, I could have a steady job. Such being the case, and as I've said before, life could get much better for all of us. So what do you say?"

No one gave JP an immediate answer, but after each took time to vent their opinions, as JP had hoped, indeed, they saw things from his prospective. Finally, they were on the same page, and his leaving for Canada was probably the best thing for him to do.

"Well JP," David's voice echoed above the rest, "thanks to Mr Price. While we are about to sever from a brother, I'll be gaining a Cadillac Car."

"David, I don't want to disappoint you, but the Cadillac car is Mom's. It should serve the family for a very long time. If you should take care of it as I do. I know Mom will make sure of it."

Now, JP did not say a word about his good fortune to his best friend Toby. He had his good reasons.

Weeks went by, close to the time of JP departure, when he received a letter from a travel agency. "We are waiting for you to come in to see us when you're ready to finalise the time of your departure and to confirm a date from available dates." He though it was odd for him to have gotten that notification because only those in the family, Mr Price and of course his wife, knew anything of his travel plan. He investigated the letter and someone at the agency told him that the agency was not at liberty to disclose who the donor was. So, at the time of his final dinner engagement with the Prices, he said, "Mr Price I received a letter from a travel agency." He told Mr Price what was in the letter and asked if he, Mr Price, had anything to do with it.

"What do you think?" Allan said.

"Sir, if it's not of your doing then I won't worry about it. Someone did and I am grateful." But all along JP was thinking no one was responsible for paying his fare, but Allan—Or, could it have been Sofia?

That evening when JP said his last goodbye to Mr and Mrs. Price, he left their residence with his last bag of goodies. Also, he was given code to use, verbally, should Charles ask for it.

Jp left Allan Price's home with something else; a sealed envelope. He wondered what was the significant, or what could be in the sealed envelope Allan Price gave him and advised him not to open it until he reached Canada.

Yes, what indeed was in the sealed envelope?

-2-

Succeeded at last

THE DAY PRIOR TO JP's departure, he packed his meagre belongings into a brown leather case that was once his father's. The night of that day, he only had cat winks. In the morning while he made his bed, fluffed his pillows, he said, "Well, bed, last night could be the last night I ever sleep in you. I am going away and I am not sure if, or when, I will ever again rest my body within the confines of this room. I'm saying goodbye to you my old, but comfortable bed. Goodbye, too, my favourite room."

Now JP was ready to leave. His family, his entourage, all sitting in his Cadillac car, David behind the wheel, the car's door lay opened for JP's entry. But instead of taking his seat in the car, he turned around to stare at the house he was leaving. He'd said goodbye to his bed and his room. He had to say goodbye to his house—the only home he ever knew. But as he stood by the car and stared at the house, his knees rubbery, he had to rest his hand on the car's roof for support. Tears formed in his eyes, his whole body became limp. He felt like pieces of shattered glass that was impossible for any one to make whole.

"What's up Jp," David asked, at his brother's hesitation to sit in the car.

JP did not respond to David's inquiry instantly. When he did, as he sat heavily on the seat, he said "Ahhh. It's not easy."

"What isn't easy, JP?" his mother asked.

"Mom, I thought it would be difficult, but not this difficult to say goodbye to the only home I ever knew."

"Well, Jp, you've made your choice. It's too late to look back."

"I suppose it is. Anyhow, David," he swung his feet in and closed the door, "let's not waste any more time. Let's get moving."

While they travelled, the two hundred or so kilometres to the designated point of his departure, JP and his family had sparse conversation. When they reached the end of their journey, they alighted from the vehicle. JP spat his last spit on the soil of his birth. Then they walked slowly into the building.

While JP sauntered to an area where those about to travel are processed, before boarding the carrier, he said, a worried expression on his face, "My family, this is it. This is where we say our goodbyes."

David, who was carrying JP's luggage, slipped the luggage off his shoulder and laid it at his feet. He hugged JP. "Take care of yourself bro." his voice sounded as if it was coming from somewhere far.

"You bet. Take care of yourself, too," JP said, with a low voice, almost a whisper.

Alvin, also Rachael took turns. As they, too, hugged him and said their parting words.

JP and his mother hugged each other, and she, with tears in her eyes, hugged him much tighter than he did. *Don't know when, if ever, I'll feel his tender hugs again.* "My son, JP, I love you. We'll miss you a great deal. God be with you. Don't forget to write as soon as you reach Canada."

"Mom,"—he was at the point of tears, "thanks. I love you very much." He felt sweat forming on his hands and on his back. "I will miss all of you. Get home safely. Goodbye. I promise I won't forget to write."

JP picked up his luggage. But just before he walked through a wide, arched doorway, to go into the processing area (custom), he turned to look back at his family. He waved at them his final goodbye.

After JP cleared custom he said, "I had better get on board and get ready to start my journey to a new beginning." He went up about five or six concrete steps, then he landed onto a long wooden walkway that led to the ship. Waist-high rails, with yellow guard ropes were on both sides of the walkway. Triangular black, gold and yellow flags danced on the guard ropes from the mild midday winds. JP stopped for a moment as he joined the orderly queue. He gazed intently at the brown and white vessel. He spit into the water, "Wow! This ship is so huge—a Monster! I guess it'll be my home on the water for a few days.

Ahead of him, at the top of the queue, and to his right, stood a guard who held onto a piece of yellow rope that stretched across the width of the walkway? He ushered folks onto the ship's deck, six at a time.

Gradually the queue nudged forward and JP, in his batch of six, went on the ship's deck. A steward greeted him and others of course. "Welcome aboard," the steward said. "May I see your travel document, please? I'll take them one at a time." He studied their documents, and as he gave each one their documents back he said, "Please, join those standing over there. Someone will take you to your berth in a short while. Next."

Before long, another steward engaged the group and asked them to follow him. As they followed, JP looked down the long passageway that seemed to close in the further he looked. The light-blue walls of both sides of the passage seemed bare. But after he had a closer look he saw there were several globes inconspicuously imbued within the paint job. One by one, JP was the third among a pack of six, the steward showed them to their berths. He briefed them on their new dwellings. The steward always left them with a few parting words. "—I hope you'll be comfortable."

"Don't worry about me," JP said. "I hope to make the best of it."

Later on that evening, JP heard the Captain said, over the PA system, "Welcome aboard. In the next half hour we'll be leaving port. I hope you have a pleasant journey."

"Well, I'm hoping we do," JP countered. "If we don't encounter storms or tidal waves we should."

Awhile after the Captain had delivered his message, JP heard the clanging of metals. Then he felt a soft jolt as the ship slowly pulled away from the harbour. He left from his cabin and walked out onto the ship's deck. The ship gradually picked up speed as it head out for open waters. JP watched as landmarks of his country slowly disappeared. He sighed, rather casually, "Thank you God. Thank you my Guardian Angel and thank you, Mr Price. Now I am on my way to a new beginning. One of these days I shall return."

Jp spent most of the first day of his journey in his bunk. Now he knew what sea sickness was all about. However, after that day had passed he felt fine. He mingled, spent considerable hours on the dance floor many evenings. Some evenings he watched movies, played pool some days, and he threw darts that became his favourite pastime as he sailed. He was not gluten, but he had his fair share of the good foods they supplied on board the ship.

Several times during his journey, and as he'd said it before and to Allan Price, too, he reminded himself that he'd said he did not mind going to a country where he wouldn't have any chance of playing the lottery. He had also told himself that he would not waste anytime in finding a job, because he felt according to the research he had done, by working hard and making the right moves, he could or indeed have a chance to become a millionaire.

He'd thought of it several times before, but more so the night before he reached Canada that, what if Mr Charles Price was not there to receive him when he reached his destination. What would he do among total strangers in a strange land? "Anyway," he said, "I should not worry myself too much about that. If he is not there for me I'll manage, and I'll try to reach him somehow. I have his phone number and his home address."

Several times JP was tempted to open the letter Mr and Mrs. Allan Price gave him, but he suppressed his urge because of his promise. When the ship docked about mid-day at Montreal, Canada, and he disembarked, he put his luggage between his legs. As he opened the envelope he was told not to open before he reached Canada, the first thing he saw was, a piece of white paper folded in a way that it had fitted snugly in the envelope. He unfolded the piece of paper that had writing on it. He saw something red. That red object turned out to be not one but eight, five hundred dollar bills. "Wow!" JP said, from his surprise, "four thousand bucks. Had I known of this before I left home I would have left half of it with Mom. Anyway, thank you very much Mr and Mrs. Price, for your gracious gift."

JP read the short note. "JP, we hope you made it safely. Here is a few bucks we thought you could use. Good luck and don't forget your dream."

"You bet, Mr Price. I promise you I won't forget. In a few days you, too, will hear from me. And thanks again a million for all you have done for me."

JP's worrying of whether Charles would be there for him was short lived. Because, in the afternoon after he had cleared custom and went in the waiting area, Charles

Price recognized him from the photographs Allan sent him.

Charles Price observed JP as he walked up to him. And, satisfied with his observation, that he knew who he was, he said, "JP?"

JP who'd formed a mental picture of him, said, "Oh, hi there Mr Price."

Also, to make absolute certain he was really in contact with the right person, Charles said, "Code please?"

JP started to recite the code Allan gave to him, "—199", and Charles joined him in finishing the rest of it—"times2=Canada?" He hugged JP, gave him a heavy slap on the shoulder, "Welcomed," he said with his choppy voice. "Welcome to Canada JP! Welcome!

"Thank you, sir."

"Let's get your luggage, then get out of here. We have a long way to go."

"My luggage, sir?" JP asked.

Charles looked at the brown bag slung from JP's shoulder, which he thought was his carryon luggage. "Yes, your luggage, where you carry your other things."

"All my things are," JP slapped the case, "right here in my case."

"All your things? That's all you have?"

"Everything is right in here." He slapped on the bag again. "Everything is right in here. I'm sure I didn't lose any of it during my journey."

Charles scratched his head. He was thinking that JP really travelled light. First thing I might have to do for him, he mused, is to get him some clothing. "JP, seeing that you have it all, lets go."

As they journey home, from Montreal to Ontario on Highway 401, they stopped only once for coffee. JP was very impressed when he walked into the opulent cafe where he noticed he had choices of different flavours of coffees, and many kinds of donuts that he perceived were fried dumplings. As they journeyed on after they left the cafe, he entertained Charles' conversations, commenting at times, being opinionated also starting his own sparse conversations. Many times he wished Charles would just shut up. He even thought Charles was chatting as a politician would, and hoped that was not a habit of his he would have to live with. But he was relieved when Charles mentioned, it was night-time then, that they'd reached Toronto and in a short while they'd be home. Nevertheless, JP had to listen to Charles chattering, for about another half an hour before Charles reached his home on Chelwood Drive.

"This is it Youngman," Charles said, as he pulled into a driveway with hedges on both sides that were about three feet tall, light aglow above the garage door of the house, "we're home. Grab your luggage and let's go in."

"Finally," JP said. *My ears, I'm hoping, should get some much-needed rest.*

They went in the house, but JP did not comment on anything as Charles showed him his bedroom, then the bathroom, and the kitchen. He asked JP if he wanted something to eat, not anything like a big meal but a snack. JP said he was not hungry. He just wanted to get himself ready for bed, and that he'll see him, Charles, in the morning. Before he went to bed he wrote his mother a letter, the first of many that he'd write. Later he'd also correspond with his friend Toby; Mr Allan Price, too.

The morning of his first day, that would be his first full day in Toronto, JP woke up early. He did not move around much. He met Josephine, Charles' wife, just before they had breakfast. She did not impress him as, Sofia, the way the other Mrs. Price did. Anyway, he thought she seemed to be a very pleasant person.

Josephine studied JP. She thought he was likeable. She also thought he was handsome and that he had a pleasant mannerism, too. In addition, if first impression was a favourable indication of measuring a person's true character then she thought she should not have any problem getting along with him.

After they finished breakfast, Josephine excused herself from the table, cleared the dishes, undid her apron and threw it to one end of the L-shaped kitchen counter. As she was about to go out the kitchen door, both men still sitting at the breakfast table, she stopped. "Oh, by the way JP," she said, "don't be afraid to ask for anything you want or need to find around here, until you are settled in fully."

"No, Mrs. Price," JP said. "I won't. Thanks very much."

Charles and JP chatter for a while. Then Charles said, "JP, I am hoping you'll make the best of the opportunity you've been given." He looked directly in JP's eyes. "JP, as long as you're here we want nothing from you, except your good behaviour."

Whew! I thought I was about to get a lecture. "You don't have to concern yourself about that, sir. I have all intention of not squandering my chances. Neither will I disappoint you regarding my behaviour." I have the feeling, JP thought, that whatever I do around here I have to do so as if I am walking on eggs.

"Sounds good to me," Charles said. He offered to take JP about the city, so he could familiarize himself.

"Sir," JP said, "I'd—first, I'd like to know where to go so I can mail a letter to my folks. Then I'd rather you take me around to search for a job, because I came here for a purpose. Familiarising myself with the city or wherever can wait. I am eager to go in search of a job; however, I'll accept your offer for just today."

"You don't have to go in search of a job," Charles told him. "I've already secured a job for you, at a factory where they make cardboard boxes. One of my friends is the boss there. Oh, is your letter appropriately stamped?"

"No, I don't have any stamp." *I don't care what they make there. Just give me a job.*

"Then I have to take you to the post office."

"Thanks, sir. Um, Mr Price, I'll start tomorrow. I have no time to waste."

"Tomorrow I'll take you to meet the manager," Charles said. "I believe he'll tell you when to start."

"I hope he'll tell me to start tomorrow or the day after tomorrow."

"That we'll find out tomorrow." *He's not missing a beat. With an attitude as that, he'll do very well indeed.*

While they were in metro Toronto, JP was impressed with the stores, in general, and the myriads of things they had to offer. As he gazed at the beautiful clothing, Charles, who noticed how excited he seemed, took the opportunity to offer to get him some new clothes. JP declined diplomatically, stating he is yet to go through the clothing he had to see how they'd help him with blending into his new surrounding. He was also overwhelmingly impressed with the grocery stores where all kinds of foods were available; also, varieties of fresh fruits and fresh vegetables that were in abundance. Most of the fruits, and vegetables, he knew were not grown in Canada, nevertheless, they were there for human to consume.

"No one should ever starve in this country," JP said, "but to afford any of these things, large or small, cares not whatever it may be you have to have money." He raised a hand to the side of his face. "You know, there's no skating around it because anywhere in the world you may go you just have to have money to live a comfortable life. There must be many millionaires in this country. I could join that rank soon. All right then, one of these days."

Charles showed JP the building in which he, JP, hoped to have his first job, the bus route he would be travelling twice each day for as long as he is in that job. Or that way of commuting could change when or if JP reached the point to afford his personal transportation.

After their rendezvous was over, they went home and had dinner. While they were relaxing, Charles told JP that in the morning, at about nine a.m, he'd take him to the workplace to meet the manager, to make the formal introduction.

I'll be ready, sir," JP said

"Oh by the way JP, I hope you don't mind fixing you own breakfast," Charles said, somewhat apologetically. "As of late, we have our breakfast about mid-morning."

"That's all right with me, sir. I don't mind fixing my own breakfast."

Awhile later, JP said goodnight to Charles. He went to his room, picked up his well-worn plaid shirt the pencil size holes a touch larger, held it up, took a good look at it and said with a wry smile, "Shirt, you were on my back the day Mr Price gave me a job. Since then, I just keep moving forward for the better. Tomorrow we are going to a place where a job is waiting for me. Where we'll meet the manager responsible for giving us our first job in this new land; you'll be on my back." He kissed the shirt. "You are my lucky work shirt. I don't remember saying it before, so I'm telling you now. Shirt, I love you."

In the morning when Charles Price was ready to take JP to the workplace, he did not have to seek out JP, because JP was sitting at the kitchen table waiting on him. So, Charles and JP, timely drove to the place where JP should start his first job. He parked his Cadillac. They went in the office.

"Hi Buster!" Charles said, to a man sitting behind a grey desk."

"Hi Charles, how are you doing today?"

"It is such a pleasant day, my friend. I am doing as well as can be."

Buster took his eyes off Charles. He fixed them on JP. "So, this is your nephew? Sit down Charles. You and you nephew sit down."

JP was astonished. *Now I am a nephew! Like his brother, have he adapted me in his heart too? Mama, I don't think you have to worry about him being good to me. We are family.*

"Yes Buster. You are looking at JP."

Buster stood up and shook JP's hand from across the desk. "Welcome to Canada!"

"Thank you," JP said.

"You're welcome, and I hope you'll be able to blend in with the work unit here . . . the family."

I think he's being presumptuous, isn't he, JP thought. I have not yet met a single person who works here, except him of course. Anyhow . . . "Sir, only time will tell," JP said, as he looked into an emotionless face he thought has seen many years past. A face that did not in the least bit exhibited any hint of welcome, as he had expressed.

Buster walked around to one side of the desk. "Come JP, let's . . . Charles why don't you get us some coffee while I show JP around."

"But I'm leaving him here!"

"Charles, please get those coffees, remember mine is black and no sugar, then we'll talk. Follow me . . . JP. Um . . . JP, it is. Right?"

"You are perfectly right. JP it is."

By the time Buster was through giving JP a tour, and came back to the office, the coffees Charles bought were almost cold.

"Charles, which cup of coffee is mine?"

"The one marked B."

"Thanks." He took the lid off the paper cup and took a sip of the coffee. JP aren't you having your coffee—Charles?"

"Mine is finished. I like mine very warm."

Buster picked up an application form. "When your nephew is through having his coffee, I'll have him fill out this application. I think he will like working here. When he's finished, finished doing the application, you can take him home and bring him back in the morning. But wait . . . today is Thursday. The week is almost done. Better yet, make it Monday morning. This coming weekend will be his first weekend here, isn't it?"

"Yes," Charles said.

"I think he needs some time to relax and unwind. While he's doing so, Charles, give him a tour of the place."

JP raised his eyes from the form. "We'd done that already," he said.

"I don't think you've seen enough. Anyhow, whatever you want to do is up to you:

"Charles, bring him back Monday morning to begin his tenure."

"He's anxious to go to work," Charles said. "He'll be here."

Ever so often, during his filling out of the form, JP pushed his hand through his shirt onto his chest to give his undershirt, his plaid shirt quick touches. And he did so one last time, only this time for a longer time before he signed the form. "Now shirt," he whispered, "that's it. To work, God's willing, we'll come Monday morning."

The evening of that day JP met the Price's children: Carol and Clifford Price. Carol made him feel as if he was really a cousin, but he could see that Clifford's welcome was not that genuine. Anyhow, Clifford's behaviour towards him was not troubling. He knew he was a new addition to the family, if only by words, and that many times not all family member gives the new member a rousing welcome. He felt they'd get to know each other better as time goes by.

Monday morning, from his anxiousness to go to work, JP woke up hours before he had to leave the house. He went to the kitchen and had his breakfast: a tall glass of orange juice. He waited for Charles Price.

When Charles came downstairs, ready to take JP to work, he'd do so via the bus route, he noticed JP was carrying a small plastic bag. "Your lunch?" Charles enquired.

"No, sir. It's my work shirt."

"Your work shirt? Um, I am certain they'll give you coveralls."

Without telling Charles the significant of the shirt to him he said, "Probably they will, sir, but I am taking my shirt."

"Well, okay then. If you are ready let's go." *I suppose almost everyone has a lucky something. What's it call? Yes, their lucky charm. Hm, his is a shirt?*

He dropped JP off, and said, "Jp have a good day. I'll pick you up after work."

"You don't have to do that, sir," JP said. "I'll make it back home by the bus."

"JP, I have the time. It's no bother."

"Sir," JP protested, "I'll be all right. I'll make it. You'll see."

"I'll do this for the rest of the week so that you become familiar with the bus route. Then we'll see what happens. Now, go to work."

"Well then, see you later, sir."

As JP walked to the building, he thought, why does he insist on taking me to work and picking me up? Is he afraid I might get lost? Doesn't he realize I am a grown man, capable of finding his way around? Anyway, I won't put up a fight. It's his call. So let him.

Jp reported to Buster. Buster gave him two pairs of coveralls. "Go change," he said. "Then come back and see me. Next weekend you'll get you own coveralls."

JP put on his worn-out plaid shirt, then his coverall. "Now shirt," he said, "this is it, the first day on this new Job for us. I'll be wearing you for awhile, then put you to rest, okay? Well, let's go and find out what Mr Buster wants us to do."

Buster assigned JP to someone who'd teach him how to operate a machine similar to the machine he would be operating daily. He was a fast learner and so in less than a few days, he was ready to operate his own machine.

During his first week of operating his own station, JP's letter reached his mother. Miriam. She opened the letter hurriedly, breezed through it once then more slowly on her second read. And she, his siblings, too, were very happy he'd reached his destination safely and he was OK.

Miriam had just replied to JP's first and she received another. She was mildly worried something was probably wrong. But when she read the letter she was very please to know JP had a job. More pleased to know Mr Chase Price embraced him as if he was a nephew. She thanked both Mr Prices'. "God's blessing," she said, "be on the both of you."

JP settled in his first job, worked hard, and he got his first promotion. More promotions followed; he became a leader. However, with all the success he was having in that job, it was not enough to cause him to lose sight of what he wanted to be . . . . *A millionaire.* Nevertheless, after a while, he found another job. Now he was able to support his mother and sibling financially, much better than he had ever done before. Life had indeed gotten much better for him and the entire family. Chicken was not a steady meal meat for them any more. Now, he could have a glass of wine, if he wanted to, and of his choice, with his meals instead of over diluted soft drinks. His family, too, had their choices of beverages.

It was a year and a half since JP moved to Canada, and he was in the process of setting up his own residence when he got the news, which saddened him greatly, that Allan Price passed away, from his bout with liver cancer. A family member represented JP, who made sure Allan got the best wreath he, JP, could possibly afford. "Although I couldn't do anything to help to cure him of that illness," JP said, "I wish he'd told me about it."

But his brother Charles knew. He kept it from JP.

Probably, JP thought, he was so good to me because he knew he did not have much time left on this earth. Whichever way it was, I am very thankful. May God bless his soul? Now that he's gone, to join my grandparents and my dad, I'll still keep in touch with Sofia."

In time, JP lived up to his promise: to help his siblings, if they wanted to immigrate.

David was the first to accept. He joined JP. Next, it was Alvin, who was always drawing objects. He went to Florida where he became an architect. And buildings they erected from his architectural designs were utterly outstanding. Rachael stayed home. She eventually became a teacher.

The three brothers remodelled the family house, took care of their mother and Rachael.

JP met five-foot-five Ruth, brown-hair, hazel eyes, who was the manager of a department store. She bore a warm smile that always gave one the feeling that he or she was always welcomed. They began dating, and the first time he went to her home he met her father, *deceased*, by his picture dressed in his marine uniform that was among a series of other pictures hanging on her living room wall. At a latter date, he met Ruth's fun loving mother who did not look her age. It took her some time before she grew to like JP.

Long before he married Ruth, he told her of his wishes, dreams . . . especially his yearning to be a millionaire, hopes and desires. And not once during any her response did she ever plant a seed of doubt in his mind. Her positive thoughts were, then, and even after they were married, that, as long as you are alive and stay healthy, anything is possible.

They, JP and Ruth, combined their funds and they bought a Kenworth rig—sleeper cab. JP instructed the dealer to paint his rig in three colours: blue, white and red. Blue, his favourite colour at the bottom section of his rig; Red, the upper colour and the colour of his writing of *I am going to be a millionaire;* White, at the mid section, which had no significance to him at that particular time—even though his long ago jalopy was red and white. The white colour, he thought, would blend in well with the blue and red colours. On the white section of both doors to his first ever office—his truck doors—was the insignia *Lucky Child* in red.

The day JP drove his rig home he did not have to explain to Ruth or David the reason for the insignia. They knew of its significance.

JP launched Lucky Child; using it to haul goods on the byways and highways throughout Canada and the United States. *Lucky Child* also became his handle. He also knew by owing only one Rig it would only make him merely independent. He would have to have a fleet of trucks, have others working for him, before he could become a millionaire. Anyhow, he was happy to have had the start he badly needed.

One day, years after JP went to Ontario, Canada,—and by then there was permanent separation between JP and the Price brothers due to their death within four years of each other, but he kept in contact with their survivors, the ones he knew—the government of Ontario introduced the lottery game to the public. JP studied the contents of the get rich scheme and thought he'd invest because, it was to his delight. He did not give much thought to where it says, your chance in winning is one in forty million, or depending on your luck. He only saw if someone had the mindset and the determination he or she could cash in. Playing the lottery was something he always wanted to do, long before he had left his land of origin. It was right up his alley. He even remembered what Allan Price had said to him, concerning playing the lottery.

JP, the splitting image of his mother, began to play the lottery with a set of six numbers, consisting of the date on which he was born; the birthdates of his three siblings; his mother's, and the date he landed in Canada. He would not leave out his mother's birth date because he believed, as he'd heard it often said that, a boy who resembled his mother was a very lucky child. The insignia on his truck reinforced his belief.

The personable man, who thought he was a lucky child, did not only share with his siblings but also with his friends. He shared with his friends by having barbecues twice each year: the first week in June and on his birthday in August. He always did so because he thought he was doing to others the way he'd like them to do to him.

One Saturday evening after one of his August barbecues, JP, and David the top furniture salesperson, sat on the black leather sofa in JP's family room. "Such a hectic day," he said to David. "The barbecue today was the largest I've ever held."

"Yes, David said. "Looking at all those guests I felt you should've called in the caterers."

"David, this time I saw so many faces, including faces I did not recognised. Anyway, I saw happy smiles on everyone's face. With your help and Ruth's, we catered well for them.

"Yes, my brother, we did, didn't we?" And for the first time, after all these years, David spoke of Allan Price's barbecues. "You know," he said, "this barbecue party reminds me of barbecues we used to attend at Mr Price's place."

Yes, my little brother, to think of it, I suppose you're right. Now, thanks to the Good Lord, we are able to share with others in the same fashion as he did for us. It makes me happy to know we accommodated them splendidly, even though I smell and feel like a barbecue pit, if you know what I mean."

JP doesn't use the term *little brother* much any more, because that *little brother* was the giant in the family.

"Me too," David said. "I could use a shower also."

David had his own residence, but he spent lots of time at JP's place. He even had clothing at JP's place he could change at any time, especially after each barbecue because of his involvement in the preparing and cooking activities. One could go through his clothing and they'd be hard-pressed not to find any of his apparel not having a touch of brown. For a few years after he went into sales, nothing was working the way he'd figured, but the day he wore a brown suit, brown pair of shoes and brown, skinny rim felt hat, he made his biggest sale up to that point. Things only got better for him from then on. If he ever got tired of selling furniture, interior decorating could be his next career. He would not accept a manager's position. Let him be a salesperson because he strives off the vibes from his interacting with customers.

"I am going to get rid of the way I smell," JP said. "Then I'll come back and watch the news, wait for the lottery result and see how I did."

"Why not," David said. "Tonight could be your lucky night."

"I hope so," JP said.

After JP refreshed himself, he put his old plaid shirt on. David also refreshed himself and suited himself with fresh clothes. They watched the news, after which the newscaster announced the winning numbers for the jackpot. JP had no luck.

"I'll keep on playing my selected numbers for as long as I breathe," JP said to David. "Do you think you had any luck tonight?"

"I did not purchase a ticket for tonight's draw. Besides, I only purchase tickets now and then. Too bad you did not win. Better luck next time."

"Thanks my brother. I know my numbers will come in one of these days."

Again, David whished his brother good luck.

"Just like you, Good Luck wish is all I get from everybody. Many times when I check my ticket and get a negative result, Mr Price's sentiments entered my thoughts. Many people, he'd said, played the lottery for years and their dreams never came through. But I feel in my bones that I'll cash in soon. Ah!" He stretched. "This old plaid shirt still feels so good on my back . . ."

"JP, I thought you'd thrown that shirt out long time ago."

"Although I have not worn it for years, because it has been retired, I am never throwing it away. Probably, if it were not for this shirt you and I would not be here in this house tonight. You . . ."

"Yep! You don't have to remind me because I remember why; that shirt, you and Mr Allan Price."

"Such a wonderful story, and like this retired shirt, I am retiring for the night. Bro., I am going to bed."

"See you in the morning," David went to bed, too.

Ruth was the first to retire for the night after the barbecue. She was also the first to get cracking Sunday morning. She went to the kitchen, made breakfast of poached eggs—three to a serving, baked beans, green beans, fried mushrooms and sautéed golden home fries, made from potatoes of course. She had another menu before the main course: of pineapple slices, strawberries, papaya and banana. She did not add any meat-kind because she remembered of the meat consumption at the barbecue the day before. She felt a breakfast excluding meat would be more appropriate.

They enjoyed the sumptuous breakfast.

As the day progressed several friends of JP's and David's, dropped in. They feasted on leftovers from the barbecue, played card and domino game until late in the evening, disbursing one at a time. David went home and did not visit his brother for about two weeks but they spoke regularly on the phone. However, on a Sunday, three weeks after the barbecue, David was in front of the computer doing some sales invoices when the phone rang.

David looked at the phone. He let it ring for a few more times before he picked it up.

The voice on the other end of the phone was his brother's.

"Hi there, my brother, I was just about to hang up. Did I wake you?"

David detected an aura of excitement in his brother's voice. "No," he said, "I am wide awake, working on some sales invoices."

"Are you sitting or standing?"

"I never worked in front of the computer standing up!"

"Well, my brother, it's good to know you're sitting because what I am about to tell you will make you weak at the knees; give you goose bumps and let your hair stand up."

I wonder what news it could be, David thought, in his moment of contemplating. Probably he found a way to purchase some new trucks.

"Are you still with me," JP said to David

"Yes, I am still with you."

"David, I am so very excited I can barely breathe . . ."

"Be careful now, my brother. That does not sound good at all. Now, take your time and tell me what it is that is restricting your breathing?"

"David, a wonderful thing happened. I know you won't believe it when you hear it." And he kept rumbling excitedly without getting to the point. Finally, he said, "My brother—"

"Yes JP . . . JP will you stop your wild chatter and tell me what it is that have you so excited?"

"All right, here we go. My brother, I won the lottery! I have won the whopping jackpot, other prizes including the encore! All prizes adds up to just over three million bucks."

"You won the lottery?" David said his voice with an aura of excitement, too.

"I told you, you wouldn't believe me!"

"You're very lucky." David said. "Much luckier than other winners I've heard of. I have never heard of anybody who had won the jackpot, also the encore. To be honest, your winning of the lottery was the farthest thing from my mind."

"Yes I did! Yes I did!" he said gleefully. He began to tell David of some of the ways he intends to spend his share of the windfall. "I'll use my portion to purchase two, maybe three trucks; set up my own trucking company; employ drivers, cut the middle man out. It feels so good knowing I won't be hauling goods for them anymore, but for myself. Tomorrow I will collect my windfall, take it easy for a few days or maybe go home for a few weeks then come back and set my plan in motion."

Meantime, while JP detailed his pragmatic plans, David was also making intriguing plans of his own. He would take the day off, maybe the week. He'd take his brother to the lottery office. Because he wanted to look at the cheque before it was lodged in the bank; hold it and maybe give it a kiss; the cheque, when cashed, would bring the entire family independence.

"Tomorrow I will go with you to collect the cheque," David said.

"You don't have to, my bother," JP said. "Terry will take me."

Ruth, who did not drive, had the week off from her job.

"Terry?"

"Yes, Terry's a taxi driver, a friend of mine. He chauffeured me around during the time I was convalescing from my accident—sometimes without any charge. He will get a new taxi."

Terry will get a new Taxi, David thought, while listening to JP. "Oh, JP, help me out here. Your friend Terry . . . is he the one who had just about everyone cracking up at the barbecue. If I remember correctly, he'd done likewise at last year's August barbecue."

"Yes that's him. Funny, isn't he?"

"He sure is. That's the man himself. Always find some ways to made you laugh."

"I've never seem him visiting you, or seen him at any of our June barbecues."

"He had said he does not socialize much. He's always on the go, because owing and operating a taxi is not an easy life."

"Life probably would be less stressful for him if he should become a comedian. Well, JP, stay strong. I will speak with you tomorrow evening. Try and get some sleep tonight."

"Don't worry my bro. I will sleep like a baby . . . . Tomorrow evening."

Terry knows about his windfall already. By the time he spreads his windfall around he might not have enough left to purchase those trucks. Anyway, they are friends.

Monday evening David did not get the call JP had promised. He began to wonder, but he was not duly worried about not getting that call. Because he knew, in due time, he'll definitely get his share. He'd leave his brother to savour his windfall.

Tuesday came and went; David did not hear a thing from JP, either. And also most of Wednesday. Filled with curiosity, he decided to call JP after he had supper. As he was walking to the phone, the phone rang. David picked it up.

"Hi there brother, how are you doing?"

"I am doing all right without hearing from you."

"If you'd call us the latter part of yesterday and anytime today, you wouldn't have gotten us. The constant ringing of the phone was annoying to Ruth. We have basic service; no add on. We plugged the phone back in when we want to make a call."

JP did not tell David what the real reason was, why he did not hear from him since Monday.

By now, too many people heard about his windfall and they are calling to get their share. That is why Alvin and Rachel could not get through to him. "JP, our brother and our sister (Rachael spoke for herself and their mother), left messages on my phone, worried they can't get through to you, but I spoke with them since I came home. They are worried you could be having second thought about sharing your windfall with them. I told them that, knowing you, I don't think so, and that I have not spoken with you since the last time we spoke late Sunday evening. I told them I am about to call you, and promised to call them back later with an update."

"David, they have no need to worry. I wouldn't cheat them. That is, if I can find my winning lottery ticket. I had bought several other tickets and had checked them first. My special numbers I checked last and discovered I was a winner. I left all the tickets on the kitchen table. All the other tickets are accounted for except the one that is the winner."

David was alarmed. "What? You can't find the winning lottery ticket?"

"Maybe Ruth hid it from me because she always tells me that investing in the lottery was a waste of time. Although she maintains that, she'd bought my ticket when asked, including the one for last Saturday night's draw, my favourite set of numbers."

"Are you sure she hid your winning lottery ticket?" David asked.

"I am not sure. I only have the strange feeling. When I asked her if she did, she laughed and said, "Why would I want to do such a thing?"

"Let me speak with her."

JP covered the mouthpiece. "Ruth!" he called out from the kitchen, to Ruth who was in the bedroom humming softly to a tune, "your brother-in-law wants to speak with you." She had just turned the Trilox Vacuum off or else she wouldn't have heard JP.

"Speak to me!" Ruth said. "Speak to me about what?"

"You'll have to talk with him then you'll find out."

"I am not in the mood for any family chatting right now. I just want to finish what I am doing and relax for awhile, while watching my favourite story. Tell him to call back later; in another couple of hours or so." She did not wait for a reply from JP, because she felt confident he would've relayed the message and it would be over with. So she went back to continue with her work. Therefore, she did not hear the next sentence, when JP had said, "He said it can't wait. He have to speak with you now!"

JP listened for Ruth to come on the extension. And when the time had elapsed, when he thought she should've been on the phone, and he heard only David sucking and exhaling air, he covered the mouth piece again and called out, "Ruth! Ruth!" He did not get any response from her. "This . . ." *I wonder what happened to her.* "Hold on," he said to David. *I wonder why she did not come on the phone. Heart attack, he mused. He* made his way to the bedroom.

However, on the way to the bedroom, and he was halfway up the blue-carpeted stairway, a hand on the varnished banister for cautionary support, he heard a rumbling noise. He listened more carefully and identified the source of the noise. "The Vacuum's?"

JP sudden appearance in the room made Ruth jump. "JP," she said over the noise of the vacuum that turned itself off when the handle was in the perfect upright position.

"Ruth, it's a matter of life or death situation," JP joked.

Ruth turned off the vacuum. "JP what . . . ? Oh, no, no, no! No time for fooling around now." She stretched her hands out defensively while taking a few short, backwards steps away from him.

"So that's the reason," he said, smiling at her behaviour, "for you not answering me. No, I am not here to fool around. David is waiting to speak with you."

"What? JP Didn't I tell you . . ."

"Ruth, he says it's a life or death situation. It can't wait. He must speak with you right now!"

It was not as if Ruth did not want to speak with David or was avoiding him. She had planned what she had to do. She did not want to be sidetracked.

"Ahhh . . . shi . . ." Ruth said, clearing her throat with a small cough as she laggard to the phone, leaned forward and grabbed it. She straightened up, phone held at the right position to hear him clearly, "High David, what's up? What is this life or death situation you want to speak to me about?"

"Ruth," David said, "my brother said you maybe hiding his windfall ticket. He can't find it."

"Why would I want to do that?" Ruth shot back. "Shame! A mighty big shame on the both of you. Besides, I am the one who bought the ticket for him, for last Saturday night's draw. The one he's claiming is the winning ticket. Although I had played jokes on him several times, I would not play a joke like that. Moreover, Sunday morning when I went to the convenience store, I brought him back the winning numbers. Saturday night he went to bed before the eleven o'clock news because he said he was tired. He did not get to check to see the winning numbers as he usually did. David, Sunday he checked those numbers and declared himself a winner."

"Ruth, he did? And then—"

"Of course he did," she said quickly. "Then he said he felt hot and flustered. He went to the freezer, took out a tub of strawberry ice cream and filled a bowl. I congratulated him. Then I went upstairs, leaving him with his ticket and his bowl of strawberry ice cream. So, whatever he did with his ticket, don't blame me."

"Ruth, I know you wouldn't. Just thought I would ask. Talk with you later" *He and his strawberry ice cream, David thought. Even when we could not afford biscuits, he always craves to satisfy his sweet tooth.* "So now I now why I did not hear from him. He hadn't gone to collect." *I wonder . . . .*

"David, is that the life or death situation?"

"Ruth, it depends on your interpretation."

The only other thing he heard from her was, "Bye David." She hung up the phone, then she walked casually downstairs, stood in front of JP who was still sitting at the kitchen table. "JP," she said with a straight face, "like I've told you before, and I'll say it again, resoundingly, I don't know where your lottery ticket is or could be. Now, I've heard it from your brother you fear I might have hidden you lottery ticket. Such a rotten thing to do . . . accusing me of hiding you ticket. Now I know why you were searching all over the place Monday and

Tuesday evenings. I was also wondering why you hadn't gone to collect your fortune instead gone to work. Oh No! I've missed my program because I've wasted so much *unnecessary* time with you and your brother."

JP apologized. "I am sorry dear. I should not have done that. But why can't I find my ticket? I've looked everywhere and can't find it . . . so strange, isn't it?"

"Yes, very strange indeed," Ruth said. "If you can't find it, it's your problem." She went back upstairs

The phone rang.

JP answered.

It was David.

"JP," David said, "I was wondering . . ."

"Wondering what?"

"Did you check the ice cream tub before you put it back in the freezer?"

"The ice cream tub," JP said sounding as if he didn't know, or had a clue what David was talking about. "Sh.t . . . . The ice cream tub . . . oh no! Good heavens! No, I did not! Hold on for a minute but don't hang up."

JP rushed to the freezer and yanked the ice cream tub out. He looked it over. "No ticket?" He lifted the tub above his eyes. The ticket was stuck frozen to the bottom of the tub. He was lucky not to have damaged the ticket.

"Good lord!, he said, shocked, "how did it get there? Ruth, Ruth!" he shouted, "I found it! I found it—stuck to the bottom of the ice cream tub."

"I am happy for you," she said. "Now you know I did not hide your *darn* lottery ticket."

JP went back to the phone. "David, I found it—"

"I know already. It is stuck to the bottom of the ice cream tub."

"Yes it is. If I should try to force it off, I might destroy it. There's no need for us to stay on the phone. I'll call you back as soon as I separate it from the tub."

"Okay, don't rush it."

JP put the ice cream tub upside-down on the kitchen counter. He watched intently as the ice that bound the ticket to the ice cream tub gradually melted, hoping the smudged numbers would still be legible. He'd force-dried it over a burner on the stove. With that done, he went over the numbers repeatedly. They were the winning numbers all right. Then he got a gut wrenching disappointment.

"What?" he said. "This can't be. Something is wrong here. Very, very, oh no, very wrong. Did the machine make a mistake?

To JP's greatest disappointment, the date on the ticket was for the next draw.

Now JP realized that winning the lottery was not as easy as he'd thought. One could come so close yet so far: missed just by a whisker.

JP called David. "Disappointment, disappointment, disappointment!" he said.

"My bro., what are you talking about? Disappointment?" David repeated. What's this disappointment thing's about? What's wrong JP?"

"According to the date on the ticket we won't be millionaires as I'd hoped. Ruth bought the ticket late, but I cannot get mad at her because I know she did not know the cut off time for purchasing lottery tickets.

"JP, I am sorry to hear that. Yes, this is grave disappointment. So we're back to square one."

"David, my heart almost stopped. All my dreams and hopes just went up like smoke."

"Mine, too," David said. *I guess Terry's, and all those others. Needless to say they, too, will be very disappointed.* "I'll pass the disappointing news onto the rest of the family."

"Next time I won't be so quick to declare myself a winner. I will follow grandpa's instruction—measure more than once before you cut. That means for you to check, check and check, and if you're not absolutely sure, double-check again."

JP hung up the phone, shook his sadly. "Look at it from the bright side,' he said. "Although I miss out by a mere hour, I still believe my luck will come through one of these days. It wasn't meant for me to win at this time."

Disappointed though JP was, he vowed to keep on playing his chosen numbers, with hoping they'll come up again. However, those numbers may never come up again, in the same sequence. Lightening never struck twice at the same place.

"Ruth," JP said, by now you know those numbers was the winning numbers all right. You bought the ticket late. I can't blame you because you were not aware of the cut off time."

"I am so sorry, my dear," she apologized.

"Sweetheart, don't worry about it. Life still goes on."

Nevertheless, one night, about a year after JP's disappointing experience, he dreamt his grandmother. He had not known her in the flesh only from her photograph. His grandmother, wearing a flowing white gown, was floating about three metres above the ground, holding a small piece of white paper in her right hand. She gave JP the piece of paper with fuzzy, red, writing.

"Here," she said, "this is a gift from me to you. Use it wisely."

As his grandmother floated away, JP jumped out of his sleep wondering, what's the meaning of the dream? He had never dreamt his grandmother, so why did she pay him this split-second visit, left him a piece of paper and that message.

JP told no one about his dream. Not even to Ruth whose head lay on the same pillow with his at nights.

In the fuzzy piece of writing, JP barely recognized three sets of numbers, numbers he figured were a six, a nineteen and twenty-seven. He had heard of people who had dreamt numbers; some had positive results from using them, others had none. Anyhow, with those thoughts in mind, JP developed another line of six numbers including some of his existing numbers and those given to him by his grandmother. Besides, seeing that those numbers came from his grandmother, which she told him was a gift, he had no doubt those numbers somehow had some significance. He was not certain, but he felt he'd amassed a possible wining combination. He kept his original six numbers in tack. Now, he was playing two sets of numbers.

JP did not depend on Ruth, either, to purchase tickets for him any more.

Eagerly, each weekend, JP checked his numbers. The result was as it always has been. Lady luck was still holding him at bay, and the only thing he could do was, to keep on playing while still hoping that someday he would get lucky.

Since the time JP had dreamt his grandmother, it was as if, to him, she was living next door and not a skeleton lying in the grave, a home from where she would never return. Many times as he barrelled down the highway in his blue, white, and red rig, he felt as though his grandma was sitting in the passenger seat, riding along with him. He even talked to her. Sometimes whenever he's having his lunch he stretch his lunch to the side he though she was sitting, or standing, for her to take a bite.

One day, about three months after JP got the message from his grandmother; he was on a trip to California, barrelling his Rig down the California desert highway. The air condition unit in his rig at full blast, the faint smell from melted tar oozing into his cab. He began to adlib: *My blue, white, and red truck and I rolling down this California highway—Hey grandma in white, how does that sound.—Not bad, he answered, give up singing and stick to driving.*

"Hey! . . . White?—I had no specific reason for including white as one of the colours for this Rig. Now I know why. There's certainly a reason for everything. My grandmother was wearing white when she'd visited me."

For about five minutes or so, JP kept up a conversation with his grandma, not really focusing on any particular subject. At some point, he asked, "Grandma, don't you think it's about time you help your grandson cash in. Ha . . . ! Not on what I believe, you could be thinking, but to be specific, I mean cash in on the lottery. So what do you have to say about it, my grandma?" He waited for a response. He got none. "Well," he finally said after a while, only the roaring sound from his Rig occupying his hearing, "I guess you have no definite answer for me. Therefore, I'll continue playing with hope as always and meekly wait and murmur not. I have proven nothing happens before it's time. Maybe I should go see my banker for funds to purchase another truck or two. That might prove to be a surer bet."

Anyhow, JP refused to give up on any of his lottery numbers. Therefore, one Saturday night, three months later after he supposedly had that chat with his grandma in the California desert, he checked his lottery numbers after the eleven o'clock news. He thought his eyes were playing tricks on him. He checked the numbers again. "No, this is not possible!" JP said. He double-checked the date. "That's it!" he said gleefully. "This time there's no mistake. My numbers including the numbers grandma gave me came through." Then he thought, I wonder how many people I have to share this windfall with, besides my family. Well, I should not worry myself about that. I will find out in due time.

This time, JP was careful not to sound the alarm bell about his good fortune . . . until he had a cheque in his hand.

Monday morning Ruth noticed he was fidgeting around in the house, like someone who was lost. "Aren't you going to work today?" she asked him, before she left for work.

"No," he said. "Today I have some business to take care of."

However, his business, which he did not disclose to her, was for him to go to the lottery office to claim his prize.

JP's hand shook as he received his cheque of the entire first prize, without the encore. He secured the cheque so much that not even the wind, cared not how strong it blew, could penetrate where it was located. He reached home, and still a bit nervous, he waited for Ruth to come home in the evening, then he said to her, calmly, "Sweetheart, take a look at this."

"Take a look at it, for wh*at?* That's a bloody cheque, isn't it?"

"Yes. It is a cheque all right; indeed a cheque in need!"

Ruth looked at JP. "I'm wondering if it's only my imagination. But he is not . . . Something is wrong. I wonder if this cheque has anything to do with it. This morning I left him here looking a bit confused. Now, the whole day had passed and he is still looking somewhat dazed. I wonder if this cheque has anything to do with his overly nervous behaviour. Is he in some kind of trouble and is hiding it from me?"

Ruth felt the cheque in his hand might have the answer. She took the cheque from him and looked at it casually. Then she opened her eyes wide— "A cheque? For five . . . what? I cannot believe what I am beholding. A cheque for five million plus? JP it's no wonder you were acting strangely, still is. Why didn't you tell me about it?"

JP beamed. "This time I wanted to be sure. I wanted to be sure we are indeed millionaires!"

"Did you tell your brother about this?"

"Except those at the lottery office, you are the first to know. Now I will call my brother and give him the mind-blowing good news."

JP relayed the news to his brother, who was very doubtful the minute he heard the news.

"Wait a minute," David said. "My brother, are you sure this time you haven't fluked?"

"I am looking at the cheque as we speak. Take the day off tomorrow. Let's go to the bank together."

"I'll think about it," David said.

Johnny Price hugged his wife affectionately. "Sweetheart, this is the happiest day in my life. Much thanks to God, my Guardian Angel; to Grandma, and of course to Mr Price and his brother. I am certain if it weren't for their help, I probably would not have realized my dream. May God bless their souls?" He let go of his wife, held the cheque above his head and said loudly, **"Mama! . . .** Oh **w**ait a minute . . ." He went away for a short while, then came back with his raggedy plaid shirt and the piece of paper, now brown, on which he had written long ago, *I am going to be a millionaire!*

His wife was astonished.

"I'll explain later," he said, as he held the cheque up again in one hand, the raggedy plaid shirt and the piece of paper in the other hand. **"Mama!"** his voice was near breaking point. **"Mama, your son Johnny Price is now a millionaire . . . We Are Millionaires! No more financial heartaches, no more financial pain."**

Johnny wept tears of joy.

"Oh, my heart," he said. He dropped the plaid shirt and the piece of paper and slammed his hand with the cheque on his chest, over the area of his heart.

"JP, JP, J . . . P!" Ruth shouted.

He opened his eyes. "Gotcha! . . . And our money, too."

CONVERSATIONS

Something in common

Isn't LIFE ON A whole unpredictable? And isn't the heart, as long as it keeps on beating the epicentre of one's emotion? The driving force (the jack hammer of the operative, Infinite Yearnings *of the hearts*), that relentlessly drives one's emotions?

As I happened to rest my eyes from my laptop screen, after I finished reading the last line in *I want to be a millionaire,* I was in a cafe on Highway #7, the city north of Toronto where I had sat and went through all my stories, but where I finished the millionaire story. The aroma of coffee of all verities was prevalent. If one walked in and was hungry, the aroma from the coffee and the aroma from other foods, would make that person salivate, while he or she waits for their orders to be filled, one could've probably choke from the accumulation of saliva.

I looked at the server of the cafe. She had her eyes planted in the flat, eggshell white ceiling. I could tell she was contemplating. I studied her. I also cast my eyes to the ceiling to see if I could see what she was looking at. I could not tell. Then I got out of my brown chair. The cafe's furniture were brown vinyl chairs and brown tables.

"Beautiful up there isn't it?"

"What is beautiful up there?' she said.

I said, "Your viewing of the ceiling is so intent. Something up there must be beautiful, that it has your undivided attention."

She looked at me, probably thinking, this guy is way out. "Nothing is up there that peaks my interest. And except for your presence, and my mate, it's so quiet in here. Of course not so quiet, because of the noise coming from the machines and from the air conditioner that is working overtime."

"If it should be forced to work any harder it might just explode."

"I hope it doesn't. With the constant heat wave in this area, I hope it doesn't because we'd get cooked."

'The human body is cooping quite adequately, and will continue to do so regardless," I said.

'Just barely under such condition, I think. Some days it's overcast, like it is now, but overcast though it gets it never rains. It stays hot as ever. I wish it would rain."

"If it should rain it'd cool things down quite a bit."

"It certainly would. Oh, by the way," she said, "what's your name? You've been coming in here quite a lot with that computer, notepad and several books. What are you? Are you a teacher; a writer; maybe a computer programmer or some scientist doing research? Or are you doing other things to keep the brain stimulated?"

"I am working on some short stories."

She asked, with a smile, "Anything 'bout me?"

"No. Nothing about you. To do that I'd have to get your permission."

"Darn," she said. "For all the time you spend in here I was hoping you were studying me and secretly writing about me. I wouldn't mind."

"No. This might disappoint you, but I never thought to write anything about you." *Perhaps until now.* "Anyway, my name is A.L. Jackson Barnes."

She extended a hand. "Well Mr Barnes, I am Stephanie Powers."

I already knew your first name, not her last name until now.

"Friends from now on, all right?"

"Yes, friends."

"All right friend, now you have my permission. Anyway, why is life so difficult?" she said.

"Difficult?"

"Yes. Difficult."

"Stephanie, that depends."

"All right Mr Philosopher, Teacher, or Writer."

"Writer, Stephanie, remember . . ."

"All right Mr Writer, depends on what?"

"Depends on what your yearning heart wants to accomplish."

"My yearning heart," she said contemplatively.

"Yes . . ."

At that yes our conversation was interrupted by Ivan, a man I was acquainted with, who pushed the entrance door open and stepped in.

"Sorry," he said. He knew he'd interrupted the conversation. "But I hope you don't mind. "Stephanie," he slapped his stomach a few times, "my usual, please? I am starving; feel like I am about to faint. Hot out there, isn't it?"

"Okay," Stephanie said. "I hope you won't faint before it is ready. Better go sit down. I'll bring it over."

Ivan's usual sandwich, he'd told me what it was, was whole wheat bread, salmon, hot pepper, brown olives, red onions, hot pepper, tomato and mayonnaise.

"Ivan, maybe it's the heath getting to you," I said.

"Could be, my man. It's been a scorcher for days."

"It has, hasn't it?"

"Sure is."

"So you're yearning for your sandwich."

Ivan looked at me curiously. "Yearning?" he said. 'Man, you say I am yearning but I'm not. I am starving. All I had to eat all day is one stinking apple, and also drank a lousy cup of coffee. Man, haven't seen you for days. Where have you been?"

It was on the cafe's patio, where Ivan spent quite a lot of time while he's at the cafe, where I first made his acquaintance.

"I've been here as usual. You're the one who hadn't come around lately."

"Well, a change of scenery is good some times."

Ivan did not go to sit as Stephanie had suggested. He looked at her from her back. "It seemed to me you two were having an interesting conversation. She's such a wonderful woman," he said of Stephanie, while she filled his order. "So beautiful! I've known her for years. No one can fix my sandwich the way she does."

"Then I have no doubt you'll enjoy it, my friend.

"You bet. Man, I enjoyed it every time."

Even though when you're outside it felt as though you're in an oven, I went out to get few whiffs of nature's fresh air, while contemplating whether my stories were completely finished or there was room for other additional texts, which I call spicing. I had to make a hasty retreat because this time the overcast cloud did deliver. It was like someone had split it wide open.

I went back in the cafe and sat at the table, facing my computer. Ivan was giving his sandwich a severe thrashing like a glutton, or as a starved raven would to its captured prey. Stephanie looked my way and smiled.

A smile darting my way all of a sudden, I thought, from someone's face that always looked so stolid?

Within a while Stephanie came and sat at my table. "Unless it gets overbearing," she said, "my mate will handle it. Now, you had started to say something about what one's heart yearns for."

"Yes. What you heart yearns for. What you'd want to gain in life . . . you know, what you'd like to accomplish."

"Hah! Accomplish? Maybe I was staring at the ceiling and yearning, which I did not actually recognize I was doing."

"Were you?"

"Look, about my life," she said. "It's nothing new."

"And."

"You can tell I am of Chinese descendants, can't you?"

"I thought so."

"They told me about how life is grand in this country, Canada. Living in the system gives you a different prospective."

"Such as?"

"Such as working as a doctor, a great accomplishment of mine. I did not know it would become so difficult for me to continue in my profession in this country. Lots of rigmarole I have to go through before I could."

"But there are standards in every country for everyone who is a doctor, or whoever wants to practice medicine in that particular country. Being a doctor is dealing with peoples' lives. People who wants to stay healthy, to get healed when they're infirmed, people who yearns to have a healthy life."

"I know that. I speak perfect English. They, authorities, say you have to go through their system before they'll allow you to practice."

"What are you doing about it?"

"Studying while I am working in a cafe. I have to become a fully fledged doctor in this country . . . that I will accomplish."

Ivan said he'd known you for years."

"Only, I might say, for about two years. That's the length of time I've been working here."

"Are you sure you'll accomplish?"

"Although it is difficult, of course I'm sure. I can't be in a coffee shop, serving coffee for God knows how long. I was a doctor, still is although I am not a practicing doctor in this country, but I shall."

"Well," I said, "I believe if you work fervently at it, with your emotion driving you yearning heart, then you'll accomplish as my characters, my close friends did in my stories."

"Yeah. Tell me about some of your characters. This yearning hearts thing of yours sounds interesting."

"Are you sure you have time for this?"

"If it doesn't get busy then I have time. Besides my only other obstacle could be, if management walked in and see me sitting with a client. I could get fired.

Anyway it's late for anybody from management to come snooping."

"Stephanie!" her mate called out.

Stephanie knew what the call meant.

"Oh gosh, I did not realize it. Suddenly it's like a circus in here. We'll talk later. You don't mind, do you?"

"Not at all."

She stood up. "See you in a while then?"

"I'll still be here."

While Stephanie went to tend to business I went back to flicking pages. But she hadn't gone for long before she returned.

"Are you all right?" she asked.

"Yes, doing okay," I said.

During this heat wave we seemed not to have enough water and ice cream. But we have yet to run out. Now, about your characters, your friends as you'd stated. Tell me about them. You don't have to relate all of the stories to me, a bit about one then the other. I'll follow."

Seeing that she wanted to learn something of my characters, step by step, from The Pilot Clipped her Wings to Johnny wanted to be a millionaire, I showed her their attitude towards going after whatever their hearts yearned for. Also given their sufferings, adversity, never one, with their resilience, did they thought of quitting because of their driving emotion—their Infinite yearnings, *of their hearts.*

"Whoa!" Stephanie said. "So I, like your friends, have something in common."

"Stephanie, most humans do; always yearning for something to make their lives better."

"You know, I was thinking as you revealed what took place with your characters that I, as with your first character, have something in common."

"You do."

"Yes."

"In what way?"

"Your character, in the pilot clipped her wings, had some serious problem with her husband. She divorced him. She also had vowed nothing would get in her way, not if she should fall in love again, would she allow it to impede her quest. And in the end she got what she'd yearned for."

"So."

"I got married at an early age. You know, arranged marriage. It did not work out for us."

"Why?"

"It's quite a long story. So let's just leave it at that. Or Let's say, I couldn't bear to be around or near him."

"So you came to this country to put distance between you and him."

"Something like that."

"But my character was living it this country. She did not have to travel half across the world to get rid of her abusive husband."

"So what's the difference? Anywhere you are in the world an abusive husband is just the same. You just have to make changes. Like her I will accomplish. The way I see it," she said, "there are always yearnings by everyone: like the haves yearning to get more. The have-nots are hoping while yearning, and also doing their best to achieve, to accomplish."

"Stephanie, life on a whole is unpredictable. But as long as human exists there'll always be Infinite Yearnings."

"Isn't that true," Stephanie said. "Humans are always yearning. By the way, the story about the Flower Queen intrigued me also. It caused me to think of my mom. She likes and grows flowers. We should get in depth about her another time. Mr Writer, tanks. We had quite an interesting conversation." She shook her head, "Yes, Yearning *of the hearts* all right. We have to close. Tomorrow, all right Mr Writer?"

"Yes Stephanie, if we are still alive, yes."

THE INVISIBLE KEY

INTRO

LINTON FELT THE WORLD was his stage. But once he walked out of his secured environment, he'd come to realize that things were not easily assessable as he'd envisioned.

Along the way upsetting and tragic events wreaked havoc on his life. Relatives and friends were not sufficient support to appease his troubled soul. However, from the day his parents reminder him of the importance of—**THE INVISIBLE KEY—,** which he'd known about but was not using it as he should, he'd realized that by using it as he really should there was nothing in comparison to its awesomeness.

PART ONE

O NE EVENING, AFTER HE had supper, Linton Barnes marched back into the dining room and made his desire known to his parents.

His astonished parents, James—Papa, and his mother Lucille—Mama Luce—asked why he had the sudden urge to go to England, knowing that he had a few semesters left to finish high school. Although his parents were displeased with his idea, they had a lengthy discussion with him concerning his sudden disclosure.

So before they gave him the green light they reminded him of the things he'd be giving up. His father also reminded him that, with no skill, finding worthwhile employment could be a daunting task. He would miss playing his favourite sport, Cricket, with his brothers and his friends. But regardless of what they'd showed him, Linton held steadfast to his resolve.

Linton told them that with the help of his brother, Mike, who'd immigrated to England a few years back, he'd coupe, and that he had no doubt he'd find others to play the game of cricket with in the land of its origin.

On the morning of his departure, the family gathered for family devotion—a custom practiced each morning throughout the year. That morning the family had devotion twice, which was done only once before, when Mike the eldest brother departed from the family to go to England. It was a sad time for the family then, and now they were reliving similar sadness. Nevertheless, they asked God through prayer, as they did for Mike, to be with Linton on his maiden flight and to help provide for him in a foreign place that would be his new home, as He, God always done for the entire family through thick and thin.

"We may never see Linton again," his mother said. "This could be the last time we congregate in this manner."

And such were the sentiment of others including his grandmother's, but her words of similar sentiments were prophetic because, after that day Linton never saw her again.

On the flight to England Linton, as were others on that airplane, had a mighty scare. He and many on the airplane felt death was imminent. During that time too, Linton relived another scary time in his life—when he fell into his neighbor's water tank and almost drowned. In those scary moments too he and many on that airplane used the Invisible Key, without being conscious of it, when they called upon the Lord to spare their lives.

On his second day in England, Linton's brother took him on a tour of London. He, Linton, saw Big Ben on the banks of the Thames River in its psychic form. He was in awe! He also saw magnificent buildings he read about in his history studies, and London's intrinsic underground railway system.

At the end of the tour, Mike told Linton they'd have English fish 'n' chips for dinner. Linton would never pass up on a fish meal. When Mike came back with their meals wrapped in newspaper, Linton said he'd rather go hungry than eat anything wrapped in newspaper.

As time went on, Linton tried but could not find a job. Now he found out the grass was not greener on the other side, as he'd thought, and during that period, the words of his dad—that without any work experience, especially not having any in England it could be difficult for you to secure worthwhile employment—kept hunting him.

After several rejections, Linton falsified an application that landed him his first job. With his conscience bothering him, he went back into the personnel's office and told him he could not accept the job because he had done something unethical, something a Christian should not have done. Eventually he secured another job. But when the Gov. told him he had to work on the weekend, which would infringe on his day of worship, he had no other alternative but to quit.

Working as a porter was not a job to Linton's liking. Because in his homeland that position was looked upon as demeaning, however he was happy to accept a position at a hospital for children in Carshalton. Being the last employee in that department, he'd deliver magazines and other reading materials from ward to ward. The children he saw in those wards seemed normal to him. He did not clean any of those wards but he swept streets and gathered leaves—a task that was humiliating to him.

One day the Gov. allocated him to work with John Thompson, the driver for the ambulance of ward C5. Linton was yet to visit that particular ward.

"Okay mate," John said, "let's go! Let's see how you like it."

How I like it? Linton thought.

At ward C5 Linton had an extremely frightening experience. Where, for the first time in his life he was in contact with Thalidomide children.

Would Linton stay on the job or would he bolt as several had done.

PARC CWO

T HAT MORNING, LINTON AND John was late getting to ward C5 late. Sister Elaine Powers were not amused. She ridiculed John. But after his explanation, why he was late, Sister Powers said she understood.

Mesmerized from those medical challenged children he saw, Linton was beside himself. He refused to go near any of them.

But after John explained why they are the way they are, Linton fear of them gradually waned. Before the first day ended he accommodated them. He learned a lot from those children. Never again would he complain about life's challenge nor take for granted his body or whatever life afforded him.

Came winter, Linton first, he experienced something he'd never seen before—small white flakes raining from the sky. That sight confused him. He had to go to work but he did not venture into the white stuff blanketing the ground until he saw someone walking in it as if it mattered not to her. He had problem coping with his first snowfall and the extreme cold, because he did not have the proper attire. As he tried to cope, slipping and sliding to stay on his feet, his body numbed, he wondered why people choose to live in such a disgusting climate. He remembered his mother telling him he would curse the weather in such a time as that.

Linton also kept a promise he made to his parents: to work and study, but that idea got disrupted when he became an outside driver of the ambulance and the coach, at the hospital.

Replies from his letters to his parents were comforting to him as he settled in this new land. As Linton made new friends, and played cricket and soccer in the summer months with those in the hospital's cricket and soccer teams, he began writing less frequent to his parents, and he believed they were replying according to his method of writing. With this in mind, he wrote a letter to his parents and apologized for his inconstancy in writing, urged them to reply to his letter as quickly as when he first arrived in England, and promised he'd write to them as often as he did in the past.

A couple of months passed and Linton did not get a reply to his last letter. He was dejected. Because of his dejection he did not show up on the weekend to participate in a very important cricket match with his team mates.

"You don't look your usual self," Mike said. "Are you OK?

"Brother Mike, I feel as if somewhere something is wrong. What could that be I haven't a clue. Besides, I am not getting replies to my letters as I'd hoped."

"I would not worry about it," Mike said. "No news is good news."

Linton went to work on Monday and promptly apologized to his teammates. Tuesday he did not go to work because of the way he was feeling. That day he listened for the mail to be delivered through the slot in the front door, and he was relieved when he saw a letter from his parents. Linton made a cup of tea, and then opened the letter. As he read the letter he was devastated from the news the long awaited letter bore. One of his bothers went to a cricket match and he was involved in a terrible accident. He's in a coma in the hospital.

Linton's tea went cold. Neither did he have a bite to eat the entire day.

Mike came home and saw his brother in a sorry state.

Linton told him about the accident.

Mike asked Linton if he'd prayed for their brother. Linton said he did not.

"Then we should pray for him," Mike said.

They prayed, and Mike's prayer was sincere but Linton's was hollow.

Several letters came from their parents, but it bore the same news. Their younger brother was still unconscious. Linton felt prayer was not working. Now Linton was not only still angry at the impaired driver of the car; he was also venting anger towards the Lord, as his parents detected in one of his letters, because he felt the Lord could've prevented the accident from happening. Furthermore, the Lord could have already healed his brother.

In his parents reply, they told Linton the Lord has a reason for everything that happens to humans, and that his brother could have died but the Lord has his reason for keeping him alive. So instead of being angry with the Lord, he should keep praying—keep using the Invisible Key—with fervent faith because, *Faith is the substance of things hoped for, the evidence of things not seen.* Keep in mind that whether your brother live or die the Lord has a reason for that too.

After Linton read that letter, he prayed regularly and with much sincerity. One day at work, he knelt in a corner of the canteen and prayed. One of his co-workers,

Len Pinkerton, jeered him. Andrew Weise noticed the taunting. He beckoned Linton to his office.

"Mate," he said, "I have never seen you do that before."

"I was praying for my brother who's at home". He told Andrew what happened to his brother.

"So that's the reason you are so withdrawn from the other day? It was brought to my attention by someone who saw you crying a couple days back. Mate, I am sorry to learn what happened to your brother."

"Andrew, I love my brother, dearly! I do not want him to die. Mind you, not only do I love my brother but I also love my entire family and my fellow humans too."

Even though Linton was hurting mentally, he and Andrew dialogued for a short while. He told Andrew that prayer is a direct link between humans and God, and if humans truly love each other, would there be wars, genocide and the likes?

A few days hence, Linton received two more letters on quick succession from his parents. The second letter bore good news: their brother had regained consciousness. Linton and Mike rejoiced exceedingly, and thanked the Lord for his wonderful mercies.

Some years went by and their mother died. Linton and his siblings went to bury her, and he, Linton, and two of his brothers were involved in an auto accident. Those who saw what was left of the car thought no one came out alive. Many say they were very lucky, but one of their cousins said it was not luck; God acted on their behalf, because of the many prayers Mama Luce had prayed asking God to take care of her children. That God have many of her prayers locked away in his vault to use whenever he wishes.

From the day Linton's parents reminded him of the importance of using the Invisible Key, he used it constantly because he'd realized the benefits of that powerful key.

IF

"**If** one is perfect in whatever he or she does, the word imperfect would not be in the dictionary.

A writer always write in two modes—the conscious and the subconscious.

Many people do write but a writer's success depends on how he or she writes.

A story begins with an idea, and the story that is told from that idea begins with the first letter on the page."

A. L. J. BARNES